JANET DEAN

The Bounty Hunter's Redemption

D0017869

⬡ **HARLEQUIN**® LOVE INSPIRED® HISTORICAL

Recycling programs
for this product may
not exist in your area.

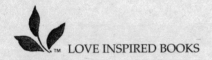

LOVE INSPIRED BOOKS

ISBN-13: 978-0-373-28343-9

The Bounty Hunter's Redemption

Copyright © 2016 by Janet Dean

www.Harlequin.com

Printed in U.S.A.

"I'll be back." He flashed a smile. "Don't let the anticipation overwhelm you."

That towering hulk of a man threatened the harmony Carly prized. Yet as she stared into those eyes, an unwelcome thrill of attraction slid through her, shooting heat up her neck and into her cheeks. She groped for a rebuke that would conceal the turmoil churning inside her. "One thing I can say for certain, Mr. Sergeant. Nothing about you overwhelms me."

He arched a brow, and then had the audacity to wink. As if he had read her mind and found her claim amusing.

Carly shut the door behind him, then leaned against it and took a deep breath. No matter what she'd said, Carly had never felt more overwhelmed. And of all things, by a bounty hunter.

A handsome bounty hunter, her heart whispered.

She pulled away from the door and steeled her spine. A handsome strong-minded bounty hunter who would stop at nothing to see that his sister owned this shop.

Janet Dean grew up in a family with a strong creative streak. Her father and grandfather recounted fascinating stories, instilling in Janet an appreciation of history and the desire to write. Today she enjoys traveling into our nation's past as she spins stories for Love Inspired Historical. Janet and her husband are proud parents and grandparents who love to spend time with their family.

Books by Janet Dean

Love Inspired Historical

Courting Miss Adelaide
Courting the Doctor's Daughter
The Substitute Bride
Wanted: A Family
An Inconvenient Match
The Bride Wore Spurs
The Bounty Hunter's Redemption

Visit the Author Profile page at Harlequin.com.

As far as the east is from the west,
so far hath He removed our transgressions from us.
—*Psalms* 103:12

For Heather: precious daughter,
loving mother, loyal friend, a strong woman of faith.
You're a real-life heroine.

Acknowledgments

To my critique partners,
Shirley Jump and Missy Tippens, a simple
"thank you" can't express my appreciation
for your savvy input and steadfast support.

To assistant editor Emily Krupin and executive
editor Tina James, thank you for all you do to
make my books the best they can be. I'm privileged
to work with you.

To my friend Mary Overmeyer, thank you for
sharing the childhood memory of your mother,
Jennie Smith, standing at the bottom of the stairs
singing the first stanza of "Father, We Thank Thee
for the Night," and of you and your six siblings
singing the second stanza back to her. I love how
this song connected your family to each other and
to God and couldn't resist using it in my book. The
author of "Father, We Thank Thee for the Night"
was Rebecca J. Weston (1818–1890),
a teacher in the Boston schools.

Chapter One

Gnaw Bone, Indiana, March 1898

A woman should mourn the loss of her husband. Or so Carly Richards once believed.

No doubt she looked the part of the grieving widow as she stood alongside Max's grave clothed in black, her gloved palm resting on her young son, unnaturally quiet and still beside her. Yet the eyes Carly bowed shed no tears. In her chest, her thudding heart beat to a steady tempo of relief.

A fearsome man to live with when he chose to make an appearance, Max had destroyed her love for him years ago.

She pulled a handkerchief from her sleeve and pressed the square of linen to her nose. Though the air carried the scent of mowed grass, spring flowers and fresh-turned dirt, the vile odors that had clung to Max filled her nostrils still, as if he stood at her side, not laid out at her feet. Stale tobacco, fresh moonshine, foul breath, permeated with the odor of sweat.

Sweat of a hardworking man, Carly admired. Sweat of a man coming off a three-day drunk roiled her stomach.

She'd never again endure the man's stench or his unpredictable temper. That knowledge purged her, freed her, promised her better days ahead.

Carly bent, cuddling her seven-year-old son close. Henry smelled of soap, innocence, the hope of new beginnings.

Across the way neighbors and members of her church had gathered to see Max into the ground. The tension that had been tangible whenever Max had been around was gone, buried with him. Now no one need keep an eye peeled for an unreasonable man itching for a fight.

Pastor Koontz closed his Bible, offered a prayer for Max's soul and then eyed his parishioners. "Thank you all for coming on this somber day." He turned to her. "God bless you and your son, Mrs. Richards," he said and then stepped aside.

Folks edged toward her, giving her and Henry a hug, mumbling condolences, avoiding her gaze, then hurried toward the wrought iron gate in quiet groups of three and four, eager to escape. Not a single soul grieved Max. He had no family. No friends. At least none Carly knew of.

Henry, his dark brown hair lifting in the gentle breeze, pointed to the hole in the ground. "Is Pa staying in there?"

Carly met his troubled eyes; eyes far too old for one so young. "Yes. Your pa's passed on."

"Like our old hound dog? Pa ain't coming back?"

"That's right."

Her son gave a nod, then stepped to the dirt piled at the edge of the grave and stomped the soil with his scuff-toed shoe.

Once. Twice. Three times.

Henry pivoted back to her, lips quivering, eyes welling with tears. "He can't hurt you now, Mama."

The heartbreaking truth sank to Carly's belly like a stone. Henry had not forgotten the last time his father had returned home. The first time Max had slapped her with more than words. The force of the blow had knocked her to the floor, terrifying her son.

Oh, Lord, why didn't I take Henry and leave long ago?
Fear.

Always imprisoned with the certainty that if she fled, Max would do as he'd threatened. Track her down, catch her unaware and kill her, leaving her precious boy at his mercy. Mercy wasn't a notion Max understood.

Nor evidently had his killer, a bounty hunter who'd come to take Max to Kentucky to stand trial for murder. Carly hadn't known Max was wanted by the law. But she hadn't found the news surprising. After almost eight years of marriage to the man, nothing surprised her.

Until now.

Even with all the prayers she'd uttered, asking God to protect her and Henry, even with abundant evidence God had protected them in countless ways, she'd never expected Max would be the one laid out in the ground instead of her.

An oppressive weight slid from her shoulders. She'd no longer dread Max's footfalls after weeks of unexplained absences. She'd no longer dread that every word out of her mouth could trigger his fiery temper. She'd no longer dread what the next day, the next week, the next month would bring.

A knot of remorse tightened around Carly's heart and squeezed. *Forgive me, Lord.* What kind of a woman found comfort in the death of anyone, much less the father of her child?

Had Max been cut down by a bullet before he'd had a chance to ask God's forgiveness for the blackness in his life? Had he gotten a moment to repent, a moment to prepare to meet his Maker? She hoped he had.

Whatever awaited Max, his eternal future was up to God. She would take care of herself and Henry. She'd run the shop. Earn a living. What she'd always done. Perhaps one day she could afford to hire another seamstress, opening more time to spend with her son.

Not that Max's death changed her finances. He hadn't supplied much except trouble. Still, she was grateful for his mother's shop and would never regret a marriage that had blessed her with this child.

Nevertheless, she'd learned a valuable lesson. She'd been a fool to hitch herself to Max Richards. She'd never trust a man again.

Never.

Carly grasped Henry's hand and then, with one last glance at the grave, at the overall-clad men already covering the casket with shovelfuls of dirt, stepped away from her past.

A woman stood between Nate Sergeant and a young boy like a petite, beautiful fortress. Pink lips, flushed cheeks, her fair complexion in sharp contrast to her coal-black hair, the delicate female couldn't outweigh a hundred-pound bag of grain. Under slashing brows, dazzling blue eyes met his, sizing him up, her expression wary, alert.

Those penetrating eyes ripped the air out of his lungs like an uppercut to the gut. "Didn't mean to scare you, ma'am," he said, doffing his hat. "I'm Nate Sergeant—"

"I'm not scared." Those cornflower blue eyes turned steely, confirming her claim. "And I know who you are."

How could she know his identity? Nate hadn't seen her before today.

Out front, a sign shot full of holes read Lillian's Alterations and Dressmaking. Lillian Richards was dead. Who was this woman? "Do you work here?"

She ignored his question and gathered the boy to her. As she ruffled her fingertips through his hair, dark like hers, her eyes softened like melted butter. "While you were in school, I made cookies. Go to the kitchen and have a couple while I talk with Mr. Sergeant."

The boy turned curiosity-filled eyes on Nate. A gentle nudge from his mother and he trudged toward the rear of the shop. At the doorway he stopped, his gaze traveling between Nate and his mother. As if he picked up on the tension in the room, his brow furrowed in a pint-size warning to treat his mother right.

In that boy Nate saw himself as a youngster. Whether he believed it or not, Nate knew the lad was far too young to wear the breeches in the family.

"Go on," his mother murmured, then watched until he disappeared into the back. With her son out of earshot, Mrs. Richards's gaze traveled to the pistol strapped on Nate's thigh. "You're the bounty hunter who killed my husband."

A chill slid through Nate, pebbling the skin on his forearms. When he'd shot Max Richards, he'd made this woman a widow and her young son fatherless. Nate had been fifteen when he'd lost his parents in a train holdup. The boy must be less than half that age.

"I'm sorry it came to that, ma'am." Nate rubbed a hand over his nape, taut as a stick of timber. "How'd you know me?"

"I'm not likely to forget the name of Max's killer." Somehow this petite woman standing across from him managed to look formidable in a prim, high-necked shirt-waist with its wide collar and tiny waist. "Even if I had, Sheriff Truitt came by earlier to warn me that he'd seen you ride into town."

Truitt was looking out for the widow's welfare. Someone needed to. As much as Nate wished things were different, that man wasn't him. He was here to protect his sister's interests, not this woman's.

How many women had suffered from actions taken

by the men in their lives? Including his? He swallowed against the sudden lump in his throat, refusing to think about that now.

"Max was known for his temper. Still, far as I know, he never shot at a complete stranger." Her eyes narrowed, filling with suspicion. "Why would he fire at you?"

"He killed my sister Anna's husband. Shot Walt in the back. That made it personal."

She winced, as if seeing the cowardly act.

"When I explained I'd be taking him back to Kentucky to stand trial for murder, he…"

"He didn't want to go."

"No, ma'am."

"So what happened then?"

Why ask? Surely she didn't want to hear the gruesome details. Still she waited for his answer. Unable to cope with a weepy female, Nate fought to keep his tone detached. "He grabbed his gun from his holster and fired. I reeled away, pulling my revolver, and answered before he got off the next round."

"Max wasn't much of a shot, leastwise not with a moving target."

Nate clutched his hat, turning the rim 'round and 'round in his hands. "No, ma'am."

Not much of a man, either. No point grinding that truth into his widow. Perhaps she already knew. She wasn't wearing widow's weeds and appeared more somber than distraught. But then, everyone handled grief differently.

Well, she'd be distraught soon enough, once he got to the point of his visit. Mrs. Richards seemed like a good woman, a good mother with a small boy depending on her. If only he could express regret for taking a life, perhaps do a chore or two and be on his way.

But he couldn't. Anna needed this chance. For once in

her life she'd have a way to handle her future, set her own course.

The widow considered him and then nodded, as if she'd accepted his lack of options. "I'm sorry about your sister's husband." Moisture welled in her eyes. "Please give her my condolences."

He shoved past the tightness in his throat. "I will."

"If that's all, I need to check on my son." Mrs. Richards turned away, as if finished with the conversation.

"Ma'am."

She turned back, eyes wide, as if surprised to find him standing there instead of heading for the door. "Yes?"

A gust of air escaped his lips. No decent man relished bringing a woman trouble. "I'm afraid I have bad news."

"Worse than killing my son's father?"

At a loss for words, Nate merely stared at her.

"I'm sorry, Mr. Sergeant. That was uncalled-for, but I have a boy who needs my attention and a shop to run." Her gaze traveled to the door, her desire for him to walk through it abundantly clear.

No point in putting off what he'd come to say. "This shop is mine," he said, settling his Stetson in place.

The air stilled, caught in the heavy hush of surprise. She took a breath, then another; in, out. Her gaze hardened. "You're mistaken. The deed to this shop is in my possession."

"My brother-in-law Walt won the deed in a poker game. Your husband killed him for it, and then terrorized my sister Anna, who had no idea where Walt had hidden it. Richards never found the deed before he rode off. But recently I did. As my sister's representative, I'm here to take possession."

"That can't be true!"

She met his gaze. As if seeing the truth in his eyes, the blazing confidence in hers ebbed.

With a gasp she whirled to a small wheeled safe on the back wall. The dial clicked right, left, right. Then, with the chink of moving tumblers and the clank of the latch, the thick door opened on quiet hinges. She knelt, reached inside, patted the interior. Came up empty.

She staggered to her feet and crossed to him, her skin ashen, eyes dazed. "It's…it's…gone," she said in a reedy, strangled voice.

Then she wobbled, as if the starch had gone out of her. In one slow motion she crumpled, limp as a rag doll.

Nate caught her before she hit the floor. With the pale woman in his arms, his mind zipped back and remembered another woman.

"Mama!"

Nate's head snapped up, his vision cleared.

Eyes wide with fear, the son ran toward them. "Is she dead?" he said.

Rachel was dead. Not this woman.

Poor tyke had lost his pa and now must believe he'd lost his mother, too. "Your ma's fine. She's fainted, that's all."

"What's fainted?"

"It's like falling asleep." Nate forced a reassuring smile. "She'll wake up soon."

Beside Nate, the little boy settled on his haunches and patted his mother's arm. "Mama, are you tired?"

Nate removed his hat and fanned the widow's face. Smelling salts would bring her around. Not something Nate carried in his line of work.

He brushed a tendril of hair off the widow's pale cheek. Under his fingertips, her skin was soft as silk.

The click of a clock's pendulum echoed in the silence. With each passing tick, the boy's bravado crumbled. "Mama, wake up! Please!" he said, tears spilling down his face.

In way over his head, Nate groped for words. He'd never been around children. How could he comfort this one?

The widow groaned, rolling her head from side to side.

Her son gazed up at him, panic sparking in his eyes. "Something's wrong with my mama. Help her! Please, mister!"

"I'll help her, I promise." As soon as the words left his lips, Nate knew he'd made a hasty promise to stop the boy's pleading. A promise he couldn't keep.

Once again. Another failure. More lives ruined.

He tamped down the remorse swirling in his gut. This woman wasn't his responsibility. How could Richards wager his family's future on the turn of a card? His wife and son deserved better.

A temptation to give back the deed slid through him. Only for a moment. Nate couldn't sacrifice his sister's future. Not after what she'd sacrificed for him.

Once Mrs. Richards had time to think about it, she would know, as he did, she'd lost the shop. Though he didn't relish the pain he would cause, Nate would not help the widow as he'd promised her son.

All he would bring Carly Richards was trouble.

Chapter Two

Where am I?

Carly closed her eyes, giving her head a little shake, and then opened them again, the scent of soap, leather and peppermint filling her nostrils. Shadows slowly came into focus.

She peered into gray eyes. Gray eyes rimmed with charcoal and filled with concern.

Intriguing eyes. Who was—?

A small face popped into view. Henry. Tears spiking his lashes and running down his cheeks. Why was he crying?

Her son's lower lip trembled. "Mama."

"I'm all right, sweetie," she said, though she had no idea what had happened.

Then the memory came rushing back. Those eyes she'd gazed into, those eyes she'd found intriguing, belonged to Nate Sergeant. Max's killer. A dangerous man out to seize her shop.

And yet she lay nestled in the varmint's arms, thinking how good he smelled. As if his touch burned her flesh, Carly jerked upright and gathered her son close.

"You're not dead!" Henry beamed up at her.

She kissed her boy's wet cheeks. "I'm fine, Henry," she said. "Just fine."

But she wasn't fine.

Carly had poured her life's blood into this shop. Found satisfaction in the work. Earned a living here. She'd made a life for herself and her child in the four small rooms at the back. Without this shop, how would she manage? Where would they go?

"I won't give up my business," she said, her voice high, thin, almost a screech.

"Don't worry, Mama." Henry pointed at Max's killer. "The man said he'd help you. He promised."

Carly's eyes darted to Nate Sergeant. Under the force of her gaze, he all but squirmed. He'd help her, all right. Help her lose her shop and everything in it.

Still, she'd lashed out at the man, not a good example for her son. "Let me up, Henry."

Her son scooted out of the way.

In one fluid motion, the bounty hunter sprang to his feet. Before she could stop him, he took her hand and helped her rise. The startling warmth and gentleness of his touch felt nothing like Max's cold, hard grip.

Chiding herself for falling for such trickery, Carly pulled herself erect and faced her enemy.

Broad-shouldered, feet apart, he towered over her, expression closed, gaze firm, as if trying to squash her with a mere look. Well, she wasn't some helpless bug.

Not with her pistol buried in the deep pocket of her skirt. She'd bought the Smith and Wesson and learned to shoot, determined to do whatever she must to protect her son.

She bit back a sigh. No matter how strong the temptation, she couldn't shoot this sidewinder for claiming her business.

Still, no one was going to take away that security. *No one.*

"I want you to leave," she said. "My son has had a scare. I won't allow you to subject him to more."

His brow furrowed. "We have to talk."

"We have nothing to talk about. Come, Henry," she said, guiding the boy toward the back. "Go to your room and close the door. I'll be right there."

Henry complied with lagging steps and backward glances.

She waited until she heard the door to their quarters click shut, then rounded on him. "The only person I will be speaking with is Sheriff Truitt. Max's name may be on the deed, but as you *well know*, my husband is dead. As his widow, everything he owned is mine. He had no right to gamble his son's future."

"I agree with you, Mrs. Richards, but the fact is he did."

"If you actually have the deed, you'd show it. I don't believe a word you've said."

"I left the deed with my sister for safekeeping. Her husband hid it so carefully, took me a month to find it."

"So you claim." She flung out a hand, pointing her forefinger at him. "I will fight you! This shop provides our living and our home. I'll do whatever I must to protect that."

"Sorry to bring more trouble to your door, ma'am, but—"

"I've faced trouble, Mr. Sergeant. All a man could throw at me." She straightened her shoulders and slapped hands on hips. "I'm not intimidated."

"I'm not trying to intimidate you." He exhaled. "I'm trying to make you understand the outcome is beyond your control. Your husband lost the deed to my brother-in-law *before* he died."

"How convenient he can't deny your claim. And *you*—" she raised a hand and pointed a steady finger at him "—did the killing."

"I had no choice. It was either him or me." Jaw jutting, face flushed, the bounty hunter clamped his hat on his head. "The law will decide who owns this property."

"Gnaw Bone doesn't have a lawyer, much less a judge—"

"At some point, a circuit judge will pass through. In the meantime, I'll bring my sister—and the deed—to town. She'll be the one running this shop. You might want to look for someplace else to live."

"I will do nothing of the sort." She stalked to the door, opened it. "I suggest you make other arrangements for your sister, Mr. Sergeant. Good day, *sir*."

As the door closed behind him, Carly wilted into a chair. "Why, Lord?" She spoke aloud. "Why, after all we've been through, have You allowed a new threat? Do You even hear my prayers?"

Nate strode out, the widow's sarcasm in the "sir" and the slamming door behind him ringing in his ears. He'd let his temper get the best of him. Still, the widow had all but called him a liar and had pointed that dainty finger at him like a gunslinger taking aim.

He unwound the reins from the hitching post, swung into the saddle and rode toward the livery he'd seen earlier. Each clop of Maverick's hooves thudded against his conscience. Why should the widow trust his word? He'd killed her husband. Claimed he had a deed he hadn't produced. When he came back with that deed, she'd fight him tooth and nail. Carly Richards wasn't a woman to take things lying down. No doubt life with that scoundrel of a husband had made her hard, tough.

If a husband's property belonged to his wife as much as to him, a judge might rule Richards had no right to gamble away shared property. But from what Nate had seen, even if that property belonged to his wife, a husband had the authority to do with marital assets as he saw fit.

Once Carly Richards realized Nate had no intention of backing down, she'd give up the fight.

Where would she and the boy live then? How would she earn an income? Who would look after them?

Nate clamped his jaw. He couldn't get soft about the widow's plight. Anna had no other means to make a living. Carly Richards was able-bodied; a good housekeeper and cook from the tidy appearance of her shop and the robust look of her son. Surely she had numerous skills to find another job in Gnaw Bone. Perhaps she had family nearby.

He had to focus on his sister, the one person he owed everything. Anna was depending on him to make things right, which he would do.

Then he'd settle the score with Shifty Stogsdill, the outlaw he hunted.

At the thought of hitting the trail, Nate's stomach twisted. He wouldn't admit it to anyone, but he was tired. Tired of huddling near a campfire and eating lousy food. Tired of sleeping under the stars on the hard, cold ground. Tired of endless hours in the saddle chasing lawless, brutal men.

As weary as he was of his life, he was a skilled bounty hunter. Bringing Stogsdill to justice would silence his loved ones calling to him from the grave.

The reward money, along with the proceeds from the shop, would set Anna up for life. Then he would have kept his promise to his parents and repaid his debt to his sister. No amount of money would compensate for the handicap she would live with her entire life.

Stogsdill's trail had gone cold, but rumor had it the outlaw was sweet on a woman living in the area. The reason Nate had ridden this way, planning to bunk with Anna and Walt while investigating the rumor.

If only he'd arrived four hours earlier, he might have

saved Walt's life. One more if-only Nate couldn't fix. A long list of regrets that plagued him.

But he could move his sister to Gnaw Bone. It meant hiring a wagon to haul her possessions. Not all that many, certainly nothing of material value, but she'd never leave family keepsakes behind.

Outside the livery Nate looped Maverick's reins to the rail. A hand-painted for-sale sign caught his eye. If the lettering over the doors meant anything, how did the proprietor, Morris Mood, hope to sell this run-down property?

Hmm, the small print indicated the sale included a vacant house. If it was habitable, perhaps Nate could work out a deal with the owner. Now that he'd met the pretty widow and her small son, he couldn't stomach the idea of evicting them from their home.

Inside the stable, he inhaled the scent of hay, leather and manure; heard the soft whinnying of horses, easing the tension in his neck and zipping him back to the time he'd wrangled horses on a Texas ranch. The pay had been lousy. Not nearly enough money to provide for Anna, but that year had taught him plenty about horses.

Maybe, just maybe, he could do this: run a livery and settle in one place. He tamped down the silly notion. He was not good at staying put, but he was good at his job.

Still, with Walt dead, Anna had no one to look after her but him. He couldn't ride off as he'd done many times before, leaving his sister behind with the hope his inept brother-in-law would make a decent living. This time he had to stay long enough to see Anna find her place in the community. Once she was settled in the rooms behind the seamstress shop, he'd be on his way.

He strolled down the aisle between the stalls, studying the horses. Unlike the dilapidated barn, the animals looked healthy, their coats groomed, their bedding clean, water buckets full. Clearly the owner cared about his horses.

Nate passed the tack room, then stopped outside the door leading into the office. A stoop-shouldered man with grizzled hair hunched over a ledger, his spectacles sliding down his nose. A broken bit and two shabby halters lay scattered on the desk, alongside a tattered saddle cinch and a rusty horseshoe. The owner and his office looked as frayed as his business.

"Mr. Mood?"

With a startled squeak, the elderly gentleman jerked up his head and then staggered to his feet, his face tinged with pink. "Didn't know anyone was about. Need a horse? Rig?"

"A wagon." He motioned toward the entrance. "And information about that sign out front."

"You're new in town." The old gent tugged at his suspenders. "Looking to buy this place?"

Why would Nate do that? "Nope, don't have the money. But in exchange for a place to live, I could work here."

The owner chuckled. "I don't have the money to pay you a wage, neither. Reckon that makes us even." He pointed to a bale of straw. "Take the weight off," he said, plopping into his desk chair with a sigh. "I wouldn't be looking to sell, exceptin' my wife needs a dry climate. If I can find a buyer, I'd take Betsy to Arizona. Good weather for consumption."

"I'm sorry your wife's sick." Nate sat, his gaze roaming his surroundings. "I could restore the place. Make the livery more attractive to a buyer."

"I can't keep up with repairs. Reckon it's as run-down as I am." He drummed knobby fingers on the desk. "All that hammering and sawing could spook my horses. You know how to handle 'em?"

"I spent a year as wrangler on a spread in Texas."

"That don't mean you'll treat 'em right."

"I'd never mistreat a horse—any animal."

Yet only minutes before, Nate had mistreated a woman.

The truth of that gnawed at him. No matter how tough she'd tried to appear, he'd seen the fear beneath Mrs. Richards's bluster. She'd reminded him of an abused horse, alert and skittish, ready to rear and kick, expecting trouble, prepared for battle. His stomach clenched. Had Richards abused his wife?

"I'll tell you what," Mr. Mood said. "I could use the help, but as I said, I can't afford to pay a wage. What if I applied what you should earn toward buying the place?" He pointed over his shoulder. "And throw in the living quarters behind the livery? Me and the missus live a few miles out now, so the house sits empty. Has two bedrooms, kitchen, small parlor—nothing fancy but it's livable and furnished."

"I'm not interested in buying the livery, but I'm moving my sister to Gnaw Bone. We'll need a place to bunk." His gaze roamed the cobwebbed corners, the glass in the window caked with dirt. "Anna is, uh, persnickety."

"The house is in better condition than the stable. I'll spiff the place up, if that's what's worrying you."

Mood's plan didn't fence Nate in. He could make improvements until the judge settled the shop ownership. Nate offered his hand. "I'm willing to try each other out, see if the arrangement fits."

The old codger reached a blue-veined hand and shook, his grip surprisingly strong. "Gives us both time. You might like working here and change your mind." He gave a nod. "If I like you, trust you with my horses, you could finish buying the livery on contract, a set amount each month."

Nate wouldn't be changing his mind. He had no interest in staying in this two-bit town tethered to a livery and half a dozen horses. Nate had spent much of his adult life wandering. He had no idea how to handle that kind of permanence. The one time he'd tried to settle down had ended in disaster. A moving target was safer for everyone.

Nate paid the rate for a wagon and team. "I'll return the rig tomorrow," he said, following Mood toward the stalls.

Anna wanted him nearby. Nate would give her that for now. He had enough money to ignore the wanted posters in his saddlebags. If the circuit judge ruled in Anna's favor, as Nate expected, she'd have a solid income to handle her bills. Then he would leave the good folks of Gnaw Bone before Stogsdill came looking for revenge and someone got hurt.

Mood tramped toward him, leading two draft horses. Nate joined him and they moseyed to the open end of the livery where a wagon waited, its green paint peeling. While in Gnaw Bone, Nate would scrape and repaint that wagon.

Perhaps if he kept busy enough, he could hold memories at bay.

A yellow, shaggy dog crawled out from under the wagon, his tail giving a slow wag.

Mood reached a hand. The dog stepped into his touch. "She's got me pegged as a softy." He raised the dog's chin. "Soon as I get this team hitched, I'll share my lunch. But I'll be moving West, too far a trip for you." Mood glanced over his shoulder at Nate. "She'd make a fine watchdog, if you've a mind to keep her."

The mutt couldn't harm a flea. "I'll be moving on, too."

"She'd be good company for your sister."

A dog underfoot might trip Anna. Mood would see that soon enough.

With slow, patient motions and gentle words to the horses, the old man hitched the team to the wagon. "This here is Mark. The other is Matthew. Named 'em after the Gospel writers. Feed, water and rub them down tonight."

As if Nate hadn't the faintest idea how to care for

horses. "Yes, sir." Nate tied Maverick to the rear of the wagon. "Once we're settled in, I'll start making repairs."

"Your coming proves the Good Lord is watching over me and Betsy, that's sure."

Mood wouldn't believe Nate was the answer to his prayer if he knew the trouble he was bringing Widow Richards.

With a nod, Nate climbed into the wagon, released the brake, and drove down the alley behind the livery, passing the cabin where he and Anna would live.

Across the alley, what had to be the backside of the seamstress shop, a female dashed out the door and across the yard as if chased by a pack of rabid dogs.

Ah, Mrs. Richards. Where was she going in such an all-fire hurry? She caught sight of him, slowed and dropped her skirts, then strode on, her mouth set in a grim line.

He hauled back on the reins. "Is something wrong?"

She gored him with her gaze. "Perhaps. I'm on my way to speak with Sheriff Truitt. About you."

"I have nothing to hide."

"So you say." She motioned to the wagon. "Glad to see you're leaving town. Don't let me hold you up."

"Only be gone long enough to bring my sister and her possessions back to Gnaw Bone."

Mrs. Richards's cheeks paled. "Morris wouldn't rent you that wagon if he knew your intentions."

"Mr. Mood has hired me to make improvements to the livery. Anna and I will be staying in his vacant house."

Chest heaving, she plopped dainty hands on her hips. A female version of David pitted against Goliath. The stones in her sling of the verbal variety. Yet the fire in her eyes made her a formidable foe. She'd stop at nothing to protect her child's future.

Nate had dealt with violent men, cagey men, the vilest of men, but he had no idea how to handle this tiny woman's colossal loathing. Of him.

What did she despise him for most? Killing her trigger-happy, back-shooting husband? Or threatening ownership of the shop? Well, he wasn't here to win anyone's approval, especially a woman trying to stand in the way of his sister's new beginning.

"If you think by working and living under my nose, you'll bully me into giving up what's rightfully mine, you're wrong."

"The judge will decide who's entitled to the shop. Until then, my sister and I need a place to live."

"In that case, I suggest you keep your distance."

She hustled off. A woman on a mission, no doubt hoping Sheriff Truitt would ride him out of town, tarred and feathered.

Well, he had no desire to remain longer than necessary. The life of a bounty hunter suited him. He had two purposes; locking up violent men who preyed on the innocent and seeing Stogsdill pay for his crimes.

"Move on, Mark, Matthew." As he turned onto Main Street, a strange, unsettling awareness sank to his gut. In the livery, for the first time in ages, he'd felt at home, at peace. The prospect of staying put dredged up a long-buried desire to belong somewhere, filling him with a yearning he didn't understand.

He shook his head, trying to dislodge the foolish notion. To stay meant settling down, letting others in. The mere idea tightened an invisible band around his neck.

Once he'd been complacent. Had believed he could be a small-town sheriff and have a wife and children. Whenever he got close and cared about others, people got hurt or...died. He'd never again take that risk.

Chapter Three

Carly gave a shove and the door rattled shut behind her. The desk was cluttered with stacks of paper, a pair of shiny handcuffs and a coiled rope, but the office chair sat empty.

"Sheriff Truitt?"

The lawman stepped from the back, a holster riding his hips, a tray in his hand. "Why, howdy, Mrs. Richards." His gaze landed on the spotless dishes. "If I didn't know better, I'd say a dog lapped these plates clean. Reckon the Harders brothers appreciated the stew, Miss Sarah's special today."

Max used to say food was good at Sarah Harvey's café, but one look at the cook gave a man heartburn. Max had a jab for every man and woman in town.

"Shore did, Sheriff," a voice called.

Through the open door, Carly caught sight of the Harders twins peering at her from a cell. Even as they sat side by side on the bunk, Carly couldn't tell Lloyd and Lester apart from here. The two went everywhere together, getting into one scrape after another. Their latest escapade—using the sign outside her shop for target practice.

"Food's way better'n Ma's, but don't you be telling her I said so, ma'am."

Carly had tasted Mrs. Harders's cooking at church potlucks and couldn't disagree. "I'd never hurt your mother's feelings."

"We're right sorry for shooting up your sign, Miz Richards."

"Yep, plumb ashamed of ourselves."

"I sometimes suspect you two get into trouble just to get some decent victuals," Sheriff Truitt grumbled. "Well, your feet will be under your ma's table by suppertime."

"Aw, can't you keep us another night, Sheriff?"

"This ain't no hotel. I aim to make your lives so miserable you'll think twice about another drunken shooting spree."

The sheriff closed the door to the brothers' groans and turned toward Carly. "They'll spend the month doing chores for you, Mrs. Richards. Work 'em hard. The nastier the job the better."

Carly gave a nod. But had no idea what they could do. The Harders brothers didn't appear to be good at much except carousing.

"They should pay for a new sign, but money's scarce and their ma—"

"Sheriff, I'm here on another matter."

"What's that?"

Carly met the sheriff's inquisitive gaze. "That bounty hunter paid me a visit."

"From the look on your face, I'd say he didn't come to apologize for killing your husband."

Anyone who hunted down outlaws for the bounty was surely driven by greed. "Could he have gone after Max for the reward?"

"Nope, no time for Max to make the wanted posters."

"Well, he's looking to make money from Max's death."

"How so?"

"He claims his sister's husband—the man Max killed in

Kentucky—won the deed to my shop in a poker game. He says his sister has the deed and that makes her the owner."

The sheriff frowned. "Do you believe him?"

"No! I don't trust the word of a killer." Carly sighed. "But I checked. The deed's not in my safe."

"Then he could be speaking the truth."

"Well, yes. But Max could've moved the deed." She paced the room, then turned to the lawman. "Sheriff, I want you to do something. You can't let some stranger ride into town and take my property," she said, unable to keep her voice from trembling.

"No need to get worked up, Mrs. Richards. No one is taking anything while I'm around, leastwise not illegally."

Carly breathed in. Out. In. Out. Until her racing pulse returned to a steady rhythm. "*If* the bounty hunter has the deed, he could've stolen it, even killed Max for it. Max can't accuse him from the grave."

"If Max anted the deed and lost—"

"He had no right to risk our livelihood and the roof over our heads!"

"No moral right." The sheriff rubbed his nape. "Not sure about his legal right."

"Are you saying I could lose the shop?" Carly shoved each shaky word from her mouth, barely louder than a whisper.

"No point borrowing trouble. Time will tell."

Easy for the sheriff to say. "I have no legal recourse?"

"If you were asking about horse stealing, I'd know the law. Property rights ain't my specialty."

The door to the sheriff's office opened. Nate Sergeant stood in the opening. Tall, broad-shouldered, a six-shooter strapped to his hip. Even from across the room, Carly could feel the power radiating from him.

He removed his Stetson and gave Carly a nod. "Sheriff, I suppose Mrs. Richards has explained the situation."

"She has."

"I'll be bringing my sister to Gnaw Bone tomorrow, along with the deed to Mrs. Richards's shop."

"If you've got that deed, I'd like to see it. Better yet, I'd like to keep it here in my safe until the circuit judge can straighten out this mess."

Nate Sergeant gave a nod. "Any idea when that will be?"

"Depends on the number of cases he's hearing."

"Sheriff," Carly said, "can you check his itinerary?"

"I'll send a wire and see what I can find out, Mrs. Richards."

"Thank you."

Carly said goodbye, then strode toward the exit. Sheriff Truitt had been no help. She heaved a sigh. The sheriff wasn't the troublemaker in town. That label belonged to Nate Sergeant, the man holding the door for her as she strode through, and then followed her out.

"Mrs. Richards…" he said.

Carly stopped and turned toward him, steeling her spine against whatever he had to say.

His gaze was surprisingly soft, gentle. "I've brought harm to way too many. I surely don't want to hurt you," he said, his eyes filling with despair so wretched Carly couldn't look away. "I wish things were different, ma'am."

Carly had an urge to try to ease his torment, to offer absolution. She reached a tentative hand toward his jaw. Close enough to feel the warmth from his skin.

At the gesture, his pupils flared into smoldering pools of black.

Carly's breath caught. She jerked her hand away.

Without a word he turned on booted heel, strode to the wagon out front and clamored aboard.

As she watched him drive off, her stomach tumbled. How could she have connected with a man determined to ruin their lives? Nate Sergeant might regret harming her, but that wouldn't stop this driven man accustomed to getting his way.

Inside her gloves, Carly's hands chilled. He had appeared confident, as if he'd known the law was on his side and she was destined to lose her shop. If the judge agreed, she'd have to move, start over. Leave everything she'd worked hard to build.

Lord, why did You allow a new threat? Hasn't my son been through enough? Why?

Well, she would handle this. Henry would be home from school soon. No time to search. After she tucked him in tonight, she'd look for that deed, proving the bounty hunter was lying through his even, white teeth.

Carly sat on her son's bed. Across from her Henry tugged his muslin nightshirt to his knees, his head bent low, revealing his slender nape and the curve of his velvety cheek.

With a grin Henry scrambled up beside her and cuddled close, gazing up at her. "Mama, is that nice man coming back?"

"What nice man?"

"The man that promised to help you. When you was asleep."

Henry thought that bounty hunter was nice? Nate Sergeant would most likely show up tomorrow with his sister in tow and try to toss them out.

Well, she wouldn't budge. "I expect he will." *I expect he will help us to the street.* But she couldn't say that without scaring her son.

She gazed into his guileless blue eyes. "Why do you call Mr. Sergeant nice?"

"You fell down and he caught you. He looked scared. Not scary like Pa."

Uninvited images surfaced in Carly's mind, of a full

head of dark hair, the shadow of beard along his chiseled jaw, gray eyes laced with regret, the pupils rimmed in charcoal. Those pupils had enlarged, and she'd felt the strangest pull.

Ridiculous.

Nate Sergeant might be handsome, manly, even uneasy about snatching her shop, but that wouldn't stop him.

"I thought you was dead, Mama. I was afraid."

"Oh, sweet boy, I'm sorry I frightened you."

His chin trembling, Henry clutched her arm. "Are you sick?"

"No, I'm healthy and strong. Why, I could wrestle a grizzly bear and win." Carly tugged him onto her lap.

He smiled up at her, his fear forgotten. "I'm strong, too," he said, fisting his right hand and gazing at the tiny swell beneath his sleeve. "See my muscle?"

"You are strong. Now climb into bed, my little monkey."

Henry grabbed the stuffed elephant she'd made for him, its trunk bent and droopy, and scrambled under the covers, pulling them up until only his eyebrows stuck above the quilt. "I'm sleepin', Mama."

"Is that so?" Carly leaned forward and peeled back the edge of the blanket with one finger. "Well, I don't see a sleeping boy. I see a pretending boy." She leaned in, pressed a kiss to Henry's forehead, pausing long enough to inhale his sweet, innocent fragrance. He filled her heart with joy, made her world complete. "I expect a story will make you sleepy."

The blanket inched down until she could see mischievous blue eyes, an impish grin. "I love stories."

Book in hand, Carly slid into the space beside her son. "That's good, because I love reading you stories."

Head cradled on his hands, Henry curved toward her, a sixty-pound bundle of energy that brought infinite happiness to her life. Moments like these were what mattered.

Moments like these filled her life with meaning. Moments like these had gotten her through the worst days with Max and had her counting her blessings twice over.

Henry listened intently to every word, only interrupting to mimic the sounds made by the animals in the story.

Carly tucked the book on the nightstand. "Time for our bedtime song." The nighttime ritual reminded Carly of her mother's faith and the memories of the happy times they'd shared.

Carly cupped her son's cheek in her palm, and then sang, "Father, we thank Thee for the night and for the blessed morning light. For food and rest and loving care and all that makes the day so fair."

Lying back on the pillow, his features sweeter than a rosy-cheeked cupid on a postcard Valentine, Henry tilted his face to the ceiling, as if singing for God Himself. "Help me do the things I should and be to others kind and good. In all I do in work or play to grow more loving every day."

Henry rolled his head toward her and smiled. "Does Grandma hear us singing?"

"She might. If she does, she's proud of her grandson."

"She's proud of you, too, Mama."

What had Carly ever done to deserve this precious boy? Her throat knotted. She was all that stood between Henry and the ugliness of this world. Was she up to the task of guiding her son to become a man who loved God, a man who thought of others, a man who lived the words of this bedtime song?

To protect Henry and ensure that happy life she wanted for him, she must first save their home and livelihood.

Help me, Lord. Please, save my shop.

She kissed Henry on both cheeks, and then walked to the door. "Sleep tight."

"'Night, Mama." Henry's eyelids were already lowering, his mouth opening in a wide yawn.

Once satisfied her son was asleep, Carly began her search for the deed. In the attic, Max's trunk was tucked in a dark corner of the back wall, off by itself. Much like the man. During the eight years of her marriage, Max had dwelled on the fringe of her life. What did she know about him, really?

Inside the trunk under a pile of photo albums, Carly found Lillian's Bible, the binding wobbly, the pages worn, verses underlined. Stuck beside the Twenty-third Psalm was an envelope addressed to Max, the flap open. She pulled out and unfolded a single sheet of paper, the words written with an unsteady hand.

Dearest Max,
I pen this letter knowing my time on earth is coming to an end. I love you, son. I will die with a prayer for you on my lips, that you will return to the Lord and one day we will meet again.
Your loving mother

Tears stung Carly's eyes. From what she knew, Lillian's prayer had gone unanswered. If she'd tried harder, could Carly have led Max to the Lord? Or would she have paid dearly for suggesting he needed God and should attend church?

The choice had been Max's to make. The consequence, his doing, yet Lillian had also paid a price for her son's rebellion.

What would Carly do if Henry made bad choices, turned his back on God? To be both father and mother to her son weighed heavily on her, but better to rear him alone than to expose him to another bad influence, another heartless man.

"I'm sorry, Lillian. So very sorry." With a sigh, Carly

returned the letter to the envelope and closed the flap. If only she could shut out her regrets as easily.

Life was never that simple.

Please Lord, if the deed is here, help me find it.

Filled with a surge of energy, Carly scoured every nook and cranny, then left the attic. She would turn the house inside out and upside down, search every drawer, clothespress and cupboard. The deed had to be here somewhere.

What could Nate say to convince his sister that her future depended upon that deed lying on the table in front of her?

Dressed in black, her tidy bun perched high on her head and her mouth set in a stubborn line, Nate knew all too well that Anna was prepared for battle. Yet Nate knew he would win. He had logic and necessity on his side. Even his softhearted sister would see she must accept reality.

Still, that deed would force another widow from her home, from her place of business. Who would help Mrs. Richards move her things? What would happen to her and her son?

Nate steeled his spine. The widow was able-bodied and strong-minded; like a cat, she would land on her feet.

"Are you ready, sis?" he said, reaching for the deed.

Anna thrust out her hand, palm up. "I don't want anything to do with that shop. Walt lost his life over that deed, same as his killer. And you could've been killed." She shook her head as if trying to rid her mind of such ugliness.

"I didn't want to kill Richards. He forced my hand."

"You'd never kill anyone unless you had to," Anna said, her tone gentle without a speck of condemnation. "But that doesn't change the fact that I don't want any part of that deed."

Nate tapped his forefinger on the document. "Anna, this piece of paper means you'll have a place to do your stitching, a business with customers ready to pay for your efforts. God's bringing good out of bad, giving you a fresh beginning."

"I know God's in control and I need to trust Him, but I hate change, you know that. I'd much rather stay here."

"The new tenants are moving in tomorrow." He grinned. "Doubt they're expecting a boarder."

Anna fiddled with her handkerchief. "What if things don't work out in Gnaw Bone? Just the name of the town makes me think twice. I've never run a shop before." She shoved the deed away. "This could be a mistake."

"Or an opportunity. Last I knew, you were mighty good with a needle. Did you make that dress?"

"Yes. I had enough black fabric to make a couple dresses and a skirt."

"To own a dress like that would give any woman confidence. Think what your talent could mean to ladies living in a town with the name of Gnaw Bone."

Anna chuckled. "You should consider becoming a salesman."

With a wink, Nate scooped up the deed and slipped it into his saddlebag before Anna changed her mind, then helped his sister to her feet and out the door.

All morning Anna had dithered here and there, cleaning nonexistent dirt from the corners and under the bed. Scoured the sink, watered the flowers and garden, straightened the curtains covering the windows, putting off the inevitable.

Nate understood it was hard to leave memories behind. "Thought we'd stop at the cemetery on our way past so you can say goodbye to Walt."

"He wanted only to give me an easier life…" Anna fell silent, blinking back tears. "Now he's gone."

The pain in Anna's soft gray eyes told of her love for Walt Hankins, a gentle, unassuming man, but not much of a provider. He'd risked and lost the family farm. Then year after year, he'd toiled on this tenant farm for half the crop, barely scrimping by. Whenever Nate earned a reward, he'd sent Anna money. Money that Walt soon lost on one fool scheme after another. More than once Nate had been tempted to knock some sense into Walt. If he had, perhaps his brother-in-law would be alive today.

He inhaled the cool morning air and let his gaze travel the shed and barn, then on to the rolling fields and budding woods beyond. The nearest farm was barely visible over the next rise. With Walt gone, Nate would rest easier knowing Anna lived in town surrounded by people. Had a doctor nearby.

At the wagon, Nate tugged the brim of his Stetson low to block the glare of the rising sun, then shoved the last trunk further into the back crammed with every item Anna owned.

She turned to him, disquiet in her eyes. "I won't know a single person in that town."

No doubt reeling from the sudden changes in her life, his sister had grown timid, not at all like her. Once they were settled, Anna would handle the move as she'd handled every hardship in her life, with strong faith in God.

"Won't take you long to get acquainted." He wrapped one arm around her shoulders. "I'll be there ready to step in should an unhappy matron complain you made her hem too short."

A gentle smile riding her lips, Anna laid a palm on Nate's cheek. "My protector," she said. "You're always looking after me. How can I thank you?"

"Make me a cherry pie, sis, and we'll call it even."

"A cherry pie it is." She accepted a helping hand onto the wagon seat. "Now, if you had a wife, she'd make all the pies you could eat."

"Why bother, when you make the best pies anywhere?"

Nate tied Maverick to the back of the wagon, then tossed his saddlebag on the seat and clambered aboard.

He shot his sister a grin, to keep her from seeing how much the responsibility for her weighed on his shoulders. Not just for her, but for all the defenseless. He'd seen first-hand how quickly life could make a detour, how quickly life could end.

He had promised God he would do whatever it took to protect Anna.

Walt had left her with no home, no money, in a mess. Nate had spent his life cleaning up the messes others left behind.

This time he'd clean up the mess created by Max Richards and see that Anna got the future she deserved.

Up ahead, Nate caught a glimpse of a small white church, void of stained glass and steeple. Not much of merit compared to the grand churches he'd seen on his travels. Except here in this simple house of worship, at the age of twelve, he'd given his heart to Jesus. He'd been young, innocent.

No longer. The path he'd chosen stood between him and God.

He drove past the church to the cemetery, following the beaten-down grass winding between the rows of gravestones. Near the back, he stopped the team with a spoken word, set the brake and helped his sister down.

As he unhitched his horse to graze, a pair of cardinals darted into the evergreens surrounding the property. From the small barn across the way, a cow lowed. A reminder of his youth when he'd helped Pa milk their Holsteins twice a day, every day, all year long.

Nate offered his arm and Anna slipped hers through the crook. They climbed a small slope and stopped in front of the simple headstone marking their parents' grave. Weeds grew at the base, tangling up and onto the engraved surface.

He knelt, ripped out the vines and tossed them aside.

"Who'll do this when we're not here?" Anna said, her voice as bleak as the black she wore.

"We'll get back."

Though he saw the doubt in her eyes, she gave a nod, then gathered the weeds and carried them to the compost.

As she walked on to Walt's grave, seeking a private moment with her husband, Nate sat back on his heels at their parents' headstone.

He traced the inscription, his fingers slipping over crevices forming the names Ephraim and Victoria Sergeant. *Beloved parents.* Good, hardworking, God-fearing people. They'd taken the first trip of their lives to visit Ma's sister in Kansas. They'd never made it. Outlaws robbed the train, killing four passengers, his parents among the dead.

For what? A few dollars and a paltry sack of jewelry.

Shifty Stogsdill had been the leader of the gang.

Nate saw Stogsdill's face in every fugitive he tracked down.

Before his parents had left, they'd asked him to look after Anna, always concerned someone would take advantage of her sweet, giving nature.

He'd tried. With everything in him, he'd tried.

A gust of air heaved from his chest. In truth, the very day Anna married Walt, Nate had left home, compelled to bring Stogsdill to justice. More than once, he'd come close to capturing the villain. But somehow Stogsdill had managed to slip away.

Then he'd met Rachel, a pastor's daughter, a sweet, gentle young woman, and he'd gotten complacent, thinking he could trade the life of a bounty hunter for a small-town sheriff's badge.

Until the day Stogsdill had come to Rachel's hometown,

gunning for Nate. As they'd crossed the street, Rachel had been chattering about their upcoming nuptials.

The thud of pounding hooves raised the hair on his nape. Drawing his gun, Nate whirled toward the road.

A flash of red, the glint of metal from Stogsdill's hand.

A blast.

Nate fired just as a bullet whizzed past.

Rachel tumbled. Down, down, down.

Stogsdill's aim had been off, a few inches to the right, and Rachel, an innocent young woman, lay on the street, her shirtwaist oozing red as life seeped out of her.

Tears stung his eyes. He'd been a fool to put aside the life of a bounty hunter for a sheriff's job, enabling Stogsdill to track him to Rachel's hometown. Even four years later, Nate could barely live with his failure to avenge her death.

If it was the last thing he did, Nate would see that Stogsdill got what he deserved. He couldn't expect God to help him. Not when he had blood on his hands and vengeance in his heart.

A gentle hand pressed into his shoulder. "You okay?"

Nate slowed his breathing. "I'm fine." He forced a smile. "And eager to see your handiwork walking the streets of Gnaw Bone."

"Walking dresses?" Anna laughed. "That's something I've got to see."

The jingle of the horses' harness brought Nate to his feet. "We'd better get going if we hope to reach Gnaw Bone by supper."

As they walked to the wagon, a blue jay squawked from a tree branch overhead. Puffy clouds inched across the topaz sky. In this peaceful moment, the earth had righted on its axis.

Yet, out there somewhere, Stogsdill waited. Armed and dangerous. Nate had given up normalcy, peace, to protect the defenseless.

His grip on Anna's arm tightened.

"Is something wrong?" Anna said.

"Everything's fine."

Or would be. Once Nate saw Stogsdill rot in jail or buried six feet under.

Chapter Four

The grand dame of Gnaw Bone, all three of her stacked chins quivering with intensity, leaned toward Carly. "Surely you can handle my daughter's wedding gown and trousseau. I'll pay you well. More money than you can earn in six months or more," Mrs. Schwartz said, her no-nonsense tone carrying an edge.

An edge that held a warning Carly couldn't miss.

The wealthiest family in town, the Schwartz women gave Carly considerable business. Business she welcomed and appreciated. But the sketch of an elaborate creation Mrs. Schwartz had laid on the counter wasn't just any dress that could be whipped up in a couple of days. This confection was to be Vivian Schwartz's wedding gown.

A spoiled young woman accustomed to the finest. In Vivian's estimation, the finest wedding gown could only be created in Paris, France. Not Gnaw Bone, Indiana. Vivian had made that abundantly clear—twice—in today's meeting.

The bride's glum expression conveyed her resentment of turning to a small-town seamstress. A miscommunication with the French fashion designer meant the gown and trousseau would arrive long *after* the ceremony. Telegrams back and forth had riled the designer, who'd refused to rush the order. Apparently the matriarch of Gnaw Bone was no match for a Paris modiste.

Her auburn hair and pale green eyes partially hidden by a flower-festooned hat, turned up in the back and held in place by two hat pins, Vivian jabbed a manicured nail at the front and back sketches on the counter. "Can you reproduce this dress *exactly* as you see it here?" she said, her young voice rising to an unladylike shrill. "And I mean *exactly*, down to the last button."

Carly forced a patient smile. "With less than a month till your wedding, there's no time to send for the exact lace and silk you specify."

"Gracious," Mrs. Schwartz said, her ample bosom heaving, setting the ostrich plumes on her hat in motion. "We would have told you sooner if we'd known about this debacle. Surely you have something similar. At least you *had* a decent array of imported lace and fabric when I made the selections for my dress."

A dress that was almost completed. Almost. And now adding a large complicated order to an already tight schedule...

Carly's smile wobbled. "I'm sure I can duplicate the Paris design. I have a bolt of white silk and several options for lace. Would you care to look, Miss Vivian?"

"Is there no other choice?" Vivian turned to her mother, as if she expected to be whisked off to Paris that very afternoon.

The melodramatic sigh sliding from Vivian's lips had Carly wondering if this young woman was mature enough to handle life's disappointments, much less enter a marriage.

For Carly they'd been one and the same.

Would things have been different if she'd waited, been older, more sure of herself and her place in the world? As she was now. She would have seen Max for what he was—a man with no sense of right and wrong—and would have known to refuse his proposal.

She didn't plan to marry again, but if she did, she'd marry a man of faith who shared her values.

Well, that thought was foolish. Besides, no such man was available.

Nate Sergeant is available.

Absurd. The bounty hunter was another Max—violent, unreliable and chasing after trouble.

"Well, are you going to show us the options?" Mrs. Schwartz asked, jerking Carly back to the task at hand.

"I'm sorry, of course."

"Mother…" Vivian whined. "Do I have to?"

Mrs. Schwartz took her daughter's emerald-bejeweled hand. "Yes, unless you want to postpone the wedding."

"No! What would people think?"

"Then you must be realistic. I'm perfectly happy using Carly for my dress. She's familiar with both our measurements, and her work is excellent."

Vivian's lower lip protruded. "I had my heart set on the wedding dress of my dreams."

"I'm sorry, dear, but your dream gown wouldn't have done you much good riding the high seas on your wedding day. To think that snobbish woman refused to rush the work, as if our order was of no consequence. The reason I prefer using Carly, thereby keeping the work in the country."

"If you'll follow me, Miss Vivian, I'm sure you'll find something just as beautiful," Carly said, leading them to her stock of the finest fabric and lace tucked inside a case, protected from sun and dust.

Across the way, Lester and Lloyd stopped scrubbing the shop window to wave at her, and then returned to the task. Even from here, Carly could see smudges they'd missed.

"This is it?" Vivian's nose wrinkled, as if picking an unacceptable pig from a poke, but then with a sigh, she begrudgingly made fabric choices from the case and cupboards.

Carly showed her several designs for gowns and day dresses, and then entered selections into a notebook under the *S* page for Schwartz. "Miss Vivian, I have a record of your measurements from six months ago."

"That should be fine. Vivian never gains an ounce." Mrs. Schwartz handed Carly a list of the number of undergarments, nightgowns, day dresses, traveling suits and evening gowns they'd discussed. "Can you finish everything in three weeks? We'll need a week to pack her trousseau."

Carly couldn't risk alienating her best customer. Yet how could she finish all these garments in time?

Somehow she'd find a way, if she had to work day and night.

What if the circuit judge ruled against her, forcing her out of the shop before she could finish this order? Carly's hands trembled. What would she do then?

She straightened her spine. She couldn't think about that now. "I'll have them ready before the wedding," she vowed.

"Thank you, Carly. You've lifted a terrible weight off our shoulders." Mrs. Schwartz patted the bride's cheek. "Now come along, Vivian, and I'll buy you a sweet cake."

The two women left the shop. Lester and Lloyd doffed their hats and bowed at the waist, as if greeting royalty. Were they poking fun? Or merely acknowledging what everyone knew? The Schwartz family ran the town.

The bell jingled. Lester stuck his head in the door. "We finished the window, Miz Richards. See you tomorrow, first thing," he said, then joined his brother.

They sauntered across the street toward home; their idea of a full day apparently included an afternoon siesta.

Actually a nap sounded good. Carly dropped onto the

settee, surrounded by a pile of tagged fabric and laces. This order was far more than she'd expected. Her pulse skipped a beat. If the judge ruled against her, perhaps with the money she would earn, she could entice Nate Sergeant's sister to sell. That is, if Carly could finish all those garments in time to earn payment.

No one else in town had the expertise to create Vivian Schwartz's wedding finery. Normally nothing would please Carly more than turning lovely fabric into fashionable gowns. But this time she might've taken on more than she could accomplish.

Lord, I asked for a big job, but now I don't know how I can manage. Please help me finish in time.

Carly sighed. She'd wanted *more* time with her son not less. But what choice did she have?

The clock on the shelf chimed three. Soon Henry's teacher would release the students for the day. She'd walk to meet her son, give herself a chance to think of how to proceed and to ease the tension knotting her stomach. Somehow things would work out.

She flipped the sign in the window from open to closed and hustled out the door.

Into a wall. A wall of hard muscle.

Large hands steadied her.

Heart thundering, she met Nate Sergeant's dark gaze. "If you came back here to coerce me into giving up my shop, you'll deal with the sheriff."

As if he believed she might bite, the bounty hunter set her away from him and took a step back. "Quite the contrary, Mrs. Richards. I brought the deed."

Carly closed her eyes and fought to slow her breathing before she again fainted on the ruffian. "Where is it?"

He waved a hand toward a wagon. On the seat sat a pretty woman dressed entirely in black. She was wearing a stunning black traveling suit befitting a well-dressed widow that immediately caught Carly's attention.

Carly's stomach dipped. The newcomer looked too much like Mr. Sergeant to be anyone other than his sister, the woman who held the deed to the shop and had lost her husband at Max's hand.

"Mrs. Richards, this is my sister Anna Hankins."

At the mention of Carly's name, Mrs. Hankins gave a tentative smile, her eyes filling with uncertainty. "I'm pleased to meet you."

With every ounce of her well-honed will, Carly fought for composure, and then said the only true and nice thing she could think of to the woman who had the power to ruin her life. "I like your dress."

"Thank you." Anna smoothed her skirt with gloved hands. "I designed and made it myself."

Tiny tucks adorned the bodice, each one exactly like the next. Covered buttons down the front and on the cuffs had not the slightest pucker. The buttonholes were neat and evenly spaced. From collar to waist, the bodice fit Mrs. Hankins's slender frame to perfection.

Apparently the woman had the skill to create exquisite clothing. Skill and time and most certainly an interest, but that didn't mean she had the know-how to operate a seamstress shop.

"I love to sew," Anna said. "I can while away an entire day making a dress. I've only done a little sewing for ladies at my church. Just pin money, really." She waved a gloved hand at the shop. "I admire your talent for running a business."

The compliment didn't match Carly's image of Nate Sergeant's sister. "Well, thank you."

"I know the circumstances are unusual, even uncomfortable," Anna said, shooting her brother a pointed glance. "I'm very sorry about all that's happened."

The bounty hunter clamped his jaw, wisely keeping his own counsel.

"Me, too. You have my sympathy," Carly said, her face heating with humiliation that Max had not only killed this woman's husband, he'd threatened her life.

"As you have mine."

Did Mrs. Hankins actually believe Carly grieved for a man like Max? "From what the sheriff said, the decision on the shop's ownership rests with the circuit judge."

"When's the judge expected?" Nate Sergeant said.

Carly shrugged, refusing to discuss the matter with him and turned to his sister.

"I'd love to spend a day in your shop," Anna Hankins said. "The idea of running a business feels a lot like jumping into a dark pool without knowing what rocks lay hidden beneath the surface." She sighed. "I know I'd be way over my head. Not that I expect to need the information," she added quickly, her cheeks flooding with color.

Without wanting to, Carly found herself connecting with Anna Hankins. Almost liking her. *Almost.*

Carly didn't want to help this woman succeed if the judge ruled in Mrs. Hankins's favor. Still, Carly well remembered those feelings when she'd first reopened the shop.

Anna Hankins had talent and a sweet spirit. Carly's breath caught. Could she be God's solution to Carly's dilemma? She'd prayed for help making the wedding trousseau, never expecting that help to come from her adversary. But no one else had the time and that kind of skill.

"You're welcome to spend a day in my shop."

From the look on Nate Sergeant's face, he found Carly's offer startling. Had he expected her and Anna to put up their fists and fight for ownership? Probably. What bounty hunter could conceive of peaceful opponents?

If the woman worked in the shop, perhaps Carly could

learn exactly what had happened at that poker game. If the judge ruled against Carly, Mrs. Hankins might agree to sell. Or as they got to know each other better, she might see that taking Carly's shop was akin to taking food out of Henry's mouth.

"I've got a big job I might be unable to manage alone," Carly said. "Since we have no idea when the circuit judge will arrive, I suggest we set aside our differences and do the practical thing. I need help. You want to learn how to run a shop. Would you be willing to work here?"

Mr. Sergeant choked out a laugh. "You want my sister to work for you."

"With me." Carly folded her arms across her middle. "Proof, Mr. Sergeant, I'm not as awful as you insinuate. Working in the shop will benefit us both." Carly arched a brow. "Maybe once your sister gets a firsthand look at running a business, she'll change her mind about wanting that pressure."

"Don't think that you can—"

"I can speak for myself, Nathanial." Anna turned to Carly. "I'd love the opportunity. Thank you."

For the first time since Nate Sergeant had walked in her door, Carly smiled. Truly smiled. If not for the obstacles between them, she could imagine forging a friendship with Anna. "Shall we discuss the particulars inside, Mrs. Hankins?"

"Anna, please."

"Call me Carly."

"I'd like that."

His fierce expression an indication of his disapproval, the bounty hunter helped Anna down. She took his arm and leaned on him as they walked toward the entrance.

With each step, Anna dipped and rose like a small sailboat on a stormy sea. Carly's heart tumbled. Anna Hankins was handicapped. Was each step as painful as it appeared?

Max had ended Anna's husband's life. Now she must fend for herself. Well, not entirely, not with that gun-toting brother at her side. Still, Anna's disability must complicate her life.

Did her lameness explain her brother's resolve to take the shop? Carly resisted the temptation to respect this man; a brother fighting for his sister's well-being. No, he was a bounty hunter, a violent man who didn't deserve admiration. But also a man with regrets. Something she understood all too well.

Inside the shop, Anna moved around, soaking up every detail, oohing and aahing as she examined cases of fabric and trimmings.

She turned to Carly. "Your shop's beautiful, prettier than I'd imagined."

"Thank you. Would you like to see a finished gown?"

"Oh, yes!"

Carly opened the armoire and motioned to the dress hanging on a hook. "It's just waiting for the bride to come in for the final fitting."

"What a sweet neckline," Anna said. "I used batiste to make my wedding gown. A cool fabric for a summer wedding."

As Anna moved on to examine the case of gloves, out of earshot, Nate leaned in. "I understand you're trying to protect your son. But I hope you don't use this job as an opportunity to talk my sister into giving up the deed."

Heat flooded Carly's cheeks. "I merely offered her a job," she said. "The judge will decide the rest."

"I'll be close by until the judge rules."

As close as now? Two feet away? Close enough to catch his fresh manly scent. To stare into those gray, deep-set eyes. To touch that chiseled jaw and those powerful shoulders.

Everything about the man shouted danger. He'd killed

Max, spent his life tracking outlaws, and now threatened her way of life. So why did she feel this strange sense of safety in his presence? As if he would allow nothing or no one to hurt her.

Had Nate Sergeant been telling the truth when the man had told Henry that he would help her?

She bit back a snort. The man would stop at nothing to see that his sister owned the shop.

Eyes sweeping every nook and cranny, a dreamy smile on her face, Anna inched toward them with hitching steps.

The bounty hunter's gaze softened. "Now you've met Anna and can see her options are limited. My sister is a good-hearted soul and doesn't want to benefit from your misfortune. It would be tempting to take advantage of her sweet nature," he said, lowering his voice.

Carly's gaze skittered away from those probing, suspicious eyes. The bounty hunter didn't trust her. Had he somehow read her mind? Suspected she wanted information, even a bond with his sister in the hope Anna would hesitate to claim the shop?

Well, she wouldn't badger Anna, but she had to find a way to protect her son.

"Anna, are you ready? I want to get settled in."

"Yes, I'm eager to see the cabin." She turned to Carly. "Thank you for giving me the job. I'll be here first thing Monday morning, before the store opens."

"If you're not too tired tomorrow, I'd like to invite you to First Christian Church. Services start at nine o'clock."

"Thank you." Anna's gaze darted to her brother. "I'll be there."

At the door the bounty hunter stepped aside, letting his sister precede him, then turned to Carly. "I'll be back." He flashed a smile. "Don't let the anticipation overwhelm you."

That towering hulk of a man threatened the harmony

Carly prized. Yet as she stared into those eyes, an unwelcome thrill of attraction slid through her, shooting heat up her neck and into her cheeks. She groped for a rebuke that would conceal the turmoil churning inside her. "One thing I can say for certain, Mr. Sergeant. Nothing about you overwhelms me."

He arched a brow and had the audacity to wink. As if he had read her mind and found her claim amusing.

Carly shut the door behind him, leaned against it and took a deep breath. No matter what she'd said, Carly had never felt more overwhelmed. And of all things, by a bounty hunter.

A handsome bounty hunter, her heart whispered.

She pulled away from the door and steeled her spine. A handsome, strong-minded bounty hunter who would stop at nothing to see that his sister owned this shop.

Chapter Five

The yellow mutt Nate had seen yesterday sprang from where she'd been napping on the cabin's front stoop, as if she somehow knew where to find her next meal.

"Oh, is the dog yours, Mr. Mood?" Anna said, running a gentle hand along the dog's ruff.

The stray leaned into her. If Nate didn't know better, he'd say the dog was smiling.

"Well, she's been hanging out at the livery, but from the looks of it, she'd like to be yours."

Nate frowned. "A dog underfoot could trip you, Anna."

Ignoring the warning, Anna lowered herself to the step and gazed into the dog's eyes. "Do you want to live with Nate and me, girl?" The wagging tail and short yip put a wide grin on Anna's face. "Do you know her name, Mr. Mood?"

"Nope. Been calling her 'dog.'"

"She needs a proper name." Anna ran her fingers through the dog's thick fur. "Her coat's the color of corn, of maize. I'll call her Maizie."

"Well, now, that's a purty name. I'll leave you and Maizie to get settled," Mr. Mood said, grinning from ear to ear. "The Good Lord is working it all out, like only He can do."

Mood had also seen Nate's construction skill as God-sent. Now he was suggesting God had brought this pooch to their door. As if every little thing fit into a master plan.

Nate's hands fisted. If the liveryman believed God was sovereign over every aspect of their lives, how would Mood explain Anna's handicap and Rachel's murder? Two women who'd never done a cruel thing in their lives.

Nothing in his life made sense except finding Stogsdill.

As soon as he got Anna settled in, Nate would make some inquiries. See what he could learn about Stogsdill's rumored girlfriend. With the hope she'd lead him to the outlaw.

As Anna preceded Nate into the house, he averted his eyes from the rise and fall of her gait, a constant reminder of what his carelessness had cost his sister.

He owed Anna his life. She'd saved him, a careless ten-year-old boy, from the stomping hooves of runaway horses. And paid a high cost. Saving his life had ruined hers, had limited her choices. Probably the reason she'd married Walt.

Anna turned back and clapped her hands for the stray waiting in the doorway. "Maizie, aren't you coming?"

A wag of her tail and the dog slipped in at Nate's heels.

"Do you mean to make her a house dog?" Nate asked. "She'll shed all over everything."

"She'll mind her manners and stay on the floor. Nothing I can't sweep up in a jiffy."

In the parlor, the afternoon sunshine flooded the room through tall windows on either side of a brick fireplace. The coat of white paint on the walls was in sharp contrast to the floor's dark wood planks, the cracks wide enough to slip a dime between the boards.

"Isn't this nice?" Anna gushed as she surveyed the room. "Why, the floors and tables don't have a trace of dust. Someone's cleaned the place. My braided rug, Mother's

Currier and Ives prints and one of Grandma's quilts draped over the sofa will make this place homey."

"You could make a jail cell cozy."

Anna cocked her head at him. "Sometimes I wonder if you perceive settling down as a prison sentence."

"Of course not." He shifted on his feet. "You know why catching Stogsdill's important."

"Could you let it go? Leave his capture to lawmen?" She raised a gaze begging him to reconsider. "We've lost them all, Nate. Promise me I won't have to bury you, too."

Nate shot her a smile. "Don't worry, sis. I'm good at what I do." Still, if Max Richards's bullet had been accurate, his sister would be alone now, fending for herself. "Once that shop is yours, I'll have peace knowing that whatever happens, you can make a living."

"What about Carly Richards? She's a widow with a child. How can I live with myself if I take the shop away from her?"

"I'm not happy about Mrs. Richards's plight, but you didn't take the shop. Max Richards lost it to Walt. Walt paid for it with his life, a high price. The shop will be your future."

That is, if the circuit judge saw things as Nate did.

Nate trailed Anna to the kitchen. Simple cupboards, large cookstove, small potbellied stove, a table and four chairs. He walked to the window over the sink with a view to the back and the alleyway beyond.

Anna clapped her hands. "Oh, look, Nate, an indoor pump!"

"Good. When I leave, you won't have to haul water."

"I thought you were certain I'd be living behind the shop."

"I am, but if I should have to leave before the ownership is settled—"

"Enough of that talk. Let's look at the rest of the cabin."

They moved on to the bedrooms, both small but adequate, each with a double-paned window, brass double bed, built-in clothespress and chest of drawers. Not fancy, but nicer than Nate had expected.

"I'll take the room next to the kitchen, if that's all right," she said.

"Fine by me."

He walked to the window and gazed at the back of the seamstress shop, the Richards's living quarters. The widow's generous attitude toward Anna had surprised him. But then Anna had a way of bringing the best out of people.

"I'll get your things," he said, "then help you set this place to rights."

Within minutes of his hauling trunks, boxes and crates inside, Anna had started building a nest. By the time he'd driven the team to the livery and returned to the cabin, Anna had made up the beds, topping the linens with colorful quilts.

Then set him to nailing bed sheets at the bedroom windows for privacy.

In the parlor, she draped another quilt over the sofa. Satisfied with her efforts thus far, she made a list of the supplies they'd need while he hung two Currier and Ives idyllic prints above it.

They moved on to the kitchen, where they unpacked jars of cherries, applesauce, tomatoes, beans—all canned by Anna—and stowed the Blue Willow dishes from their childhood in a cupboard, as well as all the paraphernalia needed to cook and serve a meal.

Anna shook out a tablecloth and let it float onto the scarred table. "If you can find two rods at the mercantile, I'll make proper curtains tonight from my stash of fabric," she said, setting a blue-striped crock in the center.

The errand would give Nate the perfect opening to ask questions. "I'll head over there now."

With a soft groan, Anna dropped into a ladder-back chair. The stray dog nudged Anna's hand and got a perfunctory pat, then curled at Anna's feet, head propped on her paws.

"You've overdone it. Now your hip's bothering you."

"I'll rest a minute and be fine." She glanced around her. "Once the curtains are made and up, this will look like home."

He suspected Anna was making a home not only for herself but for him. "Don't get too attached to the place. You'll soon be moving behind the seamstress shop."

"*If* the judge should rule the shop is mine, I won't displace Carly and her son. The boy just lost his father. I won't let him lose the only home he's probably known."

"Anna," he said, trying to make her see reason, "this cabin will sell with the livery. Where will you live then?"

As if he hadn't spoken, Anna handed him a list, then flapped her hands, shooing him out like a pesky fly. "Please. Get those rods and the items I need."

"Yes, ma'am," he said, saluting her with a grin. "I'm at your service."

Anna appeared mild-mannered, but she possessed a spine of steel. The reason she'd dealt well with her handicap, her incompetent husband and now his violent death.

"I'll fix a nice supper. Get whatever looks good from the butcher. I intend to fatten you up." She leaned down and patted the mutt. "You, too, Maizie." Tail thumping against the floor, the dog raised her head, tongue lolling.

Anna probably hoped her home cooking would entice Nate to stay, as much as food enticed the stray. He had put on weight with her delicious meals. If he stayed, living a life of ease, he'd get soft. "Be back soon as I can."

As Nate stepped onto the porch, Mrs. Richards and her son strolled toward him. The widow carried a pot, holding the handles with dishtowels, as if the metal was hot.

In three strides Nate reached her side. "Can I help with that?"

"Thank you, but I've got it."

Henry beamed up at Nate. "You came back."

"Yes, and brought my sister with me," Nate said, unable to resist rubbing a palm over Henry's cowlick. As soon as he removed his hand, the tuft sprang aloft.

Henry gazed up at his mother. "Is that the lady that's going to help you sew?"

"Yes," Carly said, her gaze darting to Nate, then away.

It didn't take a mind reader to see her disquiet about relying on the woman who held the deed to her shop. That order she'd mentioned must be a whopper.

"I thought Anna might appreciate not having to cook."

"Chicken and noodles," Henry said.

"My favorite." Nate inhaled. "Smells delicious."

"I like chicken and noodles best, too!" Henry all but danced around Nate's knees. "I could eat with you."

"It's not polite to invite yourself," Carly said, tugging her son close, obviously unwilling for Henry to spend time with a bounty hunter. "Besides, I saved some for us."

Nate didn't blame her. He wasn't someone a boy should look up to, but with Max Richards for a father, Henry had no idea what made a man admirable and might latch on to any man.

As he reached the stoop, Nate opened the door and called to his sister. He couldn't help wondering what it would be like to sit at the table with Carly and her son. To enjoy a meal and a bit of conversation, assuming they could squeeze a word in between Henry's little-boy chatter.

Anna appeared in the doorway. "Carly, what a lovely surprise." She smiled at Henry. "This handsome young man must be Henry."

"We bringed chicken and noodles for your supper."

"How thoughtful." She opened the door. "Please, come in."

At his mother's side, Henry turned to Nate. "Are you coming?"

"My sister asked me to run an errand, but I'll see you around."

The light in Henry's eyes dimmed. "Oh, okay. 'Bye," he said, taking the hand Anna offered and walking inside.

Nate tipped his hat at Mrs. Richards. "Thanks for supper. That was considerate of you."

Her sapphire eyes held a chill. "Don't be misled, Mr. Sergeant. If not for you, Anna would not consider taking my shop. That makes you and me adversaries. I'll do what I must to ensure my son's future."

"As I will with my sister's."

"We understand each other, then," she said, closing the door with a click.

Carly Richards might be hospitable to Anna, but she obviously viewed him as the enemy. She somehow knew Anna would forgo ownership of the shop if not for his insistence. And that was why he would stay until the judge ruled.

Nate strode past the livery out to Main Street. Always alert for trouble, his gaze spanned the street and buildings as he turned toward the mercantile.

Most businesses in town looked prosperous and well kept. Ruffled curtains hung on either side of the window of Sarah's Café. A red-and-white-striped pole heralded the town barbershop. First State Bank, the name hand-lettered in gold across the glass, looked as solid as its stone facade. On down the street Nate spied a grocery and doctor's office.

Apparently the livery was the only run-down building in town. Gnaw Bone was a nice place for his sister to settle. From what he'd seen, folks here had pride of ownership and weren't afraid of work.

Nate stepped through the open double doors of Stuffle

Emporium, the scents of spices, kerosene, soap and vinegar warring in his nostrils. He zigzagged through a maze of tables piled with stacks of readymade clothing, linens, pots and pans. Along the back wall he found wrought iron rods that would fit the bedroom windows. The curlicues on each end would please Anna. He gathered them up, along with supports and screws. No need to buy a hammer when Anna had Pa's metal box filled with tools.

Toting his finds, he walked to the long counter. Behind it, shelves reached from the wooden floor to the stamped-tin ceiling. J. B. Stetson hats lined a section of one shelf. A brown Stetson caught his eye. An exact replica of the hat Pa had given Nate on his twelfth birthday. "When you do a man's work, you need a man's gear," Pa had said, placing the hat on Nate's head. Though his father's praise had been overstated, Nate had worn the hat with pride and tried to live up to his words.

A lanky, tall man, his large hands folded over the apron covering his middle, stepped over and flashed a smile. "I'm Clarence Stuffle, proprietor of this here establishment. You must be new in town."

"Name's Nate Sergeant. My sister and I just moved into Morris Mood's house."

"Ah, that makes you the bounty hunter planning to fix up the livery." He thrust out a hand and they shook. "Pleased to make your acquaintance. Morris can use the help. Like an old clock, he's harder to wind and keep a'tickin'."

"I'm glad for the work."

"So what brings a bounty hunter to Gnaw Bone?"

Nate had no intention of sharing his reasons. But, word would get out. "Gnaw Bone seemed like a nice little town for my widowed sister to make a new life for herself."

"Carly Richards is doing the same. I reckon you'd know about that, having killed her husband."

Nate straightened, holding the proprietor's gaze.

Stuffle raised a palm. "Not that I'm not holding it against you, leastwise as long as you keep that revolver holstered. Most folks didn't cotton to Max."

"I'm not a threat to anyone on the right side of the law." When had Nate spoken a bigger lie?

"In that case, welcome." Stuffle motioned to the items Nate had laid on the counter. "Our blacksmith made the rods. A wooden rod, even a strong cord would do, but womenfolk like things fancy." He glanced at the paper in Nate's hand. "Anything else you need?"

Nate handed over the list. Apparently, Stuffle hadn't gotten wind of the controversy over the shop's ownership. Once the judge arrived, the entire town would know. If the judge ruled in his sister's favor, as Nate expected, would Anna be an outcast? As if his occupation didn't already bring enough censure.

Nate's jaw tightened. He might have the skill to track and bring outlaws to justice, but he had no way to protect his sister from mistreatment. If folks gave Anna a chance, they'd like her. How could they not? She always thought of others, put them first. Still, to ensure her happiness, he would come back to Gnaw Bone as much as he could while pursuing Stogsdill.

Obviously not a man to hurry, the proprietor shuffled back and forth from the shelves to the counter, piling up the items on Anna's list. Finally he rang up each on the brass cash register and told Nate the tally.

If Stogsdill's rumored girlfriend lived in the area, he might've been in this store. "I'm guessing you don't have many newcomers in town," Nate said, doling out the money.

"Not many." Stuffle shut the cash drawer, then handed Nate his change. "Reason you're big news."

Nate wouldn't show the proprietor Stogsdill's wanted

poster or give the outlaw's name. If he recognized the man, word might get out and scare Stogsdill off. Nate's best chance was to locate the rumored girlfriend.

As Stuffle boxed the purchases, Nate leaned in. "I've heard an outlaw I'm pursuing has a girlfriend in these parts."

Stuffle frowned. "Some woman from here is entertaining a criminal? What's her name?"

"Don't know. Can't describe her, either."

"Reckon finding a nameless, faceless woman is harder than locating a copper penny in a pigsty. My wife works Fridays and Saturdays. She would remember a new face in town, especially a woman. Most likely know all about her before she got out of the store." He grinned, revealing a gap between his front teeth. "My Myra's got a nose for news."

"I'll be back to speak to your wife."

"Oh, better yet, talk to Mrs. Richards. Ladies like to ogle lace and feathers while their men do business at the bank." He chuckled. "Or in the saloon."

"Thanks for your help and the advice." Nate gathered the box and strode toward the livery and the small house out back.

Tomorrow he'd stop in at Mrs. Richards's seamstress shop to ask if she'd waited on a newcomer in town. Hopefully one of these ladies would have what he sought: a lead to Shifty Stogsdill's girlfriend. That girlfriend could lead him to Stogsdill. A ruthless killer who'd taken Rachel's life—a lovely, innocent young woman who'd never harmed anyone.

Until Nate brought Stogsdill to justice, he would never be free to settle down, never have a wife and children, never have the comfort of a normal existence. Nothing would make him happier than to end the outlaw's reign of terror.

Nothing that is, except seeing Anna settled behind the shop counter with her name on the sign out front, knowing his sister had a future, even if Stogsdill saw that Nate lost his.

Chapter Six

Carly unwound the fabric, sending the bolt of silk thumping along the counter. This beautiful white fabric, surely as pretty as anything in Paris, would become Vivian's wedding gown.

On the other side of the counter, her brow furrowed in concentration, dark ringlets of her hair dancing around her jaw, Anna smoothed the fabric, while Carly pinned on the pattern pieces. Pattern pieces contoured to fit the bride perfectly.

"I've got to get this right," Carly said, setting aside the pincushion and reaching for the scissors. "I don't have extra fabric if I make an error."

Anna stretched across the table and grabbed Carly's free hand, then bowed her head. "Lord, give Carly clarity of thought and steadiness of hand to cut this dress out perfectly. Amen." With a gentle smile, Anna released Carly's hand. "Sorry for taking the lead, but I've never worked with material this fancy."

Carly had never prayed before cutting into fabric, but after hearing the simple request, she wondered why she hadn't. "I appreciate God's help. And yours."

With Henry in school, Carly and Anna worked through

the morning. Their only interruption being two customers who'd browsed through bolts of fabric, then left. By noon they'd pinned and basted the gown's bodice together. After the fitting, Carly would run up the seams on the treadle sewing machine.

Anna was a steady worker, not much for chitchat; a blessing when handling expensive fabric. Still, her quiet nature didn't give Carly an opening to seek information. She couldn't rest until she knew the details of how Walt had gotten hold of the deed.

Strands of a plan knitted together in her mind. While they ate the noon meal, Carly would bring up that poker game. See if there'd been witnesses and if so, ask Sheriff Truitt to question them. Perhaps they would deny Walt Hankins had won the deed.

Why, Anna's husband could've stolen it. The reason Max had shot him. Carly bit back a sigh, certain Max was the culprit.

"Brides have been known to gain weight. I cut generous seam allowances in case we need to let out the dress," Carly said, though with only weeks until the wedding that seemed unlikely.

"Where I'm from, a bride's wedding gown is often worn as her best dress for years. Generous seam allowances make sense."

"Not this bride. The Schwartz women rarely wear a gown twice."

Anna's jaw dropped. "Really? Seems wasteful, especially in a town named Gnaw Bone."

"I can't think of a better town to put on the dog," Carly said, then gave a wink.

Anna giggled. "You're so much fun to work with, Carly." The compliment soaked into Carly's spirit. "Thank you." At noon they stopped to reheat the pot of vegetable soup Carly had made that morning, and then sat at the kitchen table.

With aromas wafting from their bowls on the rising steam, they glanced at one another and bowed heads while Carly thanked God for the food.

Anna blew on the soup in her spoon, then ate. "Mmm, this is delicious, as good as last night's chicken and noodles."

"Thank you." How could she broach the subject? "You, uh, mentioned your husband won the deed. Was he a gambler?"

"Walt? Oh no. To hear he'd joined a poker game surprised me. And surprised the others at the table."

Carly's spoon clattered against her bowl. "There were witnesses?"

"Two men at the wake told me about the game. They felt guilty about Walt, him not being a regular. If he hadn't sat at the table, they figure one of them might've turned up dead."

These men would declare in court that Max had anted the deed and Anna's husband had won it fair and square. Any other possibility seemed farfetched, especially looking into Anna's candid gaze.

Now Carly's only hope for keeping her shop rested with the circuit judge's interpretation of the law. Her stomach lurched. If he didn't rule in her favor, Anna Hankins would be cooking in this kitchen and taking care of Carly's customers.

"I was shocked Walt won. And troubled he'd risked the money Nate sent us on the turn of a card."

"No more shocked than I was to learn Max had anted the deed." Once again, evidence her husband hadn't cared a whit about her and Henry.

Anna flushed. "I'm sorry about what happened. I don't approve of gambling."

Walt Hankins hadn't considered Anna's wishes any more than Max had considered Carly's. "It's not your fault." The fault laid with Max, a man without a sense of right and wrong. If he'd lived, his example might've led his son down that same path.

"I don't know poker, but the other players said Walt held a royal flush, the best hand there is, like that was an accomplishment instead of merely luck." Anna sniffed. "Not good luck, either. Winning that deed cost Walt his life."

"That deed didn't take your husband's life. Max did." She touched Anna's arm. "I'm sorry. More than I can say."

"Some mornings I wake and, for a moment, I forget." Moisture welled in Anna's eyes. "I can barely believe Walt's gone."

Unlike Carly, this widow grieved her dead husband. "What was he like?"

"Kind, gentle, soft-spoken. I'd call Walt a dreamer. Some might call him a failure."

"But you didn't?"

"His inventions and schemes weren't workable. Often he ran ahead of God, but Walt had this quiet way of making me feel cherished."

Max had never made Carly feel valued. Not from the first day of their marriage. "What drove Walt? A desire for wealth?"

"He had this need to give me a better life, finer things, as if I wanted a life of ease or fancy trinkets." She shoved aside her half-eaten bowl of soup. "We had a roof over our heads, food in our bellies. We had enough. Plenty."

Before meeting Anna, Carly had put Walt Hankins in the same category as Max. The two men were nothing alike. Still, even if his intentions had been good, Walt had failed his wife, just as Max had failed her.

Somehow that connected her to Anna. A connection Carly would fight with every particle of her being. She wouldn't let herself care about Anna. If she did, how could she fight for her business?

Yet fight she must. She'd paid a huge price for this shop. Nine long years under Max's thumb. Even when he'd been away from home, his presence had hovered over her. She'd never known when he'd return. Never known what mood he'd be in when he did.

"I don't know what I'll do if something happens to Nate," Anna said, her hands entwined, twisting in her lap. "I don't care about that reward money he insists on sending. I care about him." Her voice trembled. "He's all I have."

Nate Sergeant could work in the livery or in countless other jobs, but chose instead to hunt lawless men. To accomplish that, he had to be equally dangerous.

"I'm sorry for complaining." Anna wiped her damp eyes, then gave a weak smile. "I'm emotional since I lost Walt. It's a comfort to know you understand the pain and loneliness of losing a husband."

Anna's gaze landed on Carly's dress. Her eyes widened, as if just realizing Carly wasn't wearing black. Widow's weeds would chafe, be a sham. Carly had lived a lie her entire marriage and wouldn't pretend to grieve.

She lurched to her feet. "I'll make tea. Do you use sugar?"

Anna shot her a quizzical look. "Yes, please. I need to stretch my legs," she said, then rose and hobbled to the front.

Carly couldn't admit the loneliness and pain Anna spoke of had occurred during her marriage, not from her husband's death. She couldn't admit she'd married a scoundrel without faith. She couldn't admit in the past month she'd found peace and happiness as Max's widow.

That is, until Nate and Anna had showed up and put the ownership of her shop in jeopardy.

As Carly added tea leaves and poured hot water into her rose-sprigged teapot, she chastised herself for getting emotionally involved with Anna. In a matter of hours, her enemy had become a woman with whom she could empathize. That would never do. How could she fight for her son's welfare and not bring Anna harm?

She would focus on what mattered—getting the bridal finery made. She'd pay Anna the wage they'd agreed upon. Hopefully, after expenses, Carly would have enough profit to offer to buy Anna out.

Carly loaded the pot and cups onto a tray, then strode into the shop. What she saw stopped her in her tracks.

Nate Sergeant stood near his sister, filling the room with his presence. As he'd promised, he'd come to look after Anna's interests, to make sure Carly wasn't trying to convince Anna to give up the shop.

Mr. Sergeant threatened Carly's very existence. Well, the years she'd spent living under a man's intimidation had made her strong. She would not surrender the shop without a fight.

Nate leaned against the shop counter, legs crossed, trying to appear at ease, as if the conversation he wished to broach was of no consequence. Otherwise Carly might raise those defenses of hers and refuse to hear him out. But inside he was coiled tighter than an overwound spring.

Getting anywhere in Gnaw Bone required a lot of jawing. "I'm looking for someone you might know," he said, his tone casual.

"Strange as it may sound to a man like you, I don't rub shoulders with criminals."

So much for keeping this female tinderbox calm. "That's the last thing I'd think. I'm talking about a woman, not an outlaw."

Carly's stormy-sea eyes softened from forged steel to

hard-packed clay. "I'm sorry. That was rude." She took a breath. "Why do you want to find this woman? Is she a friend of yours?"

"No. An outlaw I'm pursuing supposedly has a lady friend in the area."

"In Gnaw Bone? This is a peaceful little town."

"Has a stranger come into the shop in the past several months?"

"Folks pass through. I can't know everyone." She took a sip of tea. "What does this woman look like?"

"I don't know."

"Show Carly that wanted poster," Anna said.

Nate didn't want to jeopardize his investigation, but if Stogsdill should accompany his floozy into this shop, Mrs. Richards, her son and Anna would be at risk. "Can you keep this to yourself?" he said. "If word gets out I'm looking for this rogue, his lady friend might warn him away."

"You'll just have to trust me. If he's in the area, I should know what he looks like."

Tamping down a sigh, Nate removed the wanted poster from the pocket of his vest, then unfolded and laid the crumpled paper on the table.

Carly stared at the sketch of Stogsdill's handlebar mustache, sideburns and long lashes, in sharp contrast to his lifeless, cold eyes.

"He might look different. He could've shaved off the facial hair," Nate said.

"I've never seen the man."

Anna laid a hand on Carly's arm. "I hope you never do. Shifty Stogsdill is a heartless killer."

"From reports of bank robberies he's been involved in, I don't believe Stogsdill is here now. But, perhaps you can help me track down his female friend," Nate said.

"I want this rogue caught, but I don't see how I can help."

"Do you remember a customer who looks different than most?"

"The ladies who frequent my shop are not about to be attracted to an outlaw."

"Perhaps she doesn't know he's an outlaw. Perhaps—"

"Don't pester Carly. If she knew anything, she'd tell you." Anna rose, walking to where Nate leaned against the wall, her gait more unsteady than usual. "You're obsessed with catching Stogsdill. Won't have peace until you do. Well, I won't have peace as long as you're putting your life at risk."

"You know why I have to bring him down."

"Bring him *down*?" Anna lifted a palm to his cheek. "'Vengeance is mine…saith the Lord.'"

"The law will avenge, not me." He shifted on his feet. "Once I capture him, I'll give you the reward money."

"No amount of money could take your place!" A sob escaped her lips. "I'm sorry. I…I need a moment alone," she said, then limped to the back.

Carly Richards leveled Nate with her gaze. "Are you so hard-hearted you don't care Anna fears for your safety?"

Her words battered him like an uppercut to the jaw. But he couldn't rest until he'd caught Stogsdill and knew Anna would be taken care of for life. "Of course I care. My concern for Anna is the reason I want her to have this shop."

"Paint a pretty picture if you can. But the truth is you want Anna to own this shop so you can be on your merry way, chasing after an outlaw."

Nate knew the cost the women in his life had paid for loving him. He owed them. If only he could change the past. Undo those moments searing his brain with the hot branding iron of guilt.

Why try to explain to a woman who'd use his sister as a way to save her shop?

Nate turned and stalked to the entrance. Yet the truth of

Carly's words couldn't be denied. He was a bounty hunter, not a man his sister or any woman could count on. Anna was better off without him.

At the door Nate turned back. "Once, my sister was a tomboy, running races, climbing trees, riding bareback." His voice wobbled. "Now she's crippled. Because of *me*. The reason I owe her everything." His gaze locked with Carly's. "The reason I'll make certain she gets this shop."

A chill slid through Carly, raising goose bumps on her arms. What had Nate Sergeant done to cause Anna's injury? Whatever had happened, the guilt that ate at him made him a formidable foe.

Anna slipped into the shop, her eyes swollen, but a smile firmly in place. Her gaze swept the space. "Where's Nate?"

"He left." Carly refilled their cups. "Have a cup of tea. I find it soothing."

With a sigh, Anna took her seat. "I'm sorry for making a scene in front of you."

"Don't be silly. You're recently widowed and fear for your brother's life. That's a heavy load to carry."

"You're recently widowed and with a child to rear, yet you're strong. The Good Lord is seeing you through your heartache."

"I have a lot to be thankful for," Carly said, fiddling with the lid on the teapot, avoiding Anna's eyes.

"Me, too. I'm thankful for this job and that little cabin behind the livery and a brother who cares about me." She sighed. "Even if he refuses to listen to a word I say."

"I don't understand how he can abide worrying you so. Makes me wonder if you're as close as I first thought."

"We love each other, make no mistake, but…I wouldn't say we're close." Anna's mouth twisted, as if trying not to cry. "Nate holds himself at arm's length."

"What man doesn't?" Carly sat at the sewing machine

and laid two pieces of the bodice under the pressure foot, then lowered it, guiding the fabric as she pedaled.

"Walt didn't." Anna's tone grew soft, wistful. "We'd leave the curtains open at night to watch the stars twinkling outside our window and talk. He'd share his dreams. I'd say I was sorry there'd been no babies." Anna's smile wobbled. "He'd declare I was enough. All he needed."

Anna and Walt weren't able to have children.

What would Carly do without Henry? Her precious boy gave her joy, comfort and purpose. Hope for the future.

Carly's throat knotted. How many years had Anna hoped and prayed for a baby? Month after month she'd seen that hope shattered. Yet she'd pressed on, though inside, her childlessness surely broke her heart. Anna's faith and relationship with Walt had kept her going.

Carly could barely fathom the close relationship Anna described. The men in her life had been long on orders, short on affection.

If only she could ensure one day Henry would know how to make a woman feel cherished. Why wouldn't he? He was only seven, but Henry made Carly feel cherished. Perhaps odd for a boy so young. His father's prolonged absences and unpredictable behavior had brought them closer than most mothers and sons. Good had come from bad, as Scripture promised.

"Carly, you and Nate got off to a bad start. Life has hardened him and he appears gruff, but he's a good man." Anna smiled. "He was the sweetest youngster. A chatterbox always excited about something."

From what Carly had seen, Nate Sergeant fit the pattern of all the men in her life. "Then he's changed. Hardened is an apt description for him now."

"He's considerate and devoted to me. He sees I have what I need, even if he's champing at the bit to leave." Anna heaved a sigh. "Nate's on a mission to save the world."

Or run from it? Carly fiddled with the fabric. "He said he was responsible for your injury."

"That surprises me. He usually won't talk about the accident." Anna limped to the window, gazing out. "It eats at him like a cancer."

"Would you mind telling me what happened?"

"We grew up on a dairy farm outside a small town much like this. On Saturdays farmers came in for supplies, to buy and sell. That day our folks had business in the bank. They sent us to the mercantile for stick candy." She turned toward Carly. Anna's eyes looked glazed, as if she'd traveled back in time. "A drunk banged out of the saloon, firing his six-shooters and spooking a team of horses. Eager to spend that penny clutched in his hand, Nate darted into their path and tripped in a rut, sprawling facedown in the dirt. I grabbed him by his britches and shoved him to safety."

Carly cringed, dreading Anna's next words.

"Passersby said the front hoof of the horse knocked me down. The back hoof stomped and shattered my hip. Doc did the best he could, but it never mended right. My right leg's shorter than the left."

"Does walking hurt?"

"Not enough to complain about." Tears welled in her eyes. "Nate's the one who's truly hurting."

All Anna could think about was her brother, yet could that accident somehow have destroyed Anna's ability to conceive?

Carly walked to Anna and laid her hand on her shoulder. "You're a wonderful person, Anna Hankins. I'm glad I know you."

"Thank you, Carly. I have the strongest feeling God brought us together for a reason. And not to fight over this shop."

This was the perfect opportunity to nudge Anna to forfeit the deed. But looking into those trusting, warm eyes, Carly couldn't bring herself to ask.

But, she wouldn't hand the shop over to Anna, either. This was her son's home, his security. Henry came first. Her father had never thought of her well-being. Never put her first with anything except chores.

"I'd better get back to work. Henry will be home soon."

At the machine, Carly watched the needle move up and down to the rhythm of her pumping feet. How could she go in front of a judge and testify against this woman who'd lost so much? Her husband, her home, perhaps her ability to conceive?

Yet, Carly must. Somehow she would.

A sniggle of sympathy slid through her for Nate Sergeant, imagining the torment of watching Anna hobble along, knowing he'd caused her injury.

Carly tamped down the feeling. The man was bent on displacing her and Henry and would go to any length to succeed. She suspected his desire to see his sister settled had more to do with pacifying his guilt than concern over Anna's well-being.

Her foot stilled, the hum of the machine silenced with it. Like Nate, wasn't she riddled with guilt? Guilt for marrying a man God would never have approved? She'd seen the warnings, yet hadn't taken time to pray about the decision. Hadn't trusted God to lead her to a good man.

Forgive me, Lord. I promise to never make that mistake again.

Chapter Seven

Nate wrestled the rotted board off the wall of the livery and tossed it onto the growing pile. The board landed with a thud, raising dust and a ruckus rivaling the turmoil roiling inside him.

Carly Richards had no idea what drove him to find Shifty Stogsdill. She saw him as a man like her dead husband. A man so despicable he'd shot Walt in the back, then tried to avoid paying for his crime by firing on Nate.

Nothing could be further from the truth. Yet her opinion stabbed at his pride.

Why did he care?

No point in dwelling on it. He'd concentrate on getting this livery whipped into shape. And keep alert for Anna's welfare.

In the crook of his elbow, Nate wiped the sweat from his brow, then slid the claw of his hammer under a rusty nail and pried. As the nail pulled free, the board squeaked in protest, as reluctant to let go of its purpose as he was. He should be tracking Stogsdill. Appease that all-consuming fire in his belly to rid this world of an outlaw who'd destroyed those he loved.

With a release of pent-up frustration, he grabbed the plank and tossed it in the direction of the pile.

A high-pitched voice squealed.

Nate whirled toward the sound. A mere three feet from that last flying plank, Henry stood, wide-eyed but apparently unscathed. "Are you okay? I didn't know you were there."

Nate hadn't looked. He thanked God that tossed timber hadn't hit the lad. If it had…

Nate tamped down the countless dire possibilities swarming his brain and strode to Henry. "I'm sorry for scaring you."

"I wasn't scared."

So like his mother.

"Whatcha doing?"

"Replacing rotted boards with new ones." Nate motioned toward the stack of new lumber nearby.

The boy crinkled his nose. "Stinks in here."

"I think horses and manure smell good."

Puzzled blue eyes rested on his. "Where'd you put 'em?"

"The horses? I turned them outside while I'm working."

Henry scampered to the window facing the corral and climbed onto a bale of straw, then stood on tiptoes, peering out. One strap of his overalls had slipped from his narrow shoulders. His shirttail bunched around his middle. That cowlick stood at attention. He'd obviously had an active morning.

"I wanna learn to ride." The longing in Henry's tone nudged at Nate. "But Mama sold Buck. She said Pa's horse is a mean critter." He sighed. "Mama don't have time to teach me anyway," he said, jumping to the floor.

The words had shot out of his mouth like a geyser at Yellowstone.

The boy was old enough to ride, but Nate wasn't about to interfere.

"Can I help?" Henry said, his tone brightening.

Nothing kept the lad down for long.

"This isn't a job for a boy."

Shoulders slumping, he shuffled toward the livery door.

At Henry's age, Nate had helped his pa around the farm. But, if the boy got hurt, his tigress of a mother would come after Nate with claws unsheathed.

Still, how could he let Henry go, looking as though he'd lost his best friend? As though he was of no use to anyone? The boy wanted to do more than lend a hand. He wanted to spend time with a man. Do a man's work.

"I could use help rounding up the rusty nails I dropped. If you want to help, grab that pail by the door."

Henry turned back, eyes sparkling with excitement. "Sure!"

The boy darted toward the pail while Nate turned to where he'd torn the last slat from the studs. Three more in this section and he could nail up new boards.

"I found one!" Henry said, plucking a nail from the floorboards and holding it up for Nate's inspection.

"You're sharp-eyed."

As Nate yanked out each nail, Henry stood beside him, holding out the pail, grinning ear-to-ear at the chink of the nail dropping inside. "You got big muscles, Mr. Sergeant." He made a fist and bent his arm at the elbow, grinning at his nonexistent muscle. "Me, too."

Who could resist this boy? "If we're going to work together, call me Nate."

"Yes, sir!" Henry beamed up at him, adoration shining in his eyes.

The lad would turn somersaults to please him. Nate swallowed hard against the lump shoving up his throat. Nothing about Nate warranted admiration.

"Could you teach me to ride the gray spotty horse? I like her best. I could help you work so you'd have time. I can carry this old wood outside. See." Henry tugged on a board almost as tall as he was, grappling with it, his face scrunched up with the effort.

"Be careful," Nate said, holding his breath.

"Ouch!" The board dropped from Henry's hands, teetered on the pile, and then tumbled. Landing inches shy of the boy's shins.

Nate knelt in front of Harry. "Did a nail nick you?"

Henry thrust out his right thumb. "It's a splinter. Can you get it out?"

If Nate didn't watch the youngster's every move, he'd get hurt, far worse than a splinter. "Show your ma. She'll know what to do."

"Mama uses a needle to dig 'em out. She's good at splinters and sewing stuff and baking cookies, but she can't fix our pump."

"What pump?"

"The kitchen pump." He puffed out his small chest. "Mama says I'm a big help with toting water."

Dirty clothes and a dirty boy surely required hauling lots of water. "If it's okay with your mama, I'll look at her pump."

"I'll tell her."

"Let me talk to her first." As if Carly Richards would welcome any help of his. "After I finish here."

"Thanks!"

"Better run along and get that splinter out."

"Yes, sir." Henry lifted his hand to his face, studying his thumb. "Even if she pokes and pokes with a needle, I won't cry. Us men aren't crybabies. We're tough."

Nate bit back a smile and ruffled the boy's hair. "That we are."

Henry had lost a father. Not much of a father, but a father all the same. Soon Henry would lose his home. Thanks to him.

Nate's hand fell away and he took a step back. Was there another solution? A way to avoid hurting this boy?

No, as much as Nate wished things were different, his sister's welfare came first.

With a wave, Henry raced off. At the threshold, he caught a toe and sprawled facedown in the dirt. Nate sprinted toward him, picturing a goose egg or gash on the boy's forehead.

Before Nate reached him, Henry sprang to his feet, shot Nate a sheepish grin, then ran on.

A shaky breath slid from Nate's lips. Henry was a great kid, but on the clumsy side. Without a father to teach him all the countless things a boy needed to know, Henry might not fit in with the other boys in town. Surely, with all the losses in his life, Henry should be allowed to ride.

Did he dare broach the subject with Carly?

Wasn't claiming Carly's business and her home enough? Must that bounty hunter try to worm his way into her son's life, too? The man wasn't a good example for an impressionable boy.

Hands balled into fists, Carly strode to the livery, ready to have it out with the man.

Across the alley, Nate Sergeant hauled boards on his shoulder to a barren spot near a rusty barrel and dumped them onto the growing pile, raising dust and a clatter. He then ambled toward where she waited with that loose, easy stride of his.

Carly's breath caught and her hand sought her collar. Why, he looked like a cowboy, capable of single-handedly handling a herd of stampeding cattle.

Sunlight glinted off the gun belt riding low on his hips. She stiffened. Did he wear a firearm while working around the livery? That gun could go off. A bullet could strike her son. Henry's safety was at risk. Yet another reason to keep him away from the livery.

As he drew near, Carly planted hands on hips, ready for battle.

He tipped his hat, his deep-set eyes unreadable. "Ma'am."

He swiped at the moisture beaded on his brow, then leaned against the open door. Shirtsleeves rolled, collar unbuttoned at the neck, hair damp with perspiration, he looked work-worn.

And far more handsome than a man had the right to be.

"Mr. Sergeant, I'd appreciate it if you wouldn't allow my son in this livery. It's a hazardous place."

"Figured you'd pay me a visit."

She eyed his holster. "Must you always wear a weapon, as if danger lurks behind every tree?"

"No lawman worth his salt is without his gun."

"You have no jurisdiction in Gnaw Bone. Besides, guns are dangerous," she said, wanting to add, *you're* dangerous.

He folded brawny arms across his chest and merely looked at her as if she was a pesky fly not worthy of his time.

"I spent ten minutes prodding a sliver out of Henry's thumb," she went on.

"Sorry about the splinter. Henry was just trying to help."

"You should've sent him home immediately."

"The boy's hard to resist."

The smile he turned on her softened every hard angle of her heart, every wall she'd built to protect herself and her son. Not what she intended. This man was violent, like Max.

"He's a great kid. Wants to please." He studied her. "Truth is, the boy's hungry for a man's attention."

She couldn't deny Henry needed a man in his life. A good man. A God-fearing man. Someone to show him how to lead, to work and to care for a family. Not this gun-toting drifter.

"I…I appreciate your concern for Henry's welfare, but please don't interfere. I will decide who fits that role."

"You're his mom. Decision's yours." His mouth crooked up in a cocky grin. "Not sure I can keep him away."

The truth of his words sank inside her, jarring her to the core. She had no idea why, but she couldn't deny Henry was enthralled by Nate Sergeant. All he'd talked about while Carly dug out that splinter was Nate this…Nate that. Had Henry bonded to the man when she'd fainted? And saw him as a hero?

She took a shaky breath. "Look, I've got a shop to run. A huge order to handle. A son who needs my attention." Of their own accord, tears sprang into her eyes. She willed them away, as she'd done countless times before. "I can't be worrying about Henry's safety."

"You've got a lot to deal with. Maybe I can help." He removed his Stetson, shoved a hand through his black unruly hair and then clamped the hat on his head. "Henry mentioned your kitchen pump's broken. Care if I take a look? See if I can fix it?"

She searched his face for an ulterior motive. The kind look in his eyes wasn't what she'd expect from a tight-lipped bounty hunter. Still, she didn't want him around her son. "I'll get it fixed."

He cocked his head. "But not by me."

"Not to offend you, Mr. Sergeant, but we're not on the same side." She folded her arms across her middle and nailed him with a pointed gaze. "Are you interested in fixing the pump to make *my* life easier? Or your sister's?"

"Does it matter if the job gets done?" He dared to take a step closer. "We don't have to like or trust one another, Mrs. Richards. But, from what you said, you don't need one more task to handle. Surely, Henry can't haul all the water you need."

Carly's hands fell away. She didn't want to be beholden to the man, didn't want him around her son. Still, that broken pump further complicated already complicated days. "A working pump *would* make life easier," she admitted reluctantly.

"Good, then it's settled. I'll bring my tools and be over after supper."

"I'll make sure Henry doesn't bother you again."

"I suspect Henry will sneak over here whether you approve or not." He shrugged. "Maybe he's missing his pa."

Carly sucked in a breath. "No. He isn't. No one in town misses Max."

His eyes bored into her, trying to see inside her. "I can imagine."

She looked away, avoiding his probing gaze and the unspoken questions in his eyes. Questions she had no intention of answering.

He stepped in front of her, dipped his head, forcing her to look at him. "Are you all right?"

After Max's funeral, she'd felt as if she and Henry had awakened from a nightmare. Then this man had ridden into town, intent on ruining their lives, bringing with him a new threat.

She raised her chin. "I was fine until you showed up."

"Wish I had another choice."

"We always have another choice."

"Do we?" he said, his tone soft, laden with sorrow.

The pain in his eyes rooted her in place. No matter what she'd claimed, she knew as well as this man, sometimes there were no alternatives. The reason she'd stayed with Max.

"I suspect your life hasn't been easy, Mrs. Richards. That your husband didn't treat you the way a man should."

At his gentle tone Carly again looked away, unable to bear such scrutiny.

Callused fingers tenderly tilted her face to his. "You and I have had to live with the hand we were dealt."

Her gaze locked with his. In his gray depths a flash of interest sparked and flared. Carly's mouth went dry as dust as her heart rat-a-tatted in her chest.

What was happening to her? How could she find the man responsible for Max's death attractive?

Her breath caught. She'd feared the influence Nate Sergeant would have on Henry, never once considering he might hold some unexplainable power over her.

He was a bounty hunter. He was trying to take her shop. He was a terrible example for her son.

Not admirable, not the kind of man she wanted in her life. She'd promised herself and God she'd never run ahead of Him again.

She took a step back and steeled her spine. "We may not always have a choice, Mr. Sergeant, but in this matter, I do. A gun-toting bounty hunter is a bad example for my son. I don't want Henry spending time with you."

As if a shade had been pulled, the light vanished from his eyes. His gaze grew distant, detached. "I'll fix your pump. And do what I can to keep Henry away." He huffed. "But make no mistake—I won't hurt that boy's feelings. I can't do it."

"Better to hurt his feelings than to lead him down your path."

"I'd never do that," he rasped, his jaw chiseled in anger.

"Whether you intend to or not, that's exactly what could happen. I have no idea why, but Henry admires you."

Without a backward glance, Carly gathered her skirts and dashed toward home. For a moment she'd connected with the rogue determined to take her shop. Once again, she'd been drawn in by a handsome face, a winsome smile and a string of sweet words—all meaningless. Hadn't life with Max proved where such foolishness led?

Lord, help keep up my defenses. Keep me strong. Henry's future depends on it.

Chapter Eight

Nate crossed the alley and Carly's backyard and then stepped onto the side porch, stopping by the open window of the Richards's kitchen, spellbound by the family inside.

Eyes on the McGuffey Reader she held, Mrs. Richards sat at the table, giving Henry his spelling words. "Bubbles. The sink was full of bubbles."

"B-u-b-b-e-l-s."

"No, try again," she said, her tone soft with patience.

"B-u-b-b-l-e-s."

"Good." She smiled and went on to the next word.

Mother and child—the pretty picture of a normal family, a normal family Nate had experienced as a child.

A desire to walk into that picture rose up inside him, filling him with a craving so strong his chest burned.

If only—

A cold splash of reality doused him like the frigid air of a nor'easter. For a minute there, he'd longed for the impossible. And forgotten who he was—Nate Sergeant, bounty hunter—on a mission he could not shirk. Forgotten who Carly Richards was—the obstacle to Anna's future, an obstacle Nate would thwart. Forgotten who Stogsdill was—a menace to mankind, a threat Nate would defuse.

One glance at Carly explained his loss of memory. He'd succumbed to the tantalizing pull of a pretty woman. To a pretty woman with a light floral scent that lingered in his nostrils. To a pretty woman with coal-black hair that shimmered like reflected moonlight on water. To a pretty woman with a marriage that surely had been as excruciating as walking barefoot over red-hot embers.

If that suspicion was true, Carly Richards was better off alone than tied to a cruel husband. Her son was better off fatherless than tied to a heartless pa.

A harsh truth put a stranglehold on his neck as suffocating as a hangman's noose. Carly Richards saw Nate as made from the same tattered cloth as her dead husband.

Nothing could be further from the truth. He lived on the right side of the law, seeking justice. Her opinion stabbed at his pride, scoffed at his integrity.

Again, he asked himself why he cared.

How could he feel this puzzling sense of attraction to this petite woman who was a giant nuisance? Who thought him unworthy, uncaring, a bad influence on her son?

He expelled a shuddering breath. What Mrs. Richards thought of him didn't matter.

What mattered was catching Stogsdill. Nate wouldn't rest until he'd put Stogsdill behind bars. If there was any justice, the man would rot in jail.

With his purpose clear, Nate rapped on the door. He had a pump to fix, nothing more.

Carly stood in the entrance, an apron tied around her waist. Tendrils of hair loose around her face. At the sight of him, her blue eyes filled with disquiet.

Behind her, dirty dishes, glasses and an iron skillet were stacked beside the sink. Otherwise the small space was pristine.

Not dirty like Nate, not tainted by failure and death.

He cleared his throat, then doffed his hat. "Came to fix that pump."

She stepped back to let him enter.

With a squeal, Henry scrambled off the chair and raced toward him. "Nate!"

The unreserved welcome and the sweet innocence on the boy's face knotted Nate's stomach. Children were trusting, defenseless. They needed to be protected with the same vigilance as a mother bear had for her cubs. He must do everything in his power to keep his distance from the boy.

Henry pointed at the metal box Nate carried. "What's that?"

"A toolbox. Belonged to my pa, but my sister keeps it now," he said in a tone as raspy as a door on rusty hinges.

"Wow!" The boy squatted beside him as Nate opened the lid, peering at the wrenches, hammers and screwdrivers inside. He looked up at Nate, his eyes filled with eagerness. "Can I help?"

Nate glanced at Carly. "Is that all right with you?"

"I've practiced my spelling words. Please!"

Carly's azure eyes turned stormy, revealing the battle raging inside her. She didn't want Henry getting closer to Nate. Yet she didn't want to deprive her son of the chance to learn a manly skill.

"All right, if you promise to do exactly what Mr. Sergeant says and not get in his way."

Henry beamed. "I promise!"

Nate examined the pump positioned at the end of the counter. Two missing screws in the base made the pump wobble, an easy fix, but surely not the main problem. "What's the matter with the pump?"

"Water is leaking from the pipe under the sink."

"I'll take a look."

"I'd appreciate it," she said, her tone gentle, grateful, drawing him closer.

With Carly within arm's reach, Nate found himself fumbling for the proper tool, his mind fuzzy, as if he couldn't tell a wrench from a hammer. How could this woman who couldn't abide his presence have this unsettling effect on him?

"I have paperwork to do," she said, then weaved past the table and chairs, her skirts swishing softly.

At the door she stopped, glancing back as if checking on Henry, and caught Nate watching her. Pink flooded her cheeks and she quickly turned away, proof his presence had the same strange effect on her.

While Nate assessed the pipe under the sink, Henry stuck closer than a shadow at noon, asking questions, adoration plain in his eyes. He didn't want to be important to this boy. He didn't want to care about Henry, didn't want to get involved with anyone, not even the boy's tempting mother.

Nate grabbed a box of various-size screws out of the tool kit and handed Henry a screw. "Find one more like this one," he said, setting the open box on the table.

With a nod, Henry scrambled onto a chair and spread the screws out in front of him. "Pa never let me help. He said I was…" The boy frowned, as if searching for a word. "A hinder pants."

Hinder pants? A chuckle shoved up Nate's throat, but one look at the hurt in Henry's eyes dispelled the humor. "I think you mean hindrance. Your pa probably thought you were too young to help."

"I'm a big boy. And I can hammer."

"Well, this job doesn't need a hammer, but we do need those screws."

Henry bent to the task with total absorption, wanting only to please. What kind of a man would label his son a hindrance? What other far worse names had Max Richards called his son?

Nate selected a wrench from his toolbox, worked the pump handle, then shoved the curtain aside and crouched beneath the sink. The joint in the pipe was wet and dripping, producing a puddle of water on the floor. If he couldn't tighten the joint with the wrench, he'd have to solder it.

Henry tugged at Nate's shirt. "Found it." He stretched out his hand. Two matched screws nestled in his palm.

"Thanks. You were a big help." Nate tousled the boy's hair.

"I'm a good boy," Henry said, yet his tone lacked confidence, as if trying to convince himself.

"You're a very good boy and an excellent assistant."

A giggle slipped from Henry's lips. He danced around the kitchen, unable to contain his joy at those few words of praise. Poor kid hadn't heard many from that father of his.

Nate pulled a chair over to the counter. "Want to put in those screws you found?" he said, grabbing the appropriate screwdriver from the toolbox.

With an eager nod, Henry clambered onto the seat. Nate showed him where to place the screw in the wobbly base, and then gave the screwdriver a few turns. "Hold it like this," he said, covering Henry's small hand with his own. Together they tightened the screw.

With stubby fingers, Henry jammed the second screw in place. Nate twisted the handle a few turns. "You can finish," he said, handing the boy the tool.

With each turn of the screwdriver, Henry's smile widened until he was beaming and the screw was in place. "I did it!"

"You're a fast learner."

Carly walked into the kitchen. "It's bedtime. Come along, Henry."

"Do I have to?" Henry whined. "Nate needs me."

"Wouldn't take but a minute to tighten the other two

screws and put the rest away," Nate said, turning his gaze on Carly. "He's a big help."

Her gaze bored into his. She gave a brisk nod. "All right."

"Would you put the screws we aren't using in there, Henry?" Nate said, pointing to the open box.

Henry's fingers fumbled in an attempt to hurry, and several screws fell to the floor. His gaze flew to Nate's, alarm wide in his eyes. "I didn't mean to drop 'em."

Had Max struck his son? "We men have trouble holding on to small objects." Nate searched the floor. "There's one."

As Nate gathered the rest, the lad darted under the table, then came up with a smile and his hand fisted. In seconds he'd climbed onto the chair and tucked them inside.

While Nate watched, Henry rose on his knees and poked the tip of the screwdriver into the notch. His face scrunched with effort, Henry turned the handle with a grunt. With each twist, the fastener settled deeper.

"Did you see me do it, Mama? All by myself!" Henry crowed.

"I sure did. I'm proud of you."

Henry pivoted on the chair, facing Nate, his expression uncertain. Then he flung his arms around Nate's chest and burrowed into him.

Nate tucked the boy into an awkward hug. "Thanks for your help, buddy."

Carly's brow furrowed. "Time for bed, Henry," she said in a no-nonsense tone.

Nate gently pried off Henry's arms and smiled down at him. "A wise man listens to his mother."

Henry gave a nod and then trailed after Carly, looking back with a nameless plea in his eyes Nate couldn't handle.

Once the boy disappeared around the corner, Nate knelt near the pipe and tightened the joint. Not easy to do. Most likely mineral deposits had clogged the grooves. He got to his feet, gave the pump handle a few cranks and nodded when water flowed into the sink but not onto the floor beneath.

Finished with the task, he packed the tools, then closed the chest and walked onto the porch. Sweet notes of a song floated to him, first Carly's voice, then Henry's.

Carly was an excellent mother. Much like his.

Memories of Ma paraded through his mind. Her gentle touch as she tucked him in at night. Her laugh when he'd showed off, trying to impress her with his prowess. Her warning frown when he'd fidgeted in church. All the little things she'd done to guide him, to make him feel special, secure.

When he'd met Rachel and fallen in love, he'd thought he'd found that peace he'd been missing. What a fool he'd been. The memory of Rachel dying in his arms tore through him, exploding pain in his chest, squeezing against his lungs until he couldn't breathe, as if he'd taken that bullet.

If only he had.

He gulped air, trying to ease his racing heart. Rachel, his parents, Walt had never done a cruel thing in their lives, yet all had died a violent death.

Lord, why do the good die? Why?

As long as Stogsdill ran free, Nate couldn't rest. He'd go after the outlaw as soon as he could.

The prospect of living out of a saddlebag, searching for the vilest of men, tore at the moments of contentment he'd found here in a town with the unlikely name of Gnaw Bone.

Carly joined Nate on the porch, tucking her arms around her as if warding off the night chill.

"I tightened the fitting in the pipe. Appears to have stopped the leak. If not, I'll need to solder it."

"Thank you." She laid a hand on his sleeve, then took

a hurried step back, as if she hadn't meant to touch him. "And thanks for allowing my son to help. He couldn't stop talking about it."

"The pleasure was mine. Reminds me of all the good times I had working beside my dad."

The full moon illuminated her features with a faint glow. She kept her distance. Yet even from there he caught the faintest scent of roses.

"It's a beautiful night," she said. "I don't get out here to enjoy the quiet often."

"Sometimes I forget to enjoy it at all."

She stepped to the porch railing. "I assumed a bounty hunter spent most nights under the stars."

How could he explain that his focus on capturing Stogsdill destroyed the peace of the nighttime sky? "Guess the company makes the difference," he said, taking a step closer.

He should go, yet he didn't want to leave. What could he do that would allow him to stay, something that would put distance between them yet ease Carly's burden?

Through the open door his gaze sought the stack of dirty dishes. "Maybe we should test that pump? While I wash those dishes."

She whirled to him. "You want to do dishes? Why?"

At the astonishment and suspicion in her tone, he bit back a smile, and then ushered her inside. "Yes, if you'll dry." He leaned in. "If I lend a hand, maybe you'll believe I'm not all bad."

She smirked. "This I've got to see."

"You've never seen a man clean up the kitchen?"

"Not in my house." She grabbed a dish towel from the hook by the sink. "My pa didn't do what he called 'women's work.' Max's version of a household chore was taking care of his horse." She sighed. "I shouldn't speak ill of anyone."

With a husband like Max Richards, the poor woman's conscience probably worked overtime. "Living on the trail taught me to appreciate the work women do." He smiled. "Especially a home-cooked meal."

Her face softened, slipping into the sweetest smile he'd ever seen. The sight of her stole his breath, left him standing there gazing at her with the intensity of a pup starving for affection. Her pupils dilated, luring him into their dark depths. He took a step closer.

She inhaled sharply and turned away, fiddling with the button at her collar, breaking the connection.

Telling himself her reaction was for the best, Nate walked to the sink. He pumped cold water into the dishpan hanging at the end of the counter and added hot water from the reservoir in the stove, all the while trying to tamp down an urge to pull Carly into his arms.

Carly opened a jar of soap, scooped up a blob and swished it around in the water, working up suds. She stood so near he could feel the heat from her body. Inhale her soft floral scent. See a hairpin that had worked loose from holding her bun in place.

She handed him a dishrag. As he took the cloth, their fingertips brushed. As a jolt of awareness shot through him, Carly sucked in a breath and busied herself filling another dishpan with hot water. Finished with that, she grabbed a dishrag and scrubbed the table and the counter, flitting here and there like a hummingbird in search of a place to light.

The tick of the pendulum of the kitchen clock seemed to echo in the silence. Did the knowledge they were alone in the house with only her son for a chaperone make her uncomfortable? Or was she as unnerved as he was by the attraction between them? An attraction that had roared to life with a sudden intensity that left him stunned.

With every particle of his being, he fought the pull

she had over him. Tomorrow she'd see him as an enemy. Rightly so. What could he say to ease the tension? In the room? Inside him?

"Looks like Henry licked his plate clean. Says a lot about your cooking," he said, forcing a light tone he didn't feel, trying to cover his sudden envy of a boy who had Carly's company.

"Depends on the menu. Henry doesn't like most vegetables. He prefers growing to eating them."

Nate chuckled. "Ma insisted I eat lima beans. I couldn't get them down without gagging. Finally she gave up. Said she'd forget lima beans if I ate all the others." He grinned down at her. "The reason I eat turnips to this day."

"You had a good mother." Her gaze filled with sorrow. "I did, too. My mother taught me to sew. I'd sit beside her, watch her every move and thread her needles. The older I got, the more she let me do. I cut out and hemmed a blanket for my doll, then made dishrags, handkerchiefs, aprons. By the time I was ten, I was making my own play dresses." She took the plate he handed her. "Ma said I had the knack and sent me to Mrs. Harrington, the town seamstress, to learn more, insisting I should have a trade to make my own way." Carly wiped and wiped the same plate, as if she couldn't get it dry.

She didn't say what Nate heard: *You want to take that trade away from me.*

"Your ma was a wise woman."

"I know what a cooper, blacksmith, barber, teacher, clerk and farmer does, but I can't fathom searching for outlaws," she said. "What's it like to be a bounty hunter?"

With her dislike of his occupation, the question surprised him. "Much of the time I'm in the saddle, chasing down leads or following trails. Once I nab my man, I disarm and release him into the custody of the nearest sheriff."

"Why do you want to do such a dangerous job?"

"Money's good."

"If you count the hours you spend on the trail, I doubt you're well paid." She narrowed her gaze. "I'm guessing something besides money makes a man risk his life."

"Outlaws must be brought to justice, or more innocents will die."

"I'd like to see evildoers behind bars, but I'm not out rounding up criminals. Something else drives you. What?"

"I'm after one man. Shifty Stogsdill."

"The man on the wanted poster. Why him?"

"Stogsdill was part of the gang that murdered our parents." He ground the words out between jaws so tense he could barely push the words past his lips.

Carly gasped. "I'm…I'm sorry. Anna didn't tell me. What happened?"

"Dairy farming tied our folks down. They were on their first vacation, taking the train to visit relatives in Kansas, when outlaws boarded the train, stealing jewelry, money, whatever passengers had on them. My father reached inside his coat for his pocket watch, alarming a trigger-happy bandit who fired at close range."

"Oh, no, that's horrible."

"From what passengers said, Ma lurched at the outlaw and was shot. Three outlaws fled with the loot. Stogsdill lost his bandanna in a scuffle with the conductor. The man was shot, but survived and recognized Stogsdill from a wanted poster."

"When did this happen?" Carly asked, her face pale, eyes stunned.

"I was fifteen. Anna, eighteen," he said. So long ago.

"You've been hunting their killer for…what? Five years? Ten?"

"I left home at eighteen. Eight years ago."

"That's a long time."

"It's not a life conducive to settling down."

"The reason you're not married," she said, a statement, not a question.

Nate scrubbed grease from a skillet, rubbing harder and harder, as if he could obliterate Stogsdill's face in the iron.

"Do you ever question if your parents would approve of the life you've chosen?"

He flung the dishrag into the sink, scattering bubbles. "That monster killed someone else." Head down, he laid his hands on either side of the sink, his breath coming in gasping spurts. "Someone else…I was close to."

The light pressure on his back eased the tight muscles under a gentle palm. Carly. Trying to comfort him. He turned toward her and stared into damp eyes soft with sympathy.

"I'm sorry," she said. "I wish I could help."

"Thanks, but there's nothing you can do." He took a ragged calming breath, and then returned to the chore, his eyes on the task and not on the woman at his side. When his heart had returned to a steady beat, he said, "If you want to help, think about your customers. Perhaps Stogsdill's girlfriend isn't a stranger to you. Perhaps you've made lots of dresses for her."

"None of my customers could possibly be involved with an outlaw."

"Are you sure? Folks can pretend to be something they're not."

Carly's eyes found the floor. "Yes," she said, a tremble in her voice.

"Still, I'd think she'd stick out."

"What do you mean?"

"Oh, she might talk different. Act different. Look different. Perhaps she would mention far-off places or wear flashy dresses with, uh, low necklines, like a dance hall girl."

"I've never seen a dance hall girl." A blush flooded her cheeks. "Apparently you have."

"I go where I must, to get my man."

She harrumphed, as if she believed he relished spending time in saloons. "I don't remember anyone like you describe."

Either Stogsdill's girlfriend had never stepped foot in Carly's shop, or she looked and behaved nothing in the manner he'd expect of an outlaw's woman. Surely she couldn't be a woman like Carly. Carly was refined, intelligent, hardworking. The kind of woman any man would appreciate.

Finished with the simple task, Nate dried his hands, letting his gaze roam the cozy kitchen. What would it be like to sit at that table, eat a home-cooked meal and relate the day's events surrounded by a family? What would it be like to share everyday activities like a ride in the country or painting a shed or planting a garden?

And turn away from pursuing killers and thieves?

His gaze tumbled to Carly's upturned face, then lowered to her rosy, parted lips. A desire for a wife and children gripped him, twisting inside him, squeezing against his heart.

On their own volition, his feet took him closer until the toes of his boots touched her hem. "You're so pretty," he said, the words slipping from his lips uninvited.

Her gaze skittered away, then darted back to him. "I'm plain, not one bit like those dance hall girls you mentioned."

"You're perfect exactly as you are."

In her eyes he read how much she wanted to believe him. Yet somehow didn't. Hadn't Richards told his wife she was pretty? Didn't she see the truth in the mirror each morning?

"You're a beautiful woman, Carly." He lowered his head

until his lips hovered over hers, wanting only to kiss her. Desperate to kiss her. Waiting for her permission.

Disquiet filled her eyes and she lurched back. "You should leave."

What had he been thinking? A kiss suggested permanence, a future. Something he couldn't offer. Didn't even know he had.

With a nod, he grabbed his toolbox and strode out. Each step thudding inside him, pounding in his temples until his vision blurred, strangely bereft with the sense of loss so strong his knees all but buckled.

An odd feeling swept over him. For a moment he grappled with its identity.

Need.

With every particle of his being, he tamped down the reaction. Nate had never needed anyone. Not even Rachel. He'd cared about her. Loved her, but he hadn't needed her.

And he didn't need Carly.

He had no business thinking about kissing Carly Richards. He had no business contemplating a family.

He'd never make that mistake again. His purpose came before his happiness, just as Carly put her son's well-being before her own. Some things were worth any sacrifice.

Chapter Nine

The only thing more distressing to Carly than a displeased customer was an indecisive customer who couldn't make up her mind. Or worse, kept changing it. As Vivian Schwartz was now.

Carly bit back a sigh. Wasn't she behaving the same way with her wavering feelings toward Nate? How could she be attracted to him one minute and flip to suspicion the next?

Just because the man had washed her dishes didn't make him trustworthy. Nate was a bounty hunter. When she'd asked about tracking outlaws, she'd been curious, sure, but she'd hoped that what she'd learn might give her the upper hand, give her some insight that would save the shop.

Instead, learning about the cold-blooded murder of his parents had turned the tables, fostering sympathy for the man. Now that she knew the heartache driving him.

Still, his occupation was surely not one God would approve. Nothing had changed. Nate was still determined to see his sister get this shop.

Lord, give me wisdom to know Your will. Lead me to whatever is right.

"I want lace on the skirt." Expression petulant, Vivian planted her hands on her hips.

"I'm happy to add more lace, if that's what you want." Though if Vivian kept adding lace, she'd look like one of those dance hall girls Nate had described. "I read in *Harper's Bazaar* this morning that simple lines enhance a woman's form."

The bride worried her lower lip with her teeth. "Oh, I hadn't thought of that. Too much lace could make me look plump."

Mrs. Schwartz snorted. "Nothing would make you look plump, dear. Why, you're practically skin and bones. You really should eat more."

"Mother, stop treating me like a child." Vivian swept a hand toward Carly. "I know what I like and that's what I want! Whether I look like a beanpole or an elephant."

Anna stepped between Carly and the bride. "Vivian, would you like to try on your wedding dress once more? The veil is hemmed. The white kid pumps arrived yesterday. Once you see the entire ensemble, I'm sure you'll know if the gown needs lace."

A smile brightened Vivian's stormy face. "That might help."

"We have the prettiest silk stockings embroidered with flowers at the ankle." Anna waggled her brows. "Very chic."

"I must have a pair."

As Mrs. Schwartz paced the room, Vivian and Anna disappeared behind the screen and Carly went in search of the hosiery. She found the correct size and handed them to Anna.

Thanks to Nate's sister, they'd warded off Vivian's impending temper tantrum. Anna's skill with a needle and her calm manner made her an asset in the shop. Carly had liked the woman from that very first day, but each day since, her respect and admiration for Anna had grown.

Carly refolded a stack of lace-edged handkerchiefs Vivian had been perusing into perfect alignment. How could a gentle, soft-spoken widow be kin to Nate, a tough, hard-headed bounty hunter bent on vengeance and stirring up trouble?

Her hands stilled. If someone had killed her mother or, worse, her precious son, would she seek revenge? She swallowed hard as a heavy weight of uncertainty pressed against her lungs. Truth was, she didn't know.

She'd seen a soft side of Nate, too. With his sister, with Henry, even with her. Had the conflict over the shop distorted her judgment? Or had years with Max made her suspicious of the man? Still, she knew very little about Nate.

Who had Nate been referring to in the obscure remark that Stogsdill had killed someone else he'd cared about? Had there been a woman in his life?

Across the way, Mrs. Schwartz wilted into an armchair. "Vivian is going to turn my hair gray."

Mine, too.

"We want the bride to be happy," Carly murmured. As if the perfect wedding dress could ensure anyone's happiness.

When she'd agreed to marry Max, Carly had spent hours creating the dress of her dreams. Her dreams had wilted faster than the sprig of roses she'd carried.

"Are you feeling all right, Carly?" Mrs. Schwartz asked.

"I'm fine. Would you like to try on your gown?"

Mrs. Schwartz laughed. "I almost forgot that's why we came."

Behind the screen in the opposite corner, Carly helped the matron into the dress she'd wear to her daughter's wedding. The satin skimmed her generous figure, giving the older woman an attractive silhouette.

"The lovely shade of blue complements your eyes," Carly said, adjusting the wide-brimmed hat topped with white-silk roses and a smattering of violets and ribbon matching the gown. She stood back. "You look stunning."

Mrs. Schwartz faced the mirror and inspected her reflection, the tick of the clock the only sound in the room. As she waited for her customer's reaction, Carly held her breath, her heart beating in rhythm with each swing of the pendulum.

The matron pivoted and swept Carly into an embrace. "I'm very pleased. Your creations always make me feel pretty."

Murmuring her thanks, Carly's eyes stung. *Thank You, God, for giving me talent to help women appreciate the body You gave them.*

With Anna in the lead, Vivian stepped from behind the screen. Head high, the veil sweeping the floor and trailing behind her, the white confection nipped in at her waist and scalloped at her shoulders, Vivian looked every inch the beautiful bride.

One look at her daughter and Mrs. Schwartz burst into tears. "My little girl's all grown up." She grabbed a tatted hanky from her purse and dabbed at her eyes. "And so lovely she takes my breath away."

"Mama, do you think Anthony will think I'm beautiful?"

"He's not made of stone, dear. Of course he will!"

"The gown is perfect for you, Vivian," Anna said. "I've never seen a lovelier bride."

A flush bloomed in Vivian's cheeks. "I feel like I've stepped into the pages of a fairy tale and I'm the princess."

"Anna's right," Mrs. Schwartz said. "The gown is most becoming, as gorgeous as the French design. You *are* a princess."

Vivian's gaze swept over her mother's attire. "Oh, Mama, if I'm a princess, you're a queen."

Mother and daughter turned toward the mirror, smiling at their images.

Carly met Anna's gaze, hoping the expression on her

face revealed Carly's gratitude. Anna had taken a volatile situation and turned it into a victory.

With such a nice sister, surely Nate wasn't so bad. Perhaps she'd misjudged brotherly concern for his sister as greed.

Anna slid an arm around Carly's waist, then leaned in. "You've pleased them both."

"Thanks to your tact."

Vivian gathered the veil in her arms and sashayed to them, her skirts swishing softly. "I've decided against the extra lace. I love the gown, just as it is."

The bride's decision was the right one. If Carly had added the lace, Vivian would have seen her error. Removing each stitch would have taken hours of tedious work, time they didn't have.

Within minutes, the Schwartz women had removed their wedding finery and left the shop with smiles on their faces and cash in Carly's register.

Two done and…

Carly gulped. Ten more garments to finish. "I should've charged more. We'll need to work day and night to get the trousseau made before the wedding."

"Don't worry. We'll make the deadline. I think Vivian finally trusts your judgment as a designer and won't be taking up the time we need to finish."

"I couldn't handle this order without your help, Anna. You're a wonderful seamstress, adept with customers and wise."

Anna smiled, joy flooding her eyes. "We make a good team."

"We do."

"Want to join me for a cup of tea?" Anna asked.

"I'd like to start work on Vivian's travel suit. You go ahead."

"I won't be long."

As Anna disappeared into the back, the truth of her claim slid through Carly. They did work well together, as if their personalities and traits supplied what the other needed, fitting together like pieces cut by a jigsaw.

Yet beneath their camaraderie and shared purpose lay the knowledge that only one of them would own this shop.

Carly inhaled sharply. What would happen then?

Nothing. Not a trace.

Nate had contacted every lawman he knew, looking for leads to Stogsdill's whereabouts, and once again had come up empty. It was as if the outlaw had disappeared into thin air.

At least that meant he wasn't robbing banks and trains, killing innocent bystanders. Was he avoiding anything that would attract attention to his whereabouts? If so, could he be planning to visit his girlfriend?

He pocketed the latest wire, the same message as all the others—no one's seen him—and exited the telegraph office right into the path of a woman.

To avoid her, he took a quick step back, then tipped his hat. "My apologies, miss."

She gave him a sweet smile, then averted her eyes, her demeanor as modest as her attire. "Good day."

As she passed, a flash of red drew Nate's gaze to a ring dangling from a thin gold chain around her neck, raising the hairs on the back of his neck.

A ruby ring.

A ruby ring like the one Nate had seen on Shifty Stogsdill's right hand, worn like a trophy, probably stolen from one of his victims.

A ruby ring like the one that had flashed in the sun the afternoon Stogsdill had gunned down Rachel.

Could this be the same ring?

He followed her progress down the walk. She stopped in front of the mercantile, looking at a display in the window.

The young woman had a natural beauty, looked nothing like a dance hall girl with her brown hair tucked beneath a simple hat, a demure neckline on a nondescript dress. Not the kind of female he'd expect Stogsdill to squire around.

Still, Nate had met success rounding up fugitives by noticing the smallest details and pursuing every lead, no matter how insignificant.

Ruby rings weren't rare. But the size of the gem was. And this ruby ring was worn around a woman's neck here in Gnaw Bone, the rumored location of Stogsdill's girl-friend.

A lead. The first he'd had. A lead he intended to pursue.

The young woman walked on, then entered Carly's shop.

Nate clamped his Stetson low and followed.

The shop bell jingled. Debby Pence stepped inside.

Carly covered her relief with a welcoming smile. When Debby hadn't returned for the final fitting, Carly wondered if the wedding had been canceled.

The bell jingled again. Nate ambled in, looking at ease, as if the shop belonged to him. What was he doing here? Was he checking up on her? Wasn't the situation compli-cated enough without his frequent intrusions?

Carly's breath caught. Why did she notice every detail about him? That chiseled jaw, those full lips and those dark-rimmed gray eyes that seemed to read her thoughts.

Refusing to acknowledge Nate and her pounding heart, she hurried to Debby. "I'm glad to see you."

Debby glanced at Nate. "If you're busy, I can come an-other time," she said in an uncertain tone, as if hating to interrupt.

"This is the perfect time. I'll only be a minute."

She crossed to Nate. "If you're looking for your sister, she's taking a break. I'll tell her you came by."

"I'm in no rush. I'll wait," he said, leaning against the counter and flipping through a ladies' magazine.

Was he planning on advising his sister on what supplies to carry? Why didn't he leave and come back later? Mercy, that warm smile on his face would melt butter. But his watchful gaze suggested he was up to something and that his purpose for being here had nothing to do with Anna.

Carly removed Debby's wedding dress from the armoire. "I thought you'd be back before this," she said, ushering the bride to the folding screen. "Your dress is finished, just needs the final touches. Depending on the wedding date, I should be able to finish any tucks here or there to give you a perfect fit."

Pink flooded Debby's cheeks. "I'm sorry. I wasn't sure there would be a wedding." She bit her lower lip. "I'm, uh, still not sure of the date. Things keep coming up."

How odd. Weddings required arranging countless details. Most of those details hinged on the date of the ceremony. Of course few weddings were as grand as Vivian's.

"Well, why not try on the dress?" Carly gave Debby an encouraging smile. "My mother used to say, once the dress is right, everything else will fall into place."

Keeping that smile took every bit of Carly's resolve. Nate had moved closer and was now leaning nonchalantly against the case of fine gloves, arms folded over his chest. Stetson tugged low over his eyes, as if catching a catnap.

She wasn't fooled. The man was aware of every word. What was he up to?

Why did she let Nate's presence disturb her? She'd focus on pleasing her customer, always her prime objective, and ignore the man's irksome presence.

Behind the screen, Carly helped Debby into her gown, fastening the column of tiny buttons down the back, and then stepped in front of the bride. The white batiste bodice hugged her figure, encircling her slender neck and nipping in at her waist. This young woman had evolved into a lovely butterfly.

"Debby, come see how stunning you are."

They rounded the screen and walked to the floor-length mirror. Debby faced her reflection, her shoulders hunched. "It's beautiful. The prettiest dress I've ever owned," she said, her voice falling as flat as an undercooked pancake.

"It fits perfectly. No need to alter a single dart or seam. I'll just machine stitch the basted seams." Carly smoothed the dress, gently nudging Debby's shoulders back. A touch she hoped said, "Wear the dress with pride."

"*You* look beautiful," Carly whispered.

"It *is* a mighty fine gown, not that I'm an expert," Nate said with a wry grin. "Any man would be proud to see his intended wearing that dress and looking so pretty."

Debby blushed. "You really think so?"

"Yes. Yes, I do."

Nate had called Debby pretty. While Carly stood to the side wearing her plainest dress, a blade of grass beside a slender white rose. What did it matter? Nate Sergeant was not the man for her. Now that she understood his quest, she knew he'd never settle down. Never be a man who stayed.

Carly pinned the circlet of orange blossoms to Debby's hair, and then smoothed the gauzy veil around her shoulders. "Rory is sure to be pleased."

"I hope you're right. He's been away so long this time, I'm afraid he's forgotten me."

Nate ambled closer. "Not sure what all goes into a wedding, but I'd think the groom should be around to help."

Or be underfoot. Why didn't he leave?

"Oh, it's okay. Rory's a salesman with a large territory. His company pressures him for orders, so he's on the road for long periods." Debby licked her lips as if they were dry. "I try not to bother him. He says I distract him from his job."

"That has to be hard for both of you," Carly said, though she hadn't minded Max's absences.

Carly glanced at Nate. She'd thought more about this man when he was away from her than she ever had Max. She bit back a huff. And why not? Who knew what Nate would do to see his sister installed in her shop?

"He buys me the prettiest things to show he's sorry," Debby said. "Things my grandparents would never buy." A small, pleased smile stole over Debby's face. "He's always leaving me gifts. Whenever I get upset he has to go away or he…well, wasn't as nice as he could be, he does the sweetest things." She ran a fingertip over the blood-red gem hanging around her neck. "Like this."

"Sounds like a successful, generous man," Nate said.

"Oh, he is. Very." She fiddled with the folds of her veil. "I'm so lucky." Tears welled in her eyes, belying her claim.

"Once you set a date for the wedding, let me know," Carly said. "I can finish your dress in one evening."

"I'm sure it won't be much longer. He's supposed to be back soon. Maybe even next week." Pink tinged her cheeks. "In his last letter, Rory said he couldn't wait to make me his wife. As soon as I know the date, I'll stop by. Even before I tell Pastor Koontz." She blinked several times, as if trying to dislodge something in her eyes. "Rory didn't want a church wedding. He doesn't like a lot of people around, but I told him Grandpa would never give his permission unless we were married in church."

Carly had always dreamed of a church wedding, yet Max had refused, insisting the county courthouse would be less intimidating. As if the man had ever feared anyone…well, except perhaps God.

"Pastor Koontz will perform a lovely ceremony," Carly said, yet could barely imagine what it would be like to marry a man who pledged his love in front of God and everybody.

Her gaze strayed to Nate. His face was as unreadable as blurred ink.

"Rory says churches are full of hypocrites," Debby went on. "But once he gets to know people, he'll change his mind."

Carly looked over Debby's shoulder into the girl's brown eyes staring back at her in the mirror. In those eyes, Carly saw trepidation and...hope. Hope that the decision to marry Rory wasn't wrong. Hope that the ceremony would somehow change things. Hope that a ring on her finger would turn her intended into the husband of a woman's dreams.

The same hope Carly had once held on to so tightly she hadn't seen the truth. "If you're not sure, it's okay to wait," she murmured into Debby's ear.

"It's just... Rory has been away so much." Debby nodded, then nodded again, faster this time, as if trying to convince herself all her qualms stemmed from his absence. "Once we're married, he promises it'll be different. He'll be different."

Oh, dear girl, all men say that, Carly thought but did not say.

"Nothing unusual for a groom to get cold feet before the wedding," Nate said, as casual as you please.

Why was he inserting himself into her business, into her interaction with her customer? As if he was saying, "Hey, Carly, let me show you how to ease a bride's fears."

What did Nate know about day-after regrets and bad marriages? What did he know about the inner, intricate workings of a woman's heart?

"Rory will be back soon and then we'll set a date and..." Debby let out a shaky breath. "Then everything will be okay."

Carly wanted to tell Debby marriage could be awful from the beginning. That before her wedding day was over she could realize she'd made a huge mistake. A mistake she might have to live with for the rest of her life.

But how could Carly say all that when Debby had hope shining in her eyes? Instead she said, "Marriage is a big step."

The smile broad on her face, Debby swirled to Carly. "Thank you for making this beautiful dress. I'll feel like a princess on my wedding day, like I always dreamed, and then everything will be fine. I'm sure of it," she said, slipping behind the screen.

As Carly followed to help Debby from the dress, she hoped Debby's groom *was* Prince Charming. And this sweet young woman would know only happiness for as long as she lived.

Happiness. What would it be like to fall in love with a good man? What would it be like to have a groom standing beside you, beaming with joy in his eyes, love in his heart? What would it be like to have a real wedding with all the lovely traditions of that sacred ceremony?

Carly shook off the ridiculous fantasy. She was past those romantic girlish notions. Yet no matter what Carly told herself, she couldn't stop the flicker of envy rising inside her, uninvited.

As she walked from behind the screen, her gaze locked with Nate's. In those depths she saw something bleak, remote.

"Some folks put stock in fairy-tale endings," he said. "I'm not a man that does."

Inside Carly hope for a second chance withered. She'd been foolish to think otherwise. Nate made it perfectly clear he would not be a good groom.

Yet, in the deepest part of her, Carly still believed in fairy-tale endings. The picture of her in front of a preacher rose in her mind. The groom standing beside her was smiling, handsome, his eyes filled with love. The perfect mate.

Except in her traitorous mind, the groom looked too much like Nate.

Carly's gaze darted to his, her face scorching, hoping he couldn't read her thoughts.

As if he had and couldn't abide what he saw, Nate tipped his hat and strode out, the bell overhead dancing to the erratic rhythm of her heart.

What had gotten into her? Nate Sergeant was another Max, another Rory, not a man to depend on.

Chapter Ten

Nate watched Debby Pence walk to a nondescript wagon, unhitch the team from the post, gather her skirts and climb onto the seat. She paused a moment, then released the brake and deftly backed the draft horses into the street, obviously comfortable driving a team and wagon.

Probably lives on a farm outside of town. Was the rural location the perfect hideaway for a criminal? Or was she as homespun as the dress she wore?

Nate cuffed the back of his neck. He'd learned to suspect every motive. But in this case, was he overreacting? How could this genteel young woman fall for a scoundrel like Stogsdill? How would she have met him?

Yet he couldn't tamp down the feeling her groom was the man he hunted. She was probably an innocent who believed Stogsdill's lies and had no idea the man courting her was a murderer.

Nate watched Debby turn off Main and head west until he could no longer detect the sound of clopping hooves.

Across the way, two men stood in the alley between the shop and the mercantile. One leaned on the corner of the building, a tattered hat askew on his shaggy head. The other was even more scruffy, his eyes squinting as if he'd had too late a night and too much to drink.

Nate crossed to them. "Name's Nate Sergeant," he said, sticking out a hand.

The skinny guy's gaze narrowed. "Ah, you're that there bounty hunter. I'm Lester Harders and I ain't wanted for nothing but being late to supper." He shook Nate's hand. "This here's my twin Lloyd. Iffen you need a face for a poster, he's the guilty one."

Lloyd snorted. "Ain't guilty of nothing more than shooting up a few signs after Lester talked me into tossing back one too many."

Lester waggled his brows. "If I had a sweet little wife, I wouldn't be spending my nights at the saloon with you."

"You gentlemen know the lady that just left?" Nate asked.

"Noticed your eyeballs were glued on her." Lester nudged his brother. "Told you he was interested."

Lloyd snickered.

"Better watch your step," Lester said. "She's betrothed. Her intended don't take to men ogling the promised goods, iffen you know what I mean."

That sounded like Stogsdill. The outlaw had a reputation for a jealous streak and a hair-trigger temper.

Lester craned his neck to look at the road Debby had taken. "That purty little thing would make any man a fine wife. Her grandpa's got eighty acres out on Hartzell Road and some nice horseflesh to go with it, and no one else to inherit. Reckon I'd be a welcome addition to the family if someone hadn't beat me to it."

Lloyd guffawed. "Like you'd get within ten feet of her."

Nate bit back a smile. "Sounds like a tough character."

"Rory? Only saw him once, but he made an impression." Lester rubbed his jaw. "He didn't like me working for Debby's grandpa and near knocked me out."

"I would steer clear of him, if I knew what he looked like." Nate glanced down the street, casual and calm, as if the answer didn't matter. "Can you describe him?"

"I dunno," Lester said. "Same height as me. Broad in the shoulders. Sits a horse like he was born in the saddle." He snorted. "You'd have thought he'd be grateful. I was just doing old man Pence a favor, helping out."

"Any idea where Debby met this Rory?"

"Where was she, Lloyd? That fancy place with the purty name."

"Santa Fe?" Lloyd said.

"No, that ain't it. Gotta saint in it like the town thinks it's better than most."

"St. Louis?" Nate supplied, as if helping the twin's memory, not trying to tie Debby Pence to the town where Stogsdill's sister lived.

"Yep, that's it."

Nate knew the house, had kept watch for weeks, but had never seen the outlaw. From what he'd gathered, Stogsdill and his sister weren't close.

"Debby come home with Rory on her heels. And, oh, the hullabaloo when he saw me pass the time of day with her."

Lloyd grinned. "Yep, you have a way with the ladies. Charm 'em right off."

Lester gave his brother a light jab. "Anyway, if you're a smart man, you won't even look at Debby sideways, least-ways when Rory's around."

"Thanks for the warning. Does he come often?"

The Harders brothers shrugged, then shuffled off.

Nate raised a silent victorious fist in the air. This piece of evidence, along with that ruby ring, confirmed the hunch that Debby Pence's fiancé was Shifty Stogsdill.

Perhaps if he'd showed the twins Stogsdill's wanted

poster, they'd have identified him. But the fewer people who knew about Stogsdill the better. Especially those two.

He would ride out to Hartzell Road and take a look at the Pence farm. Pick a good spot for surveillance. He'd look less conspicuous if he had an excuse, a reason to head out of town.

His gaze traveled to the dressmaker's shop. Carly sat inside, her head bent over the garment in her lap.

All Nate needed to conceal his investigation was one reason. One very pretty reason.

He heaved a sigh. Why not be honest? No matter how much he shouldn't, he wanted to spend time with Carly. Wanted to know everything about her. Wanted to bask in her goodness and, for a few moments, forget his quest.

That is if he could convince Carly that she and Henry needed a picnic in the country.

At Nate's side, Henry wiggled with excitement, asking questions about every creature they passed.

A straw hat perched squarely on her head, shading her face, Carly chucked her son under the chin. "Careful, or you'll wear out Nate's ears."

"I enjoy seeing the world through your youngster's eyes."

Carly shot Nate a stunning smile. The beauty of that smile—of her—rippled through him, soothing every weary, lonely part of him.

"Thank you for inviting us. I can't remember the last time Henry and I've gone on a picnic or, for that matter, taken a ride into the country."

Her thanks slashed at Nate's conscience. He'd used this picnic as an excuse to locate the Pence farm and possible spots to hole up. If Stogsdill was indeed Debby Pence's groom, she'd come in for that gown. A sign Stogsdill was heading this way.

And Nate would be ready and waiting.

Carly hadn't agreed to accompany him on the outing immediately. But, Anna had squelched each of Carly's objections, vowing they'd finish the Schwartz trousseau in time, and she was perfectly capable of managing the shop single-handedly.

Nate's grip tightened on the reins. If his only purpose had been staking out the Pence farm, he could've invited Anna. Truth be told, he cared about Carly and her son.

When he'd issued the invite, he'd noticed the camaraderie between Anna and Carly. Carly showed Anna a gentle side of herself. Even as she held Nate at arm's length or tried to, he couldn't deny his attraction. He admired her spunk, her fierce love for her son and her kindness to his sister.

With Henry gazing up at him as though he was some kind of hero and Carly mere inches away, the weight of his failure to bring in Stogsdill slipped from Nate's shoulders. The prospect of spending a few hours in their company had his spirits soaring like the red-tailed hawk riding the air currents overhead.

Henry edged sideways, his gaze dropping to the grip of Nate's gun sticking from his holster. "Are you a good shooter?"

Carly tugged her son closer, as if she feared Nate's pistol would leap into her son's hands.

"I've explained to Henry guns are weapons, not toys, and must be considered loaded and dangerous."

"Mama, Nate says I can't touch his gun. When I'm big, big as a man," Henry said, stretching his spindly arms toward the sky, "I can learn to shoot." He sidled closer to Nate. "Will you teach me?"

"Sorry, buddy. I won't be living in Gnaw Bone then."

A soft sigh slid from the boy's lips, tearing at the wall

Nate had built around his heart. "But I can teach you to drive this buggy. Would you like to hold the reins?"

Henry's grin stretched ear to ear. "Yes, sir!"

"See how I'm holding the strips of leather in my palm and through my fingers? I'll help you do the same." Nate threaded the reins through the boy's small hands. "Like that. The mare will likely stick to the road but you still need to stay alert for anything that might spook her."

"What would spook a big horse?"

"Anything unexpected. Like a rabbit running across her path, a snake on the road, something blowing in the wind." Nate kept alert, poised to take control, if needed. "The first time I drove my pa's team, I felt a mile tall."

"Driving's fun, but riding a horse is funner. All the boys in my grade know how to ride 'cept me. Some of the girls, too," Henry added in a whiny tone.

"Horses are expensive to keep when we don't need one," Carly said. "We can walk anywhere we want to go."

"Not clear out here, Mama."

"True, but we can rent a buggy at the livery like Nate did."

"Henry, see those buzzards hovering up ahead. Be prepared. Some horses are skittish near carcasses."

"Oo-hh. Something's dead?"

"Or dying. Buzzards could be circling for a meal."

"Ick." Henry sat straighter, his eyes darting from one side of the road to the other. "Mama, is our town named after buzzards gnawing on bones?"

Nate and Carly exchanged a smile over Henry's head.

"No one remembers how the town got its name, sweetie. Most likely with a name like Gnaw Bone, folks were happy to forget."

"When are we going to eat?" Henry said. "I'm hungry."

"All the talk about dead animals builds my son's appetite," Carly said, her eyes twinkling.

"The Harders mentioned a creek on Hartzell Road. Thought that could be a good picnic spot."

"Hartzell is at the next crossroad. Turn right. The creek's in a stand of trees beyond the Pence farm."

"Pence. Isn't that the name of the bride I met in your shop?"

"Yes. As I recall you had plenty to say to Debby about grooms and cold feet."

"Thought she might appreciate a man's perspective."

She arched a brow. "A man who'd experienced cold feet, perhaps?"

"No. Once I make a decision, especially an important decision like marrying the woman I want to spend my life with, I wouldn't vacillate."

Their gazes locked and held. The connection he'd felt between them tightened. Everything around him fell away as he focused on Carly, only Carly. The woman intrigued him as no other. He wanted to know everything about her, from her favorite food to her childhood memories, to the reason she'd married Max Richards.

Henry tugged at Nate's sleeve. "Isn't that where we turn?"

"What?" Nate jerked his gaze to the road. "Oh, you're right."

"Mama, Nate's not paying attention," Henry crowed. "He woulda missed the turn."

Heat climbed Nate's neck. "You're doing a good job driving, Henry," Nate said, helping Henry slow the horse and turn right.

In a stand of trees alongside the road, Nate spied a decrepit shed. From the looks of it, a sugar maple shack, abandoned until the first thaws in February. The perfect spot to watch the road undetected.

Up ahead, Nate spotted a house and windmill tucked behind a picket fence and nestled between several outbuildings, all painted white. Off to the side and up a rise a silo towered over a red barn. As they got nearer, he could read Pence 1867 painted above its wide double doors.

Behind the barbed wire fence, horses and cattle grazed. A narrow dirt path led up the hill toward the barn. As far as the eye could see, woods and pastures dotted the landscape. Fields of winter wheat rippled in the breeze and tender shoots of corn and beans pushed through the soil in tidy rows.

Nate's gaze roamed the area. "Nice farm. Well kept. Fine-looking stock, too. As fine as any I've seen as a horse wrangler on a spread in Texas."

"Mr. Pence breeds and sells thoroughbreds, as well as tills the land. I'm sure more than one potential suitor was disappointed when Debby fell in love."

"Understandable. A pretty girl with a well-heeled grandfather would make a fine catch."

"If you're in the mood for fishing," Carly said, a smirk riding her lips, "the creek's just around the next bend."

Nate met her amused gaze. "No need to wet a line, Carly, when I'm already in the company of the prettiest girl around."

Henry giggled. "Mama's not a girl."

"Well, not far from being a girl and far prettier than most."

Carly's cheeks bloomed pink and her gaze darted away.

"Remember, Henry, to compliment a lady. Not merely for how she looks, but for what she does. If she's cooked a good meal, tell her, and then thank her for the food."

"Pa never thanked Mama for her cooking, but he cleaned his plate."

"Reckon that's another way to show appreciation."

"'Cepting one time. Remember, Mama? You burned the biscuits. Pa knocked over his chair and throwed 'em at you."

Shoulders squared and stiff, Carly stared ahead.

"Mama, don't you remember?"

"I remember," she murmured, then glanced at Nate, her blue eyes glittering in her suddenly wan face.

Fiery-hot anger roared through Nate's veins. He'd like to teach that no-good scoundrel some manners. But Max was dead. Nevertheless memories of his cruelty lived on, still harming those who'd lived under his tyranny.

What could he say to ease Carly's humiliation and pain? "The way your pa acted had nothing to do with burned biscuits, Henry. Nothing to do with your ma."

"It didn't?"

"No, your pa was the problem. A man doesn't treat a woman like that or any human being."

"When I grow up, Nate, I'm going to be like you, not like Pa."

Nate swallowed hard. "I hope you'll live a different life than mine and settle down somewhere with a family."

"I'm gonna stay with Mama. And take care of her."

Carly ruffled Henry's hair. "You've got time to plan your life, son. No matter what you spend your life doing, you're wise to look up to a good man." She met Nate's gaze. "A good man like Nate."

The warmth of Carly's approving gaze put a lump in Nate's throat that threatened to choke him. Did Carly no longer see him as merely a bounty hunter? She'd suggested he was a man Henry could pattern himself after.

If only Nate could live up to her expectations and never let her down. But he'd experienced the uncertainty of life, of what tomorrow would bring. Those circumstances could demand actions she wouldn't approve.

As they reached the creek that wound through the woods, Nate wrapped his hands over Henry's and guided the horse to the side of the road. "Good job, Henry," he said as he swung from the seat.

"Thanks!" Henry scrambled after him and jumped to the ground.

Nate rounded the buggy and raised his hands to Carly's waist. She leaned toward him, laying her hands on his shoulders.

As he lifted her from the buggy, he marveled that this petite, delicate woman, barely weighing more than a feather in his arms, had survived marriage to a brute of a man.

He wanted to cradle her close, to shield her from everything ugly. But how could he when he held the deed to her business? When any day Stogsdill could ride into Gnaw Bone?

"Thank you," she said, avoiding his eyes as he deposited her on the ground.

Nate grabbed the picnic basket and offered Carly his other arm. With Henry skipping clumsily along in front of them, obviously a new feat needing practice, they walked to the stream drifting serenely between sloping banks.

At least Nate could give Carly this peaceful interlude from her busy life and a past that surely troubled her.

"Call me when it's time to eat." With a whoop, Henry trotted down the bank and jerked off his boots and socks, then scooted to the water's edge.

"Be careful," Carly admonished.

Nate shook out the blanket for their picnic. "I'll keep an eye on him."

"Thank you."

Nate's presence made her feel protected, safe, instead of threatened. He might not be husband material, but she admired his wise council with Henry and his patience with letting her son drive the buggy.

Humming to herself, Carly knelt at the basket and set out the food, more relaxed than she'd been in ages. Apparently she needed this time away from work more than she'd realized.

She rose, catching a glimpse of her son, dangling his feet in the water, as Nate ambled along the bank nearby. When had a man helped supervise her son? Looked out for his welfare? Nate cared about Henry. Listened to him. Taught him to do simple tasks and to treat women well. Her heart stuttered in her chest. Nate would make a good father. Something Henry needed badly.

"Spot any frogs, Henry?" Nate said.

"Yep. I scared 'em and they jumped in."

Nate chuckled, then the laugh stopped. "Henry, don't move."

The authority and urgency in Nate's voice raised the hair on Carly's nape. Heart pounding in her chest, she gathered her skirts and ran toward the creek.

An ominous click. A blast of gunfire.

Henry's wail ripped through her, squeezing the air from Carly's lungs. *Please, Lord, my son!*

Carly watched as Nate scooped up her son. Henry threw his arms around Nate's neck, whimpering against his chest.

"Is he hurt?" Carly shoved the words past the lump wedged in her throat.

Nate met her gaze. "He's fine, Carly. Scared, is all."

As his words sunk in, Carly's legs wobbled and she wilted to the ground.

"I'm sorry for scaring you, Henry. A water moccasin was slithering toward your bare feet."

"Is he dead?" Henry released the hold on Nate's neck and leaned toward the creek, peering in the water.

"Sure is. Want to see?"

"Yes!" Henry wiggled down. "Come see, Mama."

Nate followed Henry's gaze, then set Henry on a rock. "Stay put," he said.

He strode up the bank to Carly. "You okay?"

"I am now."

"For a minute there I thought you'd fainted."

"Now what would make you think that?" She forced a wobbly grin. "Just because I fainted on you once before doesn't mean I will at every provocation."

He chuckled, took her hand and helped her to her feet and down the slope.

Within minutes Nate had found a twig and retrieved the brown, venomous, now-lifeless snake, and dropped it at the edge of the bank.

Henry inched toward it, his expression rapt, clearly fascinated.

At the sight of that long, thick body, Carly shivered. Her gaze locked with Nate's. "Thank you for saving my son."

"I'm just thankful my aim was good."

She bit her lip. "I was…wrong about carrying a gun."

"Not all varmints walk on two legs, Carly."

Many did. And Nate had made it his life's work to bring them in. Not an existence she could abide. Yet she admired his strength. Strength he tempered with gentleness. He was a responsible, caring man who looked after others; something she'd not seen in her father or Max. If only he could give up his mission to catch Stogsdill—

Yet she knew he would not. Could not. That sense of duty she'd seen and admired with Anna wouldn't allow him to quit.

Nate pulled Henry onto his shoulders while Carly gathered his shoes. Together they climbed the bank to sit on the blanket and eat hard-boiled eggs, potato salad, bread-and-butter pickles and baked beans, leftovers from last night's supper.

Finished with their meal, they sat on an outcropping of rock, watching Henry toss stones into the creek, his feet shod and staying clear of the water.

"He's a great kid, Carly."

"And he might not be here if not for you." She laid a hand on his arm. "If anything had happened to him…" Her voice trailed off. "He's my life, all I've got."

"I feel the same about Anna."

Nate's love for his sister only added to the terrible burden he carried.

"Anna told me about her accident."

"Wasn't an accident. I…I caused my sister's lameness," he said, his voice hoarse, low, as if he could barely get out the words.

"From what she said, you weren't much older than Henry."

"I was ten, old enough to check the street before crossing."

"You were a child. I suspect a rambunctious, carefree little boy full of energy. That's far better than a careful child, afraid of making a mistake, of displeasing a parent."

Nate's brow furrowed. "Are you talking about Henry?"

"Yes, when Max was around," she said, studying her hands. "I shouldn't have married Max."

"Why did you?"

She gave a shrug, then stared across the creek to the far bank, eroded from years of meandering water and the occasional flood. One misstep on that thin earthen ledge and the ground could give way, as fast as the flimsy foundation of her marriage had crumbled. To share her reason was too risky, would leave her vulnerable.

"Mercy, we need to head home. Poor Anna is probably exhausted." She scrambled to her feet. "Come, Henry. Time to go."

For, if Carly stayed one more moment under the scrutiny of those intense gray eyes, Nate would surely see her true motivation for marrying Max. And would never understand the decision she'd made.

Chapter Eleven

Saturday was normally the busiest day of the week at the livery, and today was no exception. With Morris holed up in the office all morning, Nate had been scrambling to care for the horses and rent rigs.

Western Union had delivered a wire. The telegram from the lawman in Porter County had all but burned a hole in Nate's pocket. Until he'd found a moment to read the Porter City Bank had been robbed. None of the bandits fit Stogsdill's height and weight.

As customers came in, they took time to jaw with Nate, obviously not in a hurry. Would these men feel the same way when they realized he'd come to Gnaw Bone to take over Carly's shop?

Surely not. He couldn't blame them. He wasn't happy about ousting the pretty widow and her son.

Lawrence Sample, the rotund, bald town barber, had come in to rent a wagon to move his daughter, Elnora, back home. Sample had told him, sopping up the flow of tears with a red handkerchief, that Elnora had lost her husband in a logging accident and would arrive at the depot today with all her belongings and a baby. The poor man fretted if he'd make enough money cutting hair and trimming whiskers to provide for two more. By the time the barber finished the story, Nate found himself clapping Lawrence on the back and agreeing to pray for them. As if God would answer Nate's prayers. Still, his hair needed a trim. One thing Nate could do was use his services.

Then Tuffy Garfield arrived with Rosie Johnson on his arm, both of them blushing and giggling. Their happiness helped ease the sad encounter with Lawrence. They'd rented a fancy surrey for a drive in the country. With a grin, Nate had told Tuffy to return the buggy before dark, or he'd come looking for them.

All the while craving another picnic in the country with Carly. He doubted that she'd go, after the abrupt way she'd ended the day. She obviously hadn't wanted to talk about Max Richards and why she'd married him. She probably had no idea what she'd seen in the man, any more than he did. She was far too good, too gentle, to be wedded to that worthless brute.

"Anyone here?"

Nate stepped into view and greeted Mark Rowland, the town dentist. In the two weeks Nate had been working here, Rowland had come in regularly to ride Duchess, the horse he kept stabled at the livery. People said Rowland could yank a tooth faster than a gunslinger could draw. Nate hoped he'd never have to test the claim.

"I told Duchess you'd be in today," Nate said.

The grin beneath Rowland's reddish mustache revealed even, white teeth, a credit to his profession. "Would you mind exercising her next week while I'm visiting my ailing mother back east?"

"I'll see she's ridden." He clapped a hand on Mark's shoulder. "I'm sorry your mother's sick. Good of you to make the trip." If only Nate still had a mother to visit.

"I learned a valuable lesson from Max Richards."

Nate jerked up his head. "What could Richards possibly teach you?"

"His mother was a special woman, yet that worthless son of hers wasn't at Lillian's bedside when she passed. The womenfolk kept vigil so Lillian wasn't alone, but she'd hoped until she drew her last breath that Max would come." Mark shook his head. "Richards was never around when anyone needed him. Even married to a pretty thing like Carly, Richards was gone more than he was home. Why, he wasn't even here when Carly gave birth to their son."

"Where was the guy? Did he have a job that took him away?"

Rowland snorted. "No real job. Max wasn't fond of work. Everybody knew Carly paid the bills stitching clothes in the shop Max had inherited from Lillian."

Carly hadn't been able to count on her husband. Probably had seldom known his whereabouts. She deserved better. She deserved a man who would support her, a man who would stay. Nate sucked in a breath. That wasn't him.

"Well, I'd better get Duchess saddled. Appreciate the help you're giving Morris by repairing this place." He smiled. "You should consider buying the livery."

As Rowland walked to his horse's stall, Nate's stomach knotted. He was getting caught up in folks' lives, entangled in the community. Something he neither wanted nor expected.

Worse, he felt at home here. Was starting to want things he couldn't have. Not when his mission was to catch Stogsdill.

Nate pulled off his gloves and entered the office to report the morning sales to Morris.

Bent and stooped, the old man scarcely appeared strong enough to get Betsy to Arizona, yet the peace on his face was proof of his love for his business and his horses.

No, that peace ran deeper. Morris loved his wife and the Lord, and those relationships gave him peace.

If only…

"I should be done here soon," Morris said. "Then we need to talk."

The way Morris eyed him tightened the muscles in Nate's neck. "I'll be outside."

Nate grabbed the toolbox and a handful of shims, then left the office to work on the corral attached to the livery. A hard kick from a frightened horse could easily demolish the gate's wobbly slats. Nate would add a board crosswise on both sides and shims under the iron plate holding the hinges.

With each pound of the hammer, Maverick and the two remaining horses in the padlock perked up their ears and eyed him, but soon grew accustomed to the ruckus and returned to their grazing.

As Nate worked, the tension coiling inside him eased. After he finished here, he'd ride out to the shack on Hartzell Road. Perhaps he'd stock it with hardtack, a canteen of water, even a blanket.

"Hi, Nate!" Henry scampered up two rails of the corral fence, then stuck out his arms, windmilling them for balance. "Whatcha doing?"

"I'm making the corral gate stronger."

"Can I help?" Henry jumped to the ground and raced to Nate's side.

If Nate had half the boy's energy, he'd be finished here and over at Western Union sending a wire to the Porter County sheriff, thanking him for the tip, even if it had been worthless. "Mind handing me that small piece of wood?"

Henry bounced, as if he had springs in his boots. "Where?"

"There," he said, pointing to a pile of slats he'd shaved to a point of sorts.

With a pleased grin, Henry handed one to Nate.

Soon Nate was cupping his hand over Henry's and helping the boy turn the screwdriver and tighten down the plate holding the hinge, doubling the time the task would have taken alone.

But then he'd have missed the joy glowing in Henry's eyes, eyes so much like his mother's. How could he refuse and dash the boy's confidence? Still, the prospect of Henry underfoot, trying to keep him safe, tumbled in Nate's stomach.

"How's your ma?" he found himself saying.

Chin plopped in his hand, Henry sighed. "She sews and sews and sews. I can't help her neither."

"Does she know you're here?"

"She said I could play outside."

"But not here?"

"No, sir. I tried to pull weeds out of the garden, but they're stuck. Could you—" Eyes averted, Henry toed the ground. "When you're done, could you cul...cultivate the garden? I could help push the plow."

Henry's strong sense of responsibility reminded Nate of himself as a lad. Those had been carefree, simple days, milking cows, toting hay and straw, carting milk to town, selling calves. Oh, and swatting the inevitable flies. As a small boy, Nate could remember wishing for the long swishing tail of a Holstein.

"I'll come by after the livery closes," Nate said. "Now, run along. It's close to noon. Don't want your ma worrying about your whereabouts."

As if he'd conjured her up, Carly walked out back. "Henry," she called, "time for dinner!"

"Mama made cobbler," Henry said, licking his lips. Then with a wave to Nate, Henry trotted toward home. "Coming!"

If only he could put his feet under Carly's table. Eat the

food she'd prepared with her own hands. Share that moment. And leave sated. Why not be honest? Home cooking wasn't what he craved. He longed for the closeness of a family.

A growl from Nate's stomach sent him to the tack room for the dinner bucket Anna had packed. Within minutes he'd guzzled half a glass jar of water and devoured the beef sandwich and a slightly withered apple.

Outside the window the leaves on the trees didn't stir. This would be a good time to burn the rotted boards. He stowed the jar and strode out back.

As he lit and then watched the flames, Nate considered what he should do next to ready the livery to sell. He'd grown fond of Morris and wanted to help.

A glance at the roof gave his answer. He'd nail down the loose shingles. Little by little he was gaining on the work. By the time the judge arrived and ruled on the shop, Nate would have set the livery to rights and could be on his way with a clear conscience. He bit back a snort. A clear conscience was about as likely as a July snowfall in Mississippi.

"You're harder to find than a weevil in a sack of grain," Morris said, his tone trying for levity. But his furrowed brow and downturned mouth suggested the man was nearing his wit's end.

Only hours before Mood had been as peaceful as a quiet summer night. "What's wrong?" Nate asked.

Mood's thin tufts of hair stood on end from running his hands through it as he did now. "I went home to check on Betsy. Her cough's so bad she's having trouble catching her breath."

No wonder the poor man was distraught. "I'm sorry."

"We made our decision. On the way into town, I stopped at the depot and bought tickets to Arizona. We're leaving Friday, the twenty-second."

Morris and Betsy were leaving in less than two weeks. Surely with all the repairs he'd made, the livery would sell soon.

"I wired my sister and sent her a ticket. She'll come as soon as she can and stay until we can get a buyer for the house and livestock."

"Does she have a husband or son who could run the livery?"

"My sister's a maiden lady. Grew up on a farm, same as me. She lives in a boarding house, so she can come at a moment's notice." Morris lifted earnest eyes to Nate's. "She can't handle this livery, too. I'm lowering my price, but until it sells, I'd like to leave my business in your care."

Nate opened his mouth to protest, but before he could get out the words, Morris held up his palm. "Know what you're going to say—you ain't staying. Well, you're here now. No one else I can ask."

"The Harders brothers have been helping out. They'd do a decent job."

"Yeah, until they got locked up for shooting some fool sign."

How could Nate argue with that?

"Besides, Nate, you have a knack for dealing with customers. Not those two."

With Nate's experience as a wrangler on a cattle ranch, caring for Mood's horses was easy. What surprised him was how much he enjoyed chatting with clientele. But what did Nate know about running a business? He'd have to keep accounts. Order supplies. Make a profit. Or risk losing what Morris had built.

But even if he knew how to do all that, the responsibility of running the livery would tie him here. Though, if Rory was Stogsdill, as he suspected, maybe staying put was a good thing. For now.

A fire-weakened board shifted beneath the pile, collapsing the stack and shooting sparks into the air. Nate's life wasn't a good foundation for permanence any more than these rotten, scorched boards. No one should rely on him.

Nate took a step back. "Soon as my sister's settled, I'm leaving."

"You could make a good life here. Maybe settle down with one of the pretty women in town."

One face filled Nate's mind. Carly's. In his judgment, the prettiest woman in town. Anywhere. Her crystal-blue eyes stole his breath.

Another face blotted out Carly's. Shifty Stogsdill, mouth thrown wide, mocking Nate for failing to bring him to justice. If it was the last thing he did, Nate would wipe that smirk off Stogsdill's face.

"I've told you about the man I'm after and why. I have to see Stogsdill pays for killing those I loved. You can understand that, can't you?"

Morris's eyes clouded. "You're intent on vengeance. Nothing good will come from that. If you joined us tomorrow for Easter services, you'd hear about another way to live. Jesus taught us to love our enemies." He touched Nate's arm. "Don't want you to think I'm unsympathetic about your losses, but retaliation won't bring them back," he said, and then hobbled toward the livery.

With the weight of Morris's disappointment and the reminder of how far he'd fallen from his faith resting heavy on his shoulders, Nate watched the fire slowly ebb and die.

Too many innocents had died. No one understood what drove him.

He kicked dirt over the coals. More than anything, he wanted to head inside the livery, slap leather on Maverick, slip his rifle in his scabbard and head toward St. Louis.

But he'd promised Anna he'd stay until the ownership of the shop was settled. Soon the circuit judge would arrive and Nate could leave. But when he did, he wanted

the accounts in good shape with accurate records a buyer
could fathom.

From what he'd seen of Morris's books, they needed a
lot of work. Nate had no idea how to fix them. His pulse
kicked up a notch. But he knew just the person who could.

With making Vivian's trousseau and feeding her son
Carly's two main priorities, she'd put off the washing as
long as she dared. Henry attracted dirt like honeysuckle
attracted bees. Her son didn't mind. But he needed clean
clothes to wear to church, especially Easter Sunday.

*Thank You, Lord, for coming to earth and showing us
how to live, then sacrificing Your life for our sins.*

Carly added shavings of hard soap and boiled the clothes
in the rainwater she'd caught. Then, using a long-handled
paddle, she transferred them to the wooden washer, a
cradle contraption, a vast improvement from scrubbing
clothes on the washboard. Once she doused them in a tub
of cold rinse water, followed by a tub of bluing and wrung
them out as dry as she could, her apron was wetter than the
clothes she'd washed. If only she had money for a fancy
washer with an attached wringer, as she'd seen at Stuffle
Emporium.

With a wicker basket of clothes on one hip, she drudged
to the backyard, bone weary after bending over the sewing
machine most of the day, her shoulders and neck aching.

At the clothesline, she jammed pins on to the small
waistband, hanging Henry's denims along with the sailor
top and knee pants he would wear Easter Sunday. Soon
pant legs, shirtsleeves and socks danced in the brisk breeze.

Once she finished here, she'd return to the shop. Customers had been in and out all day, buying gloves, stockings and handkerchiefs. Carly didn't have time for another
interruption, for one more demand on her time.

"Can I help?"

Carly let out a gasp, dropping a pair of Henry's socks.

Nate scooped them up, offering them with a smile. "Sorry, didn't mean to scare you."

Those gray orbs of his twinkled, obviously more amused than sorry for her pounding heart. With that broad chest, those long legs and attractive face, the man was far too appealing. If she kept busy with the chore, surely he'd leave before their lives became even more entwined.

When he wasn't around, thoughts of him filled her mind and Henry's conversation. Yet Nate Sergeant was a bounty hunter. Not an occupation that encouraged putting down roots. Not a safe occupation. Far from it. Worse, Nate showed no interest in attending church. What did that say about him? What kind of example was he for Henry?

She jabbed a peg on to the toes of both socks, pinning them to the line, wishing she could pin the man in place as easily, out of her hair and her son's existence.

Henry raced to her side. "Anna sent me outside for fresh air."

Carly tousled her son's hair. Most likely Henry had been underfoot, slowing Anna's progress on the ball gown she was making.

Nate must've suspected as much, as he gave her a wink.

His gaze traveled to the weed patch she called a garden. "I'd like to cultivate your patch. That is, if you don't mind."

"Can I help push the plow?" Henry said.

Nate knelt in front of her son. "I never met a boy more eager to work."

Henry laid a palm along Nate's jaw contoured by a day's growth of beard.

Uninvited, an urge to run a palm along that bristly jaw, a very strong, very manly jaw, popped into Carly's mind and put a hitch in her breathing. Such foolishness. She'd once thought Max handsome. And look where that had led.

"Ew, you're scratchy."

"That's the stubble of my beard. Compared to yours, my face feels like sandpaper." Nate chucked Henry under the chin. "One day you'll have a beard, too."

"No, I won't!" Henry giggled.

Evidence her son hadn't watched his father shave. Not surprising with the length of Max's absences. Henry longed for a man in his life, someone to emulate.

She snatched up a wet shirt and snapped a clothespin in place. No matter how much she tried to peg Nate as a loner, he behaved more like a father to Henry than Max ever had. Nate had taught her son simple skills, showed him how a man treated his family.

Yet he'd made it abundantly clear that once the judge ruled on the shop's ownership, he'd leave. He'd spent eight years of his life chasing Stogsdill. Until he caught the outlaw, he would never settle down.

"I'm gonna watch the plants. Maybe I'll see 'em grow." Henry raced to the garden and hunkered in the dirt, his bare toes digging into the soil.

Nate chuckled. "That should keep him busy for a while."

And left the two of them very much alone.

Carly stepped behind the clothes, obscuring her view of Nate, or trying to, and fastened Henry's nightshirt to the line.

Nate stepped to the other side of the damp garment and met her gaze. "If I don't take care of that plot, the weeds will choke your plants."

"Thanks for the offer," she said, fiddling with Henry's hem. "But Lloyd and Lester Harders are doing chores to make up for damaging my sign. I'll ask them to cultivate the garden."

"I'd like to do it. In exchange for *your* help."

"Has Henry been in the way? If he's bothering you—"

"No." He grinned. "Well, not much. Henry's a special boy. I like having him around."

Nate behaved like two men housed in one body: ruthless bounty hunter and mild-tempered tutor.

She plucked a jacket from the basket, her hand brushing Nate's as he bent to assist her. She quickly looked away. "Why do you need my help?" she said, avoiding his gaze, yet his scrutiny made her fingers tremble.

"Morris and Betsy Mood are moving to Arizona in less than two weeks."

"Oh, that soon?" Carly's eyes misted. "When the Moods lived in the cabin and Max was off somewhere, they looked after me and Henry." Betsy had helped with Henry's birth. "I'm sad to see them go, but I'm worried about Betsy. I hope the drier air will heal her lungs."

"Morris is leaving the livery in my care." Nate plowed a hand through his hair, leaving furrows deep enough to plant seeds in. "The arrangement is only till he gets a buyer."

Why must Nate's actions chip away at the wall she'd built around her heart? "That's nice of you."

When he'd come claiming the shop for his sister, she'd believed him heartless. She'd been wrong. Still, the man wasn't staying. A knot twisted in her stomach. Most likely he'd wind up dead.

Carly grabbed a kitchen towel and shook it out. "Nobody in town's been interested in buying the livery. What would change that?"

"Morris is lowering the price. That, along with the repairs I've made, should lure a buyer. Until then, I'm responsible. I know horses, but not how to run a business." Troubled eyes met hers. "I'm hoping you'll teach me."

"You expect my help? When you're bent on taking my shop?"

"Please, Carly, stop blaming me. I didn't put that deed in the kitty."

She released a pent-up sigh. Everything always came

back to Max. Even dead, the man found a way to hurt her. He'd thrived on the thrill of high stakes. Not giving a thought to what would happen to her and Henry if he lost the wager. Why did the fact Henry had meant nothing to him still have the power to wound her?

"I've never ordered supplies," Nate said. "I don't know how to keep financial records. If a buyer comes along, he'll want proof the livery makes a profit. From the run-down look of the place when I arrived, I'd figured the business was failing. Now I realize Morris couldn't keep up with the livery and a sick wife."

"Morris will show you what to do."

"I took a brief look at his books…" Nate shook his head. "To put it bluntly, the records are jumbled. At least, I can't make sense of them."

"*If* I were willing, I know nothing about managing a livery."

"Your shop's orderly. I suspect your records are as meticulous." His imploring gaze bored into her. "Running a seamstress shop can't be all that different. Don't you order supplies and oversee accounts?"

The disquiet in Nate's eyes diluted her resistance. He barely knew Morris, yet cared enough to take responsibility for saving the livery. Most folks in town would do the same, if they had the time. Though she couldn't think who did. Morris clearly saw Nate as his best choice.

Nate shifted on his feet. "I shouldn't need your help long. Surely the livery will soon sell."

His words landed in Carly's stomach with a thud. Why did the possibility disturb her when she wanted him gone? "If it does sell, will you leave town?"

His gaze locked with hers. "I'm staying until the judge rules. I won't let Anna to go through the hearing alone."

Yet he had not one iota of concern about what that hearing would do to Carly. Obviously his soft, lingering looks meant nothing. No matter how much the man drew her, no matter how kind he was to Henry, and how often he handled a chore, he didn't care about her. He didn't care enough to worry what losing the shop would do to her and Henry.

Why aid her adversary? She grabbed the wicker basket, holding it in front of her like a shield. "Look, I don't have time. We have two weeks to finish making the garments for the Schwartz wedding."

"I thought the wedding was in three weeks."

"It is, but I promised to have the sewing done the week before so they can pack for the honeymoon."

She heaved a sigh. How hard-hearted had she become? If the livery failed, the Moods would lose money needed to start over in Arizona.

Plus, the desperation riding Nate's face stabbed at her conscience. When she'd reopened the shop, she'd had no idea how to run a business. The struggle to learn had kept her on edge and on her knees.

"Carly, if you help me with the books, I'll help you."

"Cultivating my garden is hardly a fair exchange."

"I'm offering something that will mean a lot to your son." Nate took a step closer. "Henry wants to learn to ride. I can teach him."

"Why would I let you teach him to ride?"

"You know I'm no threat to the boy."

She'd seen Nate's gentleness, his patience. Still, he wasn't accustomed to children. He had no idea how quickly Henry could get into trouble, or hurt. "He's too young."

"He's old enough. But he needs to learn how to care for a horse and tack, as well as how to ride. I'll keep an eye on him, I promise." He cocked a brow. "If you know he's occupied after school, you won't have to worry about his whereabouts."

"How will you have time when you have a livery to run?"

"I'll work with him late in the afternoon when things are slow." He gave a sheepish smile. "Henry stops by more than you know. He's fond of the dappled gray, a gentle mare."

Apparently whether Carly wanted Henry around Nate or not, her son found ways to spend time with him. The poor kid was attracted to the man. Much like his mother.

Where would all this lead? "I don't want Henry hurt," she said. "And I don't mean just physically."

"I would never hurt him."

"Not deliberately. But the more time you spend with him, the more likely you'll leave a hurting boy behind when you ride out of town."

He laid a callused palm over her hand that was clutching the laundry basket. "I'll tell Henry I won't be staying."

She gazed into his earnest eyes. A man with a good heart, a man with good intentions. But someone who didn't understand children. Still, Henry wanted to ride more than anything.

"All right. In exchange for teaching him, you can come in the evenings to learn how to handle the livery books," she said, pulling away from his touch. "To avoid the appearance of impropriety, bring Anna with you."

Those good intentions of Nate's didn't change the fact they traveled a collision course leading to a showdown. One of them would be a winner and one a loser.

This wasn't a game. This was her life.

Chapter Twelve

How could a man keep his mind on a column of figures when the attractive instructor at his side stole his breath away?

A couple feet from where Nate sat, Carly bent over her account books, her flawless ivory skin aglow in the gaslight. She wore her shimmering black hair pulled back into a sensible bun, exposing the soft curve of her cheek.

Carly turned to him. His stomach did a crazy little flip as his fingers itched to touch the pale skin, to tug her close. More than anything, he longed to kiss her.

Whoa, cowboy, not the reason you're here.

As if she could read his thoughts, she blushed and looked away, murmuring something about earnings.

Nate shifted in his seat, struggling to focus on her words. What had gotten into him? He couldn't get involved with Carly. To do so was cruel, would be leading her on.

Yet, despite his intentions to remember all the issues between them, he absorbed every nuance of her expression, of her tone, watched her dainty hand hovering over her financial records.

Did Carly see him as a man worthy of love?

He bit back a sigh. Hardly. She'd insisted on Anna as a

chaperone. That had more to do with Carly's lack of trust than with propriety and was the reason his sister sat nearby running stitches through the handwork in her lap, humming softly with Maizie dozing at her feet.

Could he blame Carly, when he'd swooped in and threatened her livelihood? If not for her desire to see Henry learn to ride, she would not tolerate his presence in her home.

An unbidden image popped into his mind, of coming to this cozy house with the fire crackling in the hearth, a meal simmering on the stove and Carly's welcoming smile, glad to see him at the end of the day.

"Nate? Did you hear me?"

He jerked, met the baffled expression in Carly's wide blue eyes. If she'd spoken, her words hadn't penetrated the fog that had descended on his mind. "I'm sorry. Would you repeat that?"

"I said, 'I enter sales and expenses every night, then tally the totals each week to see if I made a profit.'"

He rubbed his heated neck, trying to bring his thoughts around to the balance sheet. He'd not only let his mind wander, he'd let it wander into dangerous territory. Wander to a place where he could court Carly. A place where he could put down roots. A place where…he would surely meet defeat.

Carly tapped a pencil on the page. "The first of each month I subtract expenses from the month's earnings to see if I can afford to order supplies for the shop."

Nate folded his arms over his chest. "When it comes to the livery, I don't have much choice. Horses require feed, shoeing, bedding, occasional doctoring."

"Exactly. Some supplies *are* essential. I'd compare the horses' upkeep to the upkeep of my sewing machine. I can't stay in business without it."

"Of course," he murmured.

He straightened his shoulders, chastising himself for

behaving like a love-struck youth, not a man who'd made the wise decision to go through life alone. Yet when he left town, he'd leave behind not only his sister, but this intriguing, caring woman who made him question his very existence. And her son. A boy whose every word and deed tugged at Nate's heart.

"Some things are less vital. I can't order, say, lace and the latest fabrics until I've paid the bills," she said. "For the livery, nonessentials might be, uh, repainting the wagon or enlarging the padlock."

"Yes, nonessentials." With every ounce of his will, Nate struggled to keep his eyes off her face and on the ledger she'd parked in front of him.

"I pay myself a weekly salary," she went on. "Not much, but enough to buy food, clothing and tithe to church."

Carly tithed her income? Even with the threat of losing her business hanging over her, she remained faithful. Proof she put God first. Proof her actions lived up to her faith. Proof she trusted God with her future.

Nate didn't match her example. He believed in God, but had his actions lived up to his faith? Instead of trusting God to take care of Anna, he tried to ensure her future himself. Now that seemed foolish. A shop, a calling, friends and family—nothing or no one could guarantee the future.

Only God could.

Yet he'd avoided God. For years he'd been on the move. Even when he'd visited Anna, he'd stayed away from church. Who would want him there? Churchgoers and bounty hunters didn't mix. God wouldn't want to hear from a man bent on revenge.

"Folks at Carly's church are nice as can be," Anna said. "You were right, Nate. Gnaw Bone's a good place to settle down." The eyes she turned on him held no condemnation, only something akin to hope. "For all of us."

Once again the longing to stay seized him. Could he stop tracking Stogsdill? Run the livery and make a life here? That would make Anna happy. And perhaps for the first time since he'd taken the path of bounty hunter, he'd recover the joy of his boyhood, an innocent time surrounded by a loving family.

"The church was great to Henry and me when...when Max—" Carly cut off her words. "They helped us a lot."

Nate had been responsible for that need. That truth pressed against his lungs with such intensity his chest ached.

What would happen if the judge ruled against Carly? A town this size couldn't support two seamstresses. Would she be forced to move, to uproot her son? To lose the support of folks at church? Carly was strong, but even she might be pushed too far, to a point where she couldn't cope.

Carly rose. "That's enough for tonight." She closed the book, staring at the cover as if it held an answer she sought.

Anna struggled to her feet, then hobbled toward them, Maizie at her heels. Each awkward step treaded on Nate's conscience. To fantasize about life as a family man was foolish. For hanging over this peaceful scene was another entity, unseen, unheard but nonetheless real. Nate had a dangerous man to track. How long before the circuit judge arrived and he could leave?

"Thank you, Carly." Nate offered Anna his arm. "I'll expect Henry for his riding lesson after school Monday."

Carly gave a nod but remained at the table, opting not to accompany them to the door.

As he helped his sister cross Carly's porch and backyard, the image of a raven-haired woman rose in his mind, a competent shopkeeper, a talented seamstress, a tigress of a mother protecting her son. Carly's goodness, courage and faith in the face of difficulties affirmed she was as beautiful inside as she was out.

His stomach knotted. Carly would not allow a man like him to sully her life. Her son's life. Only a fool would think otherwise.

When he gave Henry those riding lessons, he'd hold the boy at arm's length. Far better for everyone.

The badge on his chest gleaming in the ray of sunlight streaming in the window, Sheriff Truitt doffed his Stetson. "Afternoon, Mrs. Richards."

The big man's gaze darted past Carly to Anna sitting at the sewing machine, keeping a watchful eye on the needle as she ran up a seam. "Mrs. Hankins."

The hum of the treadle stopped. Pink tinged Anna's cheeks. "Hello, Sheriff Truitt."

"Nice Easter service yesterday."

"Yes, I especially enjoyed the singing," Anna said.

Sheriff Truitt leaned near Anna's shoulder. "Looks like the Schwartz wedding has you ladies hard-pressed. Can't think when Gnaw Bone's had a bigger shindig. Good thing Josiah owns half the buildings in town."

Anna smiled up at him. "We'll make the deadline, Sheriff."

"Given name's Thor, if you've a mind to use it."

"Thor's a strong name, fitting for a sheriff."

Carly bit back a smile. Why, Sheriff Truitt actually blushed. And Anna hadn't even used his first name. If he was attracted to Anna, who knew where that could lead? Anna might choose being a contented wife over an overworked shopkeeper.

A pang of remorse nipped Carly's stomach. How could she even consider such a possibility with Anna mere weeks into losing the husband she adored?

But, perhaps one day, after the mourning period, Anna and the sheriff might suit. Why wouldn't Sheriff Truitt find Anna appealing? She never had a bad thing to say about anyone. She worked tirelessly. Had endless patience with Henry. Even patience with that brother of hers, who surely worried her half to death.

Carly's heart hitched in her chest. Would Nate survive a showdown with Stogsdill?

As she snipped the fine muslin for the last of the countless petticoats required by the bride, Carly said casually, "Sheriff, any idea when the circuit judge might arrive in town?"

Sheriff Truitt whacked his Stetson on the side of his leg. "Almost forgot why I stopped. I got a wire from Judge Rohlof. His horse threw him on his head. He's got a concussion."

Carly gasped. "Oh, no. I suppose that will delay his arrival."

"Yes, ma'am. How long of a delay depends on when his symptoms improve."

With everything in her, Carly wanted the issue decided and Nate gone.

"You and Anna might have to work things out between you."

As if Nate would agree to any solution that didn't result in Anna's ownership of the shop.

The sheriff's gaze traveled between Carly and Anna. When neither spoke, he exhaled like a train pulling into the station, the engine releasing steam. "Well, better skedaddle," he said, and then banged through the door, setting the bell overhead dancing.

"Sheriff Truitt feels caught in the middle," Carly said.

Anna's eyes filled with disquiet. "I feel the same."

Why did Carly have to like the woman who could ruin her life? "Me, too."

In truth, she and Anna probably could work something out but, like Nate, Carly wasn't confident the shop could support her and Henry, as well as Anna. Once Vivian moved to Cincinnati with her new husband, she'd find a local dressmaker there. Other than Mrs. Schwartz and a few regular customers, most women in town either made or bought factory-made clothes, except for special occasions.

"Sheriff Truitt's a nice man," Anna said.

"I think he's smitten with you."

Anna's jaw dropped. "Why would you believe that?"

"Call it female intuition." Carly studied her. "How would you feel about that?"

"*If* you're right, I'm surprised. And, well…flattered. I'm not ready for romance, you understand." A flush bloomed in her cheeks. "But, if I were, the sheriff's very nice."

"Why would you find his interest surprising? You're pretty, wise, kind. You have a lot to offer a man."

"Most men find my lameness unsettling, even repulsive. I wouldn't expect a handsome, masculine man like Sheriff Truitt to get past my disability." She sighed. "Besides, I'm always sitting when he visits. He may not realize I'm handicapped."

"Of course he does. He's seen you at church twice now."

A smile played on her lips. "Oh, I hadn't thought of that."

"Maybe you two can be a comfort to each other. A few years back Sheriff Truitt's wife and baby died in childbirth."

"Oh, my, the poor man. I wish there was some way I could help."

Anna's heartaches hadn't closed her heart, as Carly's had. But then, Anna hadn't been married to Max.

"I can name another man who's smitten," Anna said. "I couldn't help but notice a spark between you and Nate, Saturday evening."

"Are you sure you're not imagining that? I know you want Nate to settle down."

"Yes, but not with just anyone." Anna arched a brow. "Are you sure you're not deceiving yourself?"

"He's attractive, I'll admit, but I'll never remarry."

"Why? Don't you believe God gives second chances for happiness?"

If He did, why had God allowed Max to gamble the deed in a poker game? All Carly needed to be happy was this shop and Henry. "I failed my son once. I won't make that mistake again."

"Nate's patient and gentle with your son. He would never mistreat Henry."

"I don't want to upset you, Anna, but your brother is a wanderer like Max and set on vengeance. He *will* leave. And when he does, he'll hurt my son, whether he means to or not."

Tears welled in Anna's eyes. "I hadn't thought of that. I'm afraid you're right."

Never more sure of anything, Carly slid the shears through the white cambric, snipping along an invisible line, leaving a crisp, clean cut. That spark between her and Nate was stronger than she'd admit to Anna. But no matter how much she was attracted to the man, she would cut him out of her life as cleanly as she did this nightgown.

She wouldn't get involved with a man who would fail her son. A lump the size of a walnut lodged in her throat. Was it already too late? Henry followed Nate around, hung on Nate's every word, and beamed whenever Nate entered a room. Upon occasion she'd caught her son even mimicking Nate's stance, feet apart, hands in his back pockets.

Carly had tried to believe she was enough, but Henry craved a man in his life. Nate Sergeant was exactly the wrong man.

The judge's concussion not only delayed the hearing, it delayed Nate's departure. The longer he remained, the more Henry's life would get entangled with the bounty hunter.

When Nate left, he would break her son's heart.

Carly's breath caught. Perhaps even hers.

Chapter Thirteen

Henry took to his first riding lesson like a pig to clover.

Nate grinned at the boy, up on that gray-and-white mare. The brim of a tattered cowboy hat pulled low to shade his eyes, the toes of his dusty boots thrust into the shortened stirrups, Henry resembled a pint-size cowpoke.

A few feet away, Carly leaned against the corral, her shoulders barely clearing the top rail. She was a petite woman, yet carried herself tall, as if that feisty spirit of hers buoyed her spine.

Even with the deadline at the shop, she'd stayed to watch, putting her son before her job. No doubt she'd work half the night to make up for the lost time. Nate released a breath. Why not admit it? The real reason Carly had stayed was her lack of trust in him to keep Henry safe.

Between teaching him to saddle the mare and hold and use the reins, the hour had flown. At first Nate had walked alongside the horse, ready to grab Lady's bridle. But each trip around the corral with Henry directing the horse had increased his confidence and skill.

"Good job, son," Carly said as they passed. "Proud of you for listening carefully to instructions."

At his mother's praise, Henry thrust out his chest, a happy grin on his face. "Thanks, Mama!"

The mare tossed her head to look at the lightweight on her back.

"Look, Lady smiled at me. Well, kinda. Nate, do horses smile?"

"Not sure, but if they do, Lady would surely smile at you."

"Yep, 'cause she likes me."

The large hat resting on Henry's bent earlobes made him cuter than a bug's ear. "Why not? You're very likable," Nate said, turning toward Carly. "Like your mom."

"Are you fishing for an invitation to supper?"

Nate took hold of the bridle and led Lady to the fence. "No, ma'am. You don't have time to entertain with that big order to finish." He grinned. "Anna gets home so tired I've been doing the cooking."

"What are you serving your sister, hardtack and beans?"

"Nope, real victuals like fried beefsteak and potatoes."

Carly's mouth gaped.

"Careful, or you'll swallow one of those flies pestering Lady," Nate said, giving her a wink. "Not as tasty as my chow."

Carly chuckled. "Not sure that's much of a recommendation."

"I take you for a brave woman. Would you be willing to give my cooking a try?"

"I might." Her dark lashes swept her rosy cheeks, and then lifted to meet his gaze. "Remember, nothing about you scares me. Not even your cooking."

Her words were a reminder of their first meeting but, unlike then, her tone was soft and teasing. When had she looked prettier? More desirable? When had life seemed more promising?

He waggled his brows. "I find a sassy woman appealing," he said, leaning closer.

They stared into each other's eyes. Everything around them faded, leaving only the two of them. An extraordinary woman and a man captivated by her charm.

"Nate, do horses sleep standing up?"

For a moment Nate had forgotten Henry. A small boy would not be ignored for long. "Horses may lie down for an occasional nap, but they usually sleep standing up."

"If I slept standing up, I'd fall down. Why don't they fall down? Huh, Nate?"

"Guess God made them that way."

"Why?"

The boy had more questions than a mangy mutt had fleas. "For their protection. If a horse is on his feet and senses danger, he's ready to run."

Henry chattered on about the sleeping habits of dogs, Maizie in particular. The boy's delight in the world around him made Nate smile. Who wouldn't enjoy this boy? His gaze slid to Carly. And his mother? Their presence in his life had become as natural as the sun and wind.

"Nate knows everything, Mama," Henry said.

The adoration in the boy's eyes, as if Henry saw Nate as a hero—or a father figure—spiraled inside him. That would never do; wasn't part of his plan. He didn't want Henry to be hurt. The quicker he finished this lesson, the quicker he could send mother and son on their way.

Nate unfastened the gate. "Henry, real easy like, pull slightly on the right rein, the one nearest me, and Lady will head through the gate."

With a sober nod, Henry obeyed. Immediately the mare turned right and walked through the opening. "I did it! Just like I drove the buggy. Did you see me, Mama?"

Carly nodded. "Sure did."

Henry was a mirrored version of himself at that age.

Nate's mind traveled back to the first time he'd ridden his horse at a trot. "Did you see me, Pa?" Nate had called. His father had been quick to praise, and Nate had soaked it up like thirsty ground.

Every boy needs—no, deserves—approval.

"I can't wait to tell the kids at school I rode a horse."

Carly turned to Nate, amusement lighting her eyes. The tension he'd seen around her mouth when she'd first arrived replaced with a stunning smile.

That smile socked Nate like a punch to the gut. How could he remain indifferent to the woman when she looked at him that way?

Nate took hold of the bridle and led horse and rider toward the livery. Carly joined them, walking alongside her son on the opposite side of the horse.

"Henry, I like the relaxed way you hold the reins and how you sit tall and easy in the saddle," Nate said. "Lady senses your confidence and that puts her in the mood to cooperate."

"Lady likes me. She does whatever I say."

"Don't let Nate's praise go to your head, young man, and start getting careless," Carly warned in a gentle tone.

Nate set a box beneath the stirrup for Henry to dismount. "You did a fine job, but your mother's right. Horses are big and strong. They can throw you off or rub your leg against a fence post or pack a wallop with a hoof. We need to respect that and be careful."

Henry gave a nod, then threw his right leg over the saddle. As he dismounted, his boot snagged in the stirrup and he tumbled, letting out a shriek, his arms pinwheeling.

Whinnying and tossing her head, the mare sidestepped.

"Whoa," Nate said, swooping in and scooping up the boy.

Henry wrapped his arms around Nate's neck, burrowing into his chest. Nate didn't see Henry's big brown eyes or seven-year-old frame. He saw Anna crumpled in the road. The horse's back hoof coming down. The horrifying, sickening crack. Anna's cries. In those few seconds, his sister's life forever changed.

"Nate? You okay?"

Carly was looking at him with a mixture of confusion and gratitude in her eyes.

"Yeah, yeah. I'm fine."

As Henry clung to his neck, a strong desire seized Nate. To protect the boy, to make sure nothing ever harmed Henry as it had Anna. "You're okay," Nate murmured against Henry's ear.

"You seemed in a daze for a minute there," Carly said. "What happened?"

"Nothing. I'm…just relieved Henry didn't get hurt." Nate put the boy on his feet and knelt in front of him. "It's good to be confident, but carelessness can get you injured. You got in a hurry dismounting."

Tears sprang into Henry's eyes. "I'm sorry."

Nate gave the boy's too big hat a tug. "No damage done. Just remember to move slow and easy around a horse. So you won't get hurt."

Henry looked up at him. "Did a horse hurt you?"

"No," Nate said. "But a horse hurt someone I cared about."

"Who?" Henry asked in the direct way of a child. A child who didn't know the painful scar a simple question could open.

Nate could feel Carly watching him, no doubt recalling that he'd caused Anna's limp. Nate couldn't tell Henry the truth, the one person in Nate's life who thought Nate could do no wrong.

"That's nothing to worry about. Just remember horses are powerful, at times unpredictable." Nate chucked Henry under the chin, then eased to his feet.

"Yes, sir."

As Nate stripped leather and double-tied the mare, he explained each step to Henry, then they cleaned and stored the gear. With each trip to the tack room, Nate felt Carly's gaze upon him. Her smile, the gentle approval in her eyes, suggested she'd absolved him of responsibility for Anna's injury.

The strangest sense of elation filled him. As if he'd found a rare treasure that could be his for the asking.

"Run the brush like this," Nate said, showing Henry how to curry the mare's coat, then handing him the tool.

Henry ran the bristles along Lady's back. "Next time, can we ride someplace funner than inside the corral?"

"One step at a time. Once you've had more experience, we'll ride out a piece."

Henry beamed. "We could have another picnic."

What would it be like to follow Carly up the trail? Or ride companionably side by side? Did she even ride? He wanted to know everything about her.

"How can you leave the livery?" Carly asked.

"The Harders give me a hand."

"I'm surprised you'd leave them in charge."

"For all their foolishness, they're good with horses. The responsibility is making men of them and is giving me some freedom. Freedom for another picnic, perhaps."

Nate lost himself in the depths of her eyes, bluer than the brightest summer sky. A flush bloomed in her cheeks, and her gaze skittered away. Whether she'd admit it, Nate affected her.

That awareness drew him closer, until he stopped mere inches from her skirts. "Are you willing?"

"If you're providing the food," she said, "I might be."

"I'm game, if you are."

A soft smile curved her cheeks. "We'll see." She touched his forearm. "Thanks for protecting my son earlier."

"He would've been okay, even if I hadn't intervened."

"Perhaps. You know, you're Henry's hero. Well, except when he's the hero," she added with a chuckle.

"As a kid, I was the hero, too…in my imagination."

"Well, for saving my son twice, today you're mine."

His gaze lowered to her lips, rosy, soft, kissable. "Just for today?" he murmured.

"With the issue over the shop, I'd say that's more than generous."

Her words doused him like a bucket of cold water, ripping him back to reality. He'd been thinking about kissing her, not appropriate with Henry looking on. Besides, too much divided them. If only Carly could keep the shop…

For that to happen, he'd have to sacrifice Anna's security, her happiness. How could he do that when she'd taken to the shop and this town as though she'd been born to it?

If only the shop could support Anna as well as Carly and Henry, but from what he'd observed, except for this big order, business was slow. The reason Nate would ensure his sister got what she deserved.

"Time to go," Carly said, turning to Nate, "Thank you for your patience with Henry." She ruffled the boy's hair. "It's not something…he's seen much of."

"Pa got real mad when I got near his horse," Henry said. "I wasn't s'posed to touch him."

"Your father probably worried if you weren't careful, you'd get hurt." Nate bent to Henry's level. "Horses can get spooked, remember?"

His expression somber, Henry nodded. "Is that why Pa got mad at you, Mama? So you'd be careful?"

"Henry, I don't think—"

"'Cuz he knocked you down. He was so mad, he scared me. Why did he do that?"

Nate sucked in a breath, his gaze darting to Carly's. Sudden tears welled in her eyes; tears that shredded

Nate's heart. She laid a shaky hand on Henry's shoulder and the boy leaned into her. "We'll talk about it later, sweetie."

If only Nate could've had the chance to talk some sense into Max Richards before he'd harmed his wife, a defenseless woman, and branded his innocent son with that terrible memory. The more he heard about Richards, the more Nate understood those walls Carly erected.

"I wish I'd been there," he grumbled from between clenched teeth.

Alarm filled Carly's eyes. As if the man could come back from the grave and hurt her still. Or did she believe Nate was just another violent man like Max?

Nate longed to prove otherwise, to tug her and Henry close, to promise he'd never allow anything bad to happen to them again, but he couldn't. Not when Stogsdill ran free.

Nate ushered mother and son toward the door. At the entrance to the livery, Henry stopped abruptly. Nate grabbed Carly before she plowed into her son. She thudded against him, every soft curve fitting up against him, shooting shivers along his spine.

Startled blue eyes flashed to his. Then, as they lowered to his mouth, a blush climbed into her cheeks. She took a hurried step back. "Thank you for Henry's lesson."

He cleared the lump from his throat. "You're welcome."

"He'll be back tomorrow. I won't," she quickly added. "Too much to do."

Carly was running scared. How could he blame her, after being tied to that low-down husband of hers? Well, keeping her distance was better for everyone.

As Carly headed toward the shop, Henry lagged behind, his gaze lingering on Nate, his big blue eyes filled with longing.

What the boy wanted was a father. The poor kid hadn't known, as Nate had, the kind and patient love and instruction of the man who gave him life. Max Richards had cheated his son and his wife out of far more than losing that deed.

Nate watched Carly and Henry walk away hand in hand. If only he could be that man, could be that father, that husband. But inside he was hardened, a driven man. They deserved better.

"Mighty pretty woman, isn't she?"

Nate reeled to the speaker. He'd been so wrapped up in Carly that he'd forgotten his job, hadn't been aware anyone was around.

Well-dressed in a suit, vest and bowler, sporting muttonchop whiskers, the stranger extended his hand. "Josiah Schwartz."

"Nate Sergeant, Mr. Schwartz. What can I do for you?"

"I'm here to reserve Mood's fanciest carriage for my daughter's nuptials."

The bride's father. An image slid through Nate... Of Carly walking up the aisle toward him, her eyes shining at the prospect of becoming his wife.

With every ounce of his will, Nate forced away the notion. "Your daughter's wedding has the seamstress shop humming," he said, his voice gravely. He quickly cleared his throat.

"A little less than three weeks till the big day." Mr. Schwartz hooked his thumbs into his vest pockets and rocked back on his heels. "Can't say I'll be sad to see it come and go. The ladies have been in a tizzy for weeks."

Nate murmured some mindless comment, but in his mind he calculated the days. Anna had told him about the circuit judge's concussion. Surely, he would be mended enough to arrive and settle the dispute before the Schwartz wedding. And Nate could leave before he got more wrapped up in a life he couldn't have.

"Come with me," Nate said, leading Mr. Schwartz to

the barn alongside the stable and the only fancy carriage on the premises, a white brougham that had seen better days. Perhaps he could repair that small rip in the cushions. "This work? It'll look better once it's polished."

"Guess it'll have to do. We've got our carriage and the groom's but need another to haul guests and their luggage from the depot."

A good job for the Harders twins. The more they worked, the less time they'd have to carouse. "I can get all the drivers you need to deliver your guests and their baggage."

"Appreciate it. Some will stay with us. Others, at the hotel."

"Let's go back to the office and get the particulars on paper." In case Nate had to leave town suddenly. Or the livery sold and the responsibility rested with another man. Though they hadn't had inquiries by prospective buyers.

"Do you have any interest in buying the livery, Mr. Schwartz? It's solid and profitable."

He held up a hand. "Sorry. I got too many assets tied up in property." Mr. Schwartz leaned against a post, obviously not in a hurry to transact business. "Why not buy it yourself? From the moony way you were looking after Mrs. Richards, I suspect you've got designs on her." He removed a pipe from his coat pocket and fiddled with it. "Could work out nicely for you both. Assuming gossip's correct and you won the deed to her shop from that worthless husband of hers."

Small-town secrets didn't remain secret long. He sized up the older man. Was Schwartz insinuating Nate would fake affection for Carly to ensure he got the shop? "My sister's husband won the deed, not me. Richards killed him for it."

"Is your sister planning to take ownership?"

"The circuit judge will decide who the rightful owner is."

"Folks won't cotton to Mrs. Richards losing her business."

Nate didn't miss the point. He and Anna were seen as outsiders, intent on bringing harm to one of the town's own.

"Still, a bounty hunter in town could discourage some unsavory characters."

Something about the expression on the man's face made Nate ask, "Have you seen someone of that ilk?"

Mr. Schwartz shrugged. "A few weeks back, I was west of town looking for that five-point buck. With the scarcity of deer, hunters for miles around are trying to bag him. Never saw the buck, but I spotted two men cooking rabbits on a spit, their horses tethered nearby."

West of town. In the general area of the Pence farm. Could those men be members of Stogsdill's gang? Or Stogsdill himself? "Did you talk to them?"

"No. Something about them looked unsavory. With one of me and two of them, I opted to skirt their encampment."

"How long ago was that?"

"March twenty-fifth. I remember the date because we'd had a late snowfall. Good time to track deer." Mr. Schwartz eyed him. "Are they trouble?"

"Doubt they're still around." If Stogsdill was Debby Pence's fiancé, she had indicated the outlaw hadn't been in these parts for weeks. Perhaps around that same date. "I'll ride out and have a look."

"Appreciate it."

"What's the nearest landmark?"

"I was in the woods across from the Pence and Slater farms out on Hartzell Road. Both men had given me permission to hunt. The men I saw weren't far from a run-down shack Slater stored maple syrup spigots and buckets in, so they might've been bunking there." The older man pocketed his pipe and pulled away from the post. "Better reserve that brougham and get back to the bank."

Nate followed Mr. Schwartz to the office. The special moments he'd had with Henry and Carly, a peek at family life, had been shaken loose by the report of strangers outside of town. A reminder of Nate's purpose.

A reminder that no matter how nice folks in town were and how much he enjoyed time with Carly and Henry, he dared not trust that cozy picture and get complacent.

Even now, evil might be lurking.

Chapter Fourteen

W‍ould Carly's fried chicken and mashed potatoes tempt her son to listen to reason and knock Nate Sergeant off that pedestal Henry had him on?

For a while today, toward the end of Henry's riding lesson, the three of them had seemed like a nice little family, living one of those moments she'd craved and never had with Max.

But then Henry had started talking about his dad and she couldn't leave the livery fast enough. What must Nate think of her for living with the man, for subjecting her son to Max's temper?

Then Nate had showed up at their door an hour ago with a brand-new Stetson; a gift for Henry that had thrilled her son.

No wonder Henry revered Nate. Nate never had a sharp word. Never made a threatening move. Never disappeared for weeks on end.

Oh, but he would.

Nate would climb down from that pedestal and leave town. If she didn't prepare her son, Henry's heart would be broken.

Beside her, Henry stood on the stool, wearing the new

cowboy hat, pounding the potato masher into the creamy mound as Carly held the crock in place to ensure her energetic son didn't knock the bowl off the counter.

"I'm getting the lumps, Mama." Head bent, Henry attacked those potatoes with all of his strength, but his hand wobbled.

Carly leaned toward him, intending to ask if he'd like help. Just as a glob of potatoes shot into her face.

Her son's eyes rounded in surprise, and then he crowed with laughter, his shoulders shaking with mirth.

"You little monkey. We'll see how you like it." She scooped two fingers into the bowl and dabbed mashed potatoes on his left cheek.

Henry swiped a finger across his face and stuck it in his mouth. "Mmm, good," he said, leaning into Carly, laughing up at her. "Try 'em, Mama."

Carly slid the potatoes off her cheek and tasted them. "Needs a little salt."

Henry made a dive for the shaker, but Carly was faster. "I'll do that." A couple shakes, a dash of pepper, a quick stir and Carly pronounced the mashed potatoes perfect.

"Can I put the taters on the plates?"

As Henry plopped potatoes on the plates, leaving a trail on the counter, even a blob on the floor, Carly dished up the fried chicken and sliced beets, a vegetable Henry disliked. But an occasional taste wouldn't hurt him.

She grabbed both plates, set them on the table and sashayed toward her son, singing, "All around the cobbler's house, the monkey chased the people. And after them in double haste, Pop! goes the weasel."

With a squeal of laughter, Henry raced around the kitchen with Carly chasing after him. Just as she reached him, he plopped onto his chair, grinning up at her.

"One day I will catch you, Henry Richards."

"Next time I'll be the monkey and catch you."

"You can try," she said with a smile, waggling her brows. "Are you hungry?"

At the mention of their second silly game, Henry giggled. "Yep, hungry enough to eat worms."

"That's hungry!"

"Are you hungry?" he asked, leaning toward her.

"Yes, hungry enough to eat spiders."

He shivered, his eyes twinkling. "That's hungry!"

Carly set Henry's plate in front of him, then took her seat. "No hats at the table."

"Do I have ta take it off?"

"Yes, you do. Want to say grace?"

With a nod, Henry removed his hat and hung it on his chair back, then folded his hands and bowed his head. "Hi, God. Thank You for the chicken and taters. Thank You for making Mama a good cook. Amen."

Carly smiled at him. "One of these days you'll thank God for the beets."

"Beets are pretty," he said, screwing up his face, "but taste icky. God didn't make 'em wrong. I'll like 'em when I'm big like Nate."

"How do you know Nate likes beets?"

"'Cuz he's a grown-up."

Here was the opportunity to prepare Henry for Nate's fall off that pedestal. "You know, Henry, grown-ups aren't perfect. They can disappoint us. Make mistakes."

"You don't," Henry said, then shoveled in a spoonful of mashed potatoes.

Carly bit back a sigh. If she tried to count the mistakes she'd made, she'd need all her fingers and toes several times over. "Yes, me, too."

"Pa said I was a mistake."

Carly's beet-loaded fork clattered to her plate, splattering juice. A few droplets landed on her son's face. "I'm sorry, sweetie, that was clumsy of me."

Henry grinned. "You made a mess."

"Yes." Carly rose and scrubbed Henry's cheek with her napkin, and then got the dishcloth and wiped the table.

Her son glanced at the empty seat where Max had sat. "If beet juice splashed on Pa, he'd be real mad." Henry rested his elbow on the table and plopped his chin in his hand. "Why didn't he like us?"

If only Carly knew the answer to that question. But she did know how things had been, how she'd walk on eggs, careful not to do or to say anything to cause trouble, living in a quiet house with no laughter, no singing. Not when Max was home.

Max's death had freed her from his threats, freed her son from his bad example. Life was peaceful. Until Nate Sergeant arrived, threatening her livelihood and the walls that sheltered them. Threatening her son's happiness.

"You're a wonderful boy, Henry." She groped for the right words to comfort her son. "You're not a mistake. Your pa wasn't good with praise."

The flash of skepticism in Henry's eyes knotted her stomach. Why had she whitewashed the truth?

His chin resting on his chest, Henry laid his hands in his lap, the meal forgotten. "Nate likes me," he said with a sniff.

"Yes, he does." No wonder Henry had put Nate on a pedestal. A kind word, a thoughtful gift, a small deed were huge to a boy starving for a man's approval. Now Nate was teaching Henry to ride, the highlight of her son's young life, increasing his regard.

Henry sighed. "I wish Nate was my pa."

Carly's pulse tripped. "Nate isn't planning to live in Gnaw Bone. He's here…visiting Anna. He might have to leave soon."

"He's gotta get the bad guys, Mama." Henry sat straight,

a smile on his face. "When he does, he'll come back. Know why I know?"

"Why?" she whispered.

"God bringed him to us."

"Why do you say that?"

"'Cuz I prayed for a new dad. Nate's him."

Henry's words churned inside her. Not only had Carly failed to convince her son Nate wasn't a man to count on, she had failed to realize how desperately Henry wanted a pa.

Every muscle in Carly's body tightened, turning her stomach into a queasy, quivering mess. Matrimony was out of the question. No matter how much she tried to put Max Richards out of her mind and move on with her life, she couldn't. She'd been married to a polecat and couldn't get rid of his stench.

If one day she was ready for a new beginning and could find a man worthy of her son, a good man who loved God…

Her shoulders sagged. If that good man existed and knew the mistakes she'd made, he would not want her.

Hadn't Pa taught her at every turn she wouldn't be enough? Not for a truly good man?

Gnaw Bone Christian Church cast a morning shadow, the steeple's silhouette pointing right at Nate like the finger of God. His steps lagged. He didn't belong here, and wouldn't consider stepping inside, if not for the opportunity to question Debby Pence and put faces with the names of her grandparents.

Anna tugged at Nate's arm. "Mercy, you're slower than cold molasses. Why, you're barely keeping up with me." Her brow puckered. "Are you feeling awkward about missing church?"

No point in trying to explain to Anna that God wouldn't welcome him into His house, not with the hate Nate carried and the relentless need to settle the score with Shifty Stogsdill.

"What's awkward is not wearing my gun." Anna had insisted he leave his weapon at home. Without his firearm, he felt exposed. Vulnerable.

"God will be glad to see you. So will Carly and Henry," Anna said, beaming at him like a ray of sunshine in August.

The prospect of facing the Almighty in church had Nate's heart pounding as wildly as if he'd stumbled into a showdown without a loaded gun.

And Carly... She knew, the same as he did, that his life didn't mesh with the will of God.

"You're going to enjoy the sermon. Pastor Koontz makes me take a hard look at myself."

As if Anna had ever done a mean-spirited act in her life.

Nate took his sister's arm and helped her climb the steps. Inside the sanctuary, he removed his hat, his mouth dry as gunpowder.

In a pew on the outside aisle midway back, Nate spotted Carly and Henry. Exactly where Anna headed, leaving him to trail behind. Folks craned their heads to watch their progress. Were they offended at a bounty hunter in their midst? Or merely wary of the outcome of the hearing?

Lawrence Sample stepped out of a pew. "Good to see you sporting that new haircut."

"You give a good cut," he said, though he still felt shorn like a sheep.

"Want you to meet my wife, Bertie, and our daughter, Elnora Watkins, and her baby, Bonnie Sue."

This must be the daughter who'd lost her husband in a logging accident and had moved in with the Samples. Nate smiled, then introduced Anna.

She leaned past him. "Mrs. Watkins, I'm recently widowed. Perhaps you could join me for tea one afternoon."

"Thank you, Mrs. Hankins. I'd like that."

Nate glanced at the drooling baby the young widow jiggled on her knee. Bonnie Sue grinned, revealing three tiny teeth, and reached out chubby arms.

To him.

Elnora Watkins's eyes welled with tears. "You resemble her daddy," she murmured in a raspy voice, as if speaking the words had cost her.

Inside his chest, something as strong as a noose tightened around Nate's heart. He'd never be a daddy. Never know the touch of his baby's small, chubby hands.

"I'm…I'm sorry about your loss, ma'am," he said, then turned tail and strode up the aisle after Anna.

Henry scrambled out of the pew and raced to them, a welcoming grin on his face. "Wanna sit with us?"

Nate tousled the boy's hair and looked for permission in his mother's startled blue eyes. With a nod and a smile, Carly scooted down, leaving room for him and Anna.

At the pew, Henry grabbed Nate's hand. "I wanna sit beside Nate."

"That's fine if you behave." Carly met Nate's gaze.

In her eyes he saw warmth, as if she was glad to see him. Probably what a good woman like Carly would feel about any backslider.

As Nate settled between Anna and Henry, he noticed the Stetson on the other side of Carly, taking up space in the pew.

"He'd sleep in it if I let him," Carly whispered, shooting him a grin.

"My father gave me a hat like that when I was just a boy."

She smiled, as though she understood the importance of the gift, then picked up the hymnal and leafed through it.

Nate searched the congregation for Debby Pence. He caught folks staring at them, whispering. No doubt surprised Carly would share a pew with the interlopers claiming her shop.

No more surprised than he was. Though he wasn't misled into believing this was more than Christian kindness.

He put thoughts of Carly out of his mind and scanned the sanctuary. Debby Pence sat up ahead on the right between an older man and woman, surely her grandparents. He studied the couple's features and filed the information in his brain, then turned his attention to Debby.

Her head was angled toward him, an unfocused, dreamy look in her eyes and a half smile on her lips. Was she thinking about Rory?

As far as Nate knew, Stogsdill had never used Rory as an alias. He was too smart to give Debby a name plastered on wanted posters. Before Nate left church today, he would lead the conversation around so he could learn Rory's last name and when Debby had last seen him.

A robust man rose from the front pew, an open hymnal in one hand, his bald head gleaming. He welcomed visitors, his gaze leaping to Nate, apparently the only newcomer. "Turn to page thirty-one in your hymnals," he said and nodded to the pianist.

Notes of "The Old Rugged Cross" filled the sanctuary, and the congregation joined in. Carly's soft soprano mingled with his sister's alto. Nate remained silent. Each additional hymn, each one familiar and as suffocating as a tightly bound gag, exposed how far he'd drifted from a life God could commend.

Pastor Koontz stepped to the podium and opened his Bible. "Good morning," he said, looping the curled ends of his wire-rimmed glasses around his ears. "Our passage today comes from the book of Romans, Chapter Twelve." Then he read, "'If it be possible, as much as lieth in you, live peaceably with all men.'"

All men? Shifty Stogsdill gave no more thought to taking a life than Nate did to killing a mosquito. His parents, Rachel, Walt—

Didn't God care about these innocents?

Yet, not long ago, Nate had taken a second life. As his bullet had sunk into Max Richards's chest, the sneer on Richard's lips had given way to a surprised *O*. He'd stumbled back and toppled to the ground like a rotten tree in a windstorm.

As it had the first time, it had been either Richards or him. Still, Nate had blood on his hands.

"'Avenge not yourselves, but *rather* give place unto wrath. For it is written, Vengeance *is* mine, I will repay, saith the Lord.'"

Nate glanced at Henry leaning against his mother, his eyes closed, exposing his soft vulnerable nape. The top of the boy's head barely reached Nate's elbow. With her arm wrapped around her son, Carly listened attentively to the pastor's words, the two of them the picture of innocence.

His gut tightened. If he waited on God to avenge Stogsdill, how many others would die?

Carly glanced over at him then, a pucker between her brows, as if she knew the inner workings of his mind and disapproved.

"'Therefore if thine enemy hunger, feed him. If he thirst, give him drink. For in so doing thou shalt heap coals of fire on his head,'" the preacher said, his gaze roaming the congregation, then resting on Nate.

Nate ran a finger under his collar, suddenly too tight, the room too hot. Someone coughed. In the stillness of the sanctuary, the harsh sound careened through him like a bullet.

Too many bullets. Too many he cared about murdered.

Heaping coals weren't sufficient. Heaping coals didn't bring back the dead.

"'Be not overcome of evil, but overcome evil with good,'" the pastor read.

Any man fool enough to expect Stogsdill to be overcome by good had no concept of the man's true nature. Stogsdill would shoot first and ask questions later.

Why had he come? He didn't belong here.

At the final song, the call to forgiveness, Nate rose with the others then tried to slip from the pew.

"What's wrong?" Anna whispered.

"I need some air."

In the aisle, he glanced at Carly and found her gaze upon him, a question in her eyes. Did she believe he was going forward to ask for forgiveness? To make himself right with God?

He would do no such thing.

Instead he'd walk out the back, Scripture grating on his conscience, abrasive as a coarse metal file against flesh and bone.

He didn't have it in him to wait on God to exact justice. He would see that Stogsdill paid for his crimes.

Eyes straight ahead, Nate fled through the double doors at the back. As much as he wanted to escape the churchyard, he'd wait on Anna. But his plan to question Debby Pence would have to wait.

As parishioners exited the church, Nate crouched and fiddled with the hub of the back wheel facing the street.

"Why did you leave?"

Nate lurched to his feet and faced his sister. "I don't belong in church. You heard that sermon."

"We're all sinners."

"Most of these folks don't feel compelled to hunt killers," he said, helping her into the buggy.

"Nate, give that up. Start over."

"No." He gulped air, tamping down his impatience as

he clambered up beside her. "No matter what the preacher said, I have to get Stogsdill."

"That won't bring back our parents or Rachel." Anna laid a palm on his hand gripping the reins. "There's another choice."

Nate opened his mouth to speak.

"I know what you're going to say. But, what kind of life is chasing after outlaws, never having a family? Stop fooling yourself. I can see you're not happy, that you hate what you do."

"Perhaps, but once I bring Stogsdill to justice, this world will be a little safer."

"I can't help but wonder if catching Stogsdill's just an excuse to not have to look at my injury day after day and remember what happened."

A lump formed in his throat. He stared at the road ahead, away from those gray, perceptive eyes. "That's not true."

"So why can't you look at me when you say it?"

Every time he saw the hitch in Anna's gait, Nate was reminded of how he'd failed his sister. He'd failed Rachel, too. If he settled down, how many more would he fail?

"Answer me."

He groaned and turned the horse toward the livery. "If not for me, you wouldn't be lame."

"It was an accident. You tripped in the street, like any small boy. You didn't do anything wrong."

"Look what you lost."

"Look what I gained."

"Like what?" he all but bellowed.

"My lameness has taught me to depend on God, not on myself. To slow down and savor each moment of each day."

"There are easier ways to learn that lesson."

"Perhaps, but saving your life was worth any sacrifice. Even as a small boy, you were my champion. You're still looking out for me." Her voice caught. "Don't you know I'd do it again in a heartbeat?"

Every cold crevice inside him filled with the warmth of his sister's amazing mercy and love. "If only I could change that day."

She tossed him a saucy grin. "If you're determined to take responsibility, I'd say giving up bounty hunting is a fair trade."

"I'd do anything for you. Anything but *that*."

"I lost Walt. I can't bear to lose you. Give it up, Nate, if not for me, for yourself." She thumped him on the knee. "You'll never find happiness until you make peace with God."

How could he make peace with God when his heart burned for revenge? How could he make peace with God when he'd become Stogsdill's judge and jury? How could he make peace with God when he wanted Stogsdill dead?

He wouldn't confide in Anna, but tomorrow he'd ride out to the Pence place. Pretend an interest in Debby's grandfather's thoroughbred horses. See what he could learn about Rory.

Chapter Fifteen

If only Carly had the courage to ask the pastor the reason God hadn't guided her better. Why He'd put such intimidating men in her life. First her father and then Max.

But with Henry beside her and others waiting to shake hands with Pastor Koontz, this wasn't the time or place.

She looked forward to a quiet day with her son. He was growing up before her very eyes. In a few years he'd leave home. Perhaps after dinner she'd take Henry on a walk or play a game.

As they crossed toward home, she avoided the little knots of parishioners scattered on the church lawn. From the furtive glances coming her way, the topic of conversation was probably the controversy over her shop.

The day Nate had delivered the news she no longer had possession of the deed, she'd cried out to God, asking Him to save the shop. Yet she didn't sense His support in the dispute. Was it fair to expect God to take her side when the deed would provide for the woman Max had made a widow?

She bit back a sigh. She'd married Max impulsively. She hadn't taken the time to pray. She hadn't trusted God to lead her. Instead, despite her qualms, she'd jumped into marriage. Her hasty actions had brought consequences. No wonder her marriage had been a nightmare. Still, if not for her marriage to Max, she wouldn't have her son.

And you wouldn't know Nate, her traitorous mind whispered.

Her heart skipped a beat. When had she come around to believing Nate's presence in her life was a good thing?

"Carly! Wait up." Rosalie Harders, hat askew, her full cheeks flushed, dashed toward them, huffing and puffing with the effort. "Mercy…you're harder…to catch…than a greased pig at the county fair."

"Sorry, I didn't realize you were looking for me."

"Of course I would be. The whole church is talking about it."

"About what?" As if Carly didn't know.

"Why, about you and that bounty hunter and his sister sharing a pew." She laid a gloved hand on her chest. "I'll admit I was surprised, too, what with the disagreement over your shop and all. Then I figured you were doing what the Good Book says and heaping burning coals on your enemies' heads."

Carly stiffened. Enemies? Anna? Nate?

Perhaps once. But Anna had become a mainstay in the shop, a friend to both her and Henry. And Nate…

Well, he had become important to her son. Henry believed God had sent Nate to be his father. A child couldn't be expected to understand the impossibility of such a hope. Carly certainly did. Still, Henry's trust in the man didn't make Nate her enemy.

"You should get to know Anna, Mrs. Harders. She's an excellent seamstress and a wonderful woman."

"Well, that's what my boys say. They claim she's sweeter than syrup-soaked bread. But what about that brother of hers? Doesn't he keep you on edge?"

"Not in the least," Carly said, asking forgiveness the moment the lie left her lips.

In truth, she wasn't afraid of the man. She was afraid of the effect he had on her. Her attraction was hardly surprising, considering her other bad choices.

"Reckon there's good in him. He's given my boys work. Kept them so busy they're too tired for Saturday night sprees. Come Sunday morning, they're up in time for church."

"I'm glad."

"Well, I'd say you're in a pickle, Carly, over that shop, but the Good Lord's a master of messes. He'll take care of you and Henry like He's taken care of me and my boys."

Carly's shoulders tightened. Rosalie's husband died around the time Carly had moved to Gnaw Bone. Without their father's guidance, her sons had become unruly. Hardly encouraging, but she had seen the difference in the twins of late. They'd come into her shop clean-shaved and sporting haircuts. They fulfilled their obligations. "Gotta get home and feed my boys. They always tell me not to bother, they'll get something at the diner, but what kind of mother would that make me?"

Behind their mother's back, the Harders twins edged toward the café.

Rosalie turned in the direction of Carly's gaze. "Oh, there you are! Come along. I'll have food on the table in no time."

Lester and Lloyd lumbered over, dragging their feet as if mired in mud. They tipped their hats at Carly and Lloyd chucked Henry under the chin.

"What you, uh, cooking, Ma?" Lester asked, stumbling over the question.

"Fried chicken."

The color drained from the twins' faces. Shoulders

slumped, they tramped after their mother as downcast as men going to their own hanging.

No doubt Rosalie's fried chicken would be burned to a crisp on the outside and, on the inside, as red as Carly's geraniums.

Carly had to offer Lester and Lloyd a reprieve. "Mrs. Harders," she called, "I'm frying chicken for dinner. Why don't you and the boys join us?"

The smiles erupting on Lester's and Lloyd's faces outdazzled the noonday sun.

"That's right nice of you, Miz Richards," Lloyd said.

Rosalie shook her head. "Goodness, I can't put you to the trouble, Carly."

"Ma, that's no way to answer an invitation," Lester said. "Why, you'll hurt Miz Richards's feelings."

"Oh, mercy, and on the Lord's Day, too." Rosalie gave a nod. "We'd love to come. What time do you want us?"

"Give me an hour."

"What can I bring?"

"Only your appetites."

"I can't come empty-handed. I'll bring a jar of my bread-and-butter pickles."

Lester bent down to Henry. "Ma makes the best pickles, Henry. They took first prize at the country fair."

They moseyed off toward home, but Lester lagged behind. "We're beholden to you, Miz Richards. We'll burn your trash all summer," he whispered, then jogged after his ma.

Suppressing a giggle, Carly took Henry's hand and strolled on. She couldn't undo the past and all the mistakes she'd made, but she could give the Harders brothers a decent meal, perhaps ensuring they would never again use her shop sign for target practice.

In truth, Nate was responsible for the positive change in the twins. When he moved on, would that change stick?

"Mama, will I still get a chicken leg?"

"Company chooses first," Carly said, patting Henry's shoulder.

"But there are three of them and a chicken's got only two legs. I'm gonna pray I get one."

"Henry, God wants us to share our best, not just what we don't want."

Henry's crestfallen face put a lump in Carly's throat. How had she dared to rebuke her son when she'd prayed for God to let her keep the shop? Even though Anna held the deed and was also a widow in need of a livelihood.

"You know," Carly said, "sometimes trusting God with the outcome is hard. But that's what He wants us to do."

"Then I'll get a chicken leg, Mama. 'Cause God loves me more'n Lester and Lloyd."

Carly gasped. "Henry Austin Richards. Why would you say such a thing?"

"They shooted our sign. They're bad."

"Sweetie, God loves everyone. Even when they do things they shouldn't."

Henry turned wide blue eyes to hers. "Even Pa?"

"Yes. God loved your father, too."

Hadn't Carly questioned that very thing? Not just with Max, but also with Nate? Yet hadn't she seen Nate's underlying decency with her and Henry? With Anna? Even the Harders?

When he'd stepped into church, the vulnerable, wounded hurt in his gaze echoed her own struggles and tugged at her heart.

But then, he'd left before the service ended, as if issues with his faith separated him from God. Did Nate even understand God's love?

Her breath caught. Hadn't she questioned God's love for her? Hadn't she struggled to trust Him?

It had taken a small boy's desire for a chicken leg to

remind her that God's love was unconditional. Deserved or not. Even when she made mistakes and didn't trust His provision. That assurance flooded her with peace.

She leaned down and hugged Henry to her. "You know, this once, I'll let you choose the piece of chicken first. I'm sure the Harders won't mind."

"I got me the bestest mama in the whole wide world!"

"God loves you and I love you." She tapped him playfully on the tip of his upturned nose. "God loves me, too. Do you know one reason I'm sure that's true?"

Eyes somber, lips slightly parted, Henry shook his head.

"Because He gave me you."

Without throwing a single punch, Mood packed quite a wallop, his words slamming into Nate's conscience with one-two precision.

As if Nate needed a reprimand after the fruitless meeting with Debby Pence's grandfather. Either Pence knew nothing of importance, or was in cahoots with Stogsdill.

"Me and Betsy leave Friday. Didn't plan on those two lamebrains running the livery," Morris said, picking up speed.

Brow furrowed, his faded blue eyes drilling into Nate like an auger, Morris paced the livery office. One pant leg was caught in his boot, his suspenders in a twist as if he'd dressed in a hurry.

Nate suspected Mood's reaction had more to do with fear for his ailing wife than with the Harders twins' incompetency. "They're good with horses."

"I'll give you that, but they got a lazy streak a mile long and a reputation in this here town that puts the good name of my business at risk."

"Morris, the responsibility is good for them, is making men out of them."

"Ain't got a problem with them caring for the horses

and mucking stalls, but I don't want them dealing with the public."

"All right. But you know I've got to ride out upon occasion. I can't promise."

He huffed and threw up his hands. "Reckon you're driven to find that there outlaw. And can't understand the importance of building a business, a home, a family. Taking care of those you love."

At the barely veiled censure, Nate exhaled. "That's why I'm here. To make sure Anna gets the seamstress shop and can provide for herself, no matter what happens to me."

"Son, it don't work to take what ain't rightfully yours. God ain't gonna bless that."

"I didn't ante the deed in a poker game."

"Max deserves the blame, that's sure. But the Good Book says to love your neighbor like yerself. That ain't just words. That's a call to action."

"As I see it, Anna *is* my neighbor." He owed her everything.

"Gotta be another way to help your sister. Think about it. Pray about it."

Prayer or no prayer, Nate couldn't do what Morris wanted.

The older man laid a knobby hand on Nate's shoulder. "After we leave, the livery earnings are yours. Work hard and you can make a go of this. You'll have no problem taking care of Anna without hurting a widow with a boy to feed."

Nate's gaze found the floor. The boards were dusty, worn. The gaps between the boards wide enough to lose a Morgan silver dollar in, yet these boards, this office, the livery, had served Mood well. The man had provided a vital function in the community while providing for him and his wife.

If Nate owned this livery, he could handle his and Anna's

expenses. If Anna continued to work for Carly, she could save her earnings and build a nest egg for the future, if anything happened to him. Morris saw the plan as an easy solution for all of them.

But Stogsdill might come soon to marry Debby. If Nate settled in, wasn't vigilant, those he cared about could be in danger. "Morris, I'm a bounty hunter not a liveryman. This town can't support two seamstresses. Even if Carly kept Anna on, where would my sister live once the livery sells and the cabin along with it?"

Mood sighed. "You're good at putting up obstacles."

"This mess isn't my fault. Richards should've thought of his family before anteing that deed."

"A reprobate like Max Richards don't know nothing about duty." Morris's eyes snapped with anger. "I've seen him in action. Heard him, too. The way he treated Carly and Henry weren't right."

The thought of Carly and Henry living under Richards's thumb sent a wave of fire cascading through Nate's veins. His hands fisted. If only he'd been here to protect them.

Piercing blue eyes met Nate's. "Now you're aiming to hurt them, too."

Morris's words cut like an ax, chopping at Nate's purpose. Carly deserved better than that scoundrel she'd married.

He admired her spunk, her work ethic, her love for Henry and kindness to Anna. She drew him like a mirage lured a thirsty wanderer in the desert. But a mirage was no more real for him than the life Morris touted.

If only things were different...

Even if he could find Stogsdill and put that behind him, he wasn't a family man. He'd taken a different path at fifteen years of age when he'd buried their parents, then spent the next three years taking care of the farm and practicing with a gun.

The day Anna and Walt had married, he'd ridden out to find the men responsible. Eight years later, he'd brought in all but one member of that gang. *Stogsdill.*

Nate's throat clogged. By neglecting to bring down Stogsdill, he'd signed Rachel's death warrant. The outlaw was determined to rid this world of the bounty hunter dogging him. That put anyone close to Nate at risk.

"I respect you, Morris. Admire your unfailing love for your wife. Your gentle nature with your horses. Your kindness to me and Anna. Even your confidence in my ability to run this livery. But you have no concept of the enormity of what you're asking."

With a defeated nod, the liveryman drudged to the door, then turned back, his gaze roaming the cramped livery office. "I've spent my adult life here. This place matters to me. I'm giving it up for my Betsy. Her welfare's more important than mine. More important than the plans I'd made for my life." His moist gaze landed on Nate. "That's love, son. I'm praying one day you'll understand that undoing the past ain't possible. You gotta let it go and move on. I hope by the time you see that, it ain't too late," he said, and then shuffled off.

Perhaps one day Nate would.

One day when Shifty Stogsdill no longer roamed free. One day when Nate had paid his debt to Anna. One day when Nate had patched up the mistakes he'd made.

Maybe then he could look to the future. Maybe then he could allow himself to love Carly and Henry, who were becoming as vital to him as the very air he breathed.

If Debby Pence's face hung any lower, she'd surely trip over her jaw. Carly didn't blame her. The bride had come into the shop to pay for her gown, yet she still had no date for the wedding. Her groom's indecision had to be humiliating.

"There's no need to pay now, Debby. Why not wait?"

"I don't feel right tying up your money in my dress."

Better to tie up money than spend her life tied to a no-account man. "If Rory can't set a date, business must be good."

Or the man didn't love her. At least not the way he should.

Debby's lower lip trembled. "Grandpa says Rory's as reluctant as my mother's beau."

Had Debby been born out of wedlock? The reason her grandparents had raised her?

Tears welled in Debby's eyes. "Rory's in love with me. Not like my pa at all. Grandpa doesn't understand Rory wants to succeed so he can give me a nice place to live and money in the bank."

Material blessings hadn't saved her marriage to Max. "Those are good goals, but a lot of couples marry with less."

"Grandma's upset Rory won't go to church. She doesn't understand he's tired from his travels." She sighed. "They keep planting all these doubts in my mind. If he were here, I'd feel better."

"Your grandparents want to make sure you don't marry outside of God's will." As Carly had.

"Oh, they think everything's wrong." Debby harrumphed. "Like God's just waiting to rain down fire and brimstone."

Debby's grandparents were known to disapprove of square dancing, ice-cream socials, hayrides, most everything that brought young people together. Debby would probably find any man who could sweep her away from their rigid view appealing.

"When's the last time you saw Rory?"

"Four weeks ago tomorrow. He rode in one morning to surprise me." She smiled. "He's always doing the unexpected."

"Was he able to stay long?"

"He had to leave the next morning to ride to Louisville in time to catch the evening train."

"Must've been disappointing to have him leave so quickly."

"Yes. But, he doesn't like me to complain. Says it takes the fun out of surprising me."

"Are you afraid of Rory's reaction?"

Debby blinked. "No. I, uh, just don't want to upset him when our time together is so short."

The same excuse Carly had made for not speaking up about Max's actions. "Debby, marriage isn't always a ticket to freedom." Hadn't Carly learned that the hard way?

"What do you mean?"

"A husband can be in control, same as a parent or grandparent." She took a fortifying breath. Perhaps, if she confessed her poor choices, she could help this girl. "You've probably heard my husband was…difficult."

Debby's eyes widened, then her gaze dropped to the floor. "Yes, ma'am."

"My father was strict, disapproving, not an easy man to live with. To get out of the house, I married Max. He didn't attend church and didn't value me any more than my father did." Carly heaved a sigh. "If Rory is hard to get along with before you're married, he could treat you far worse afterward."

"I'm at fault, really. I upset him with my nagging, with asking too many questions. Rory hates being badgered."

Carly bit back a sigh. Debby wasn't listening, didn't want to hear the warning. "I know you. You're a sweet girl. I'm sure your questions are what any prospective bride would ask her groom. If you can't talk to him now, how—"

"I need to go," Debby said. "Grandpa's probably finished with his errands and waiting for me in the wagon."

Debby hustled toward the entrance and met Nate strolling in. He tipped his hat and held the door for her, then turned his gaze on Carly, a smile on his lips, warmth in his gaze.

The solid strength of the man gave her hope good men existed. If only Debby would examine the facts before it was too late. For, in her bones, Carly knew Rory was trouble.

Carly's welcoming smile drew Nate to her like a well-aimed lariat. He longed to take her hand, to pull her close.

Instead he would focus on the reason he'd come. "From the way she scurried out, I'd say Miss Pence is upset." He searched Carly's upturned face. "Know what about?"

"Rory hasn't set a wedding date. The more I hear about the man, the more I hope and pray she doesn't marry him."

If Rory and Stogsdill were one and the same, the lack of a wedding date meant the outlaw wasn't in the area. Yet.

"I don't understand what Debby sees in him." He glanced around the shop. "Where's Anna?"

"She looked exhausted when she came in this morning so I insisted she get away from the shop awhile," Carly said, stacking the bolts of fabric on the counter and straightening their edges with precision, as if avoiding him. "She's having tea with the Sample's widowed daughter, Elnora."

"That was thoughtful of you."

"You sound surprised." She looked up at him from re-aligning bolts of fabric.

Aware they were alone in the shop, Nate's heart tripped in his chest. He took a step closer.

"Do you need to speak with Anna?" she said, gathering up the bolts and carrying them to a cabinet. "I'll tell—"

"No, I came in to, uh, let you know I talked with Debby's grandfather," he said, struggling to stay focused on his mission, not on those mesmerizing eyes, not on her smile, not on the sunny, warm day outside the window, perfect to whisk her away on a picnic.

"What did Mr. Pence have to say?"

"I mentioned I'd met Debby at the shop and eased the conversation around to her engagement. Pence opened up, admitted he has little use for Rory, but suspects his granddaughter would run off if she's forbidden to see him."

Carly nodded. "I agree."

"Why would she want to marry this guy? How much could she know about him?"

"I'm sure she has qualms but is ignoring her better judgment. She sees Rory as exciting, as a man who will take her away from a tedious life."

"Better tedious than terrifying."

"Undoubtedly, Rory has made Debby grand promises." Carly sighed, the sound wrenching. "Too many women make that mistake. They want more, they want…to move forward in life. Sometimes when they want something so badly, they ignore the warning signs."

Nate's stomach tightened. "You speak as if you know this firsthand."

She averted her gaze. "I just see Debby making a mistake. It worries me. I suspect Rory doesn't treat her right, but she's blaming herself and her grandparents, instead of putting the blame on him, where it belongs."

"Why would a woman blame herself when a man doesn't know how to be a good man?"

A bittersweet smile crossed Carly's lips. "Sometimes in the rush to have her dream, a woman forgets to look at the truth."

"What dream?"

A spark flickered in her eyes. "Oh, you know, having a kind, caring man to love and cherish her. Her personal White Knight. Her hero. They'd live in a pretty little cottage in the woods and he'd promise her they'll fill it with flowers and babies and laughter…"

Carly looked at him hard, as if seeing inside him, extinguishing the light in her eyes. She smoothed a palm over a bolt of cloth, over and over again, as if seeking comfort in the soft fibers.

He laid a hand over hers, stopping her frantic movements. "Do you still believe in that dream?"

She raised her eyes, eyes filled with hurt. "We're both too old for such nonsense, don't you think?"

Nate wanted to agree. Knew deep in his heart that he did agree, but right now, staring into Carly's soft, wounded gaze, he wanted to hold on to that dream. Hold on to the notion of flowers and babies and laughter. "I think we're never too old to have that kind of happiness." She tried to look away. He gently turned her face toward his. "Maybe there's hope for us yet, Carly."

"Maybe." The word escaped her lips on a breath.

"You're a remarkable woman."

"I'm not someone to admire."

He gaped at her. "You're not serious." But the misery clouding her pretty eyes said she was dead serious. "Why would you say that?"

She heaved a sigh. "All that's happened are the consequences of the poor decisions I made."

Carly didn't blame him or Max for possibly losing the shop? "What do you mean?"

Her gaze darted away, focusing on some spot over his shoulder. "When my mother died, I was eleven. I took over the chores, but wasn't much of a cook or housekeeper."

"That's a big job for a child."

"I didn't mind the work as much as…" She fiddled with her sleeve, as if looking for answers in the cotton.

"Tell me."

She lifted her face to his. "My father treated me like

a hired hand. No matter how hard I tried, nothing I did pleased him. By the time I was eighteen, I had perfected my skills as a seamstress and was desperate to escape." Her eyes misted. "When I met Max, I, ah…"

"Saw him as the answer."

"Yes, but more than that, I—" Carly sighed.

"You can tell me anything."

"I…I was wooed by the shop. Got caught up in Max's talk about what a success I'd make of the business. How his mother's shop would live on. I disregarded the uneasy feeling I had about marrying him." She gave a shaky laugh. "I see myself in Debby. The reason I know she's making the same mistake."

He pulled her into his arms. "Richards put on a phony face and manipulated you."

"I worked hard and tried to be enough." Her head drooped against his chest. "I was never enough. Not for my father. Not for Max."

Her shoulders shook with a sob. As she quietly wept, her tears soaking the front of Nate's shirt, his eyes stung, sharp and hot.

He held her close, stroking her hair, murmuring words of comfort, wanting to take away her heartache.

How could this wonderful, strong woman have believed such nonsense? "They were at fault, not you."

She straightened, pulling away from his arms, avoiding his gaze. "I see now I settled for Max because underneath I didn't believe I was enough for a truly good man."

The pain in her voice told him she still believed those lies. He lifted her face to his and spoke past the lump in his throat. "I've never known anyone more deserving of a good man than you. You deserved to be treated with respect. I'm sorry you weren't."

She gave a nod and wiped at the tears on her cheeks. Nate brushed two fingertips over her lips, so soft, parting now, rosy and beckoning. He wanted to kiss her badly. He wanted to be that good man she sought. He wanted to give her everything.

"You smell good," she said, leaning in, as if she couldn't get enough of his scent.

He touched the silky, fragrant strands of her hair. "You're beautiful, Carly, inside and out." He lowered his head, looking into her eyes for permission.

Her eyelids drifted closed. "Nate," she whispered.

His name, rolling off her lips, filled with longing, was all the invitation he needed.

With a moan, he pulled her to him, brushing his lips over hers. With Carly in his arms, the years of loneliness fled. As he deepened the kiss, Carly rose on tiptoe and slid her arms around his back. The touch of her soft curves shot through his veins, igniting the wild beat of his heart.

With a sigh, she broke away. "I…I have to work. I can't get wrapped up in…"

"In what?"

She raised her forlorn gaze to his. "In foolish dreams."

Her words extinguished the wild hope surging through him for a future with Carly. Nate wanted to do whatever he could to keep that happy look she'd worn, but she was right. It was a foolish dream—a foolhardy dream—to think he could be any woman's knight.

"I should get to work, too." He settled his hat in place and pivoted back. "You need to be careful, Carly."

"Careful? Of what?"

Of men like me, he thought. *Of men who could fall for you and break your heart.*

"Of Rory. I suspect Rory's the outlaw I'm after."

Carly gasped. "Stogsdill?"

"Mr. Pence said Rory's last name is Cummins, not one of the aliases Stogsdill uses. Still, Sheriff Truitt's checking his stash of posters to see if Rory Cummins is wanted by the law. If he isn't, it doesn't mean he's the salesman he claims."

"Surely you don't think Debby would knowingly marry an outlaw. She's innocent. I'd stake my shop on that."

At her claim, an awkward silence hung in the air, as they both realized the shop might not be Carly's to wager.

"Normally, I wouldn't tell you about my suspicions without definite proof, but with Debby coming into the shop, you and Anna need to be alert for any information about her fiancé, and let me know the minute you hear they've set a wedding date."

"Does Anna know?"

"I told her this morning." He leaned closer. "If Rory and Stogsdill are the same man, make no mistake about it, he's dangerous. Should Rory accompany Debby to the shop, make an excuse and close, then find me or Sheriff Truitt."

"But if you're wrong and Rory's not Stogsdill—"

"Assume he is." Nate's voice deepened to a rumble. "Promise you'll come to the livery."

"I will." Carly bit her lip. "I hope Debby hasn't fallen in love with a criminal."

"Evil men prey on the innocent. The helpless. The naive. Outlaw isn't stamped on their foreheads."

Carly bit her lower lip. "A woman wants to believe the best in a man," she said, then turned away, walked to the window, fleeing the question in his gaze. "If you're right, what can we do to stop Debby from marrying him?"

"We won't do anything to alert Debby and warn Rory away."

She whirled to face him. "And what? Let her marry the man and ruin her life?"

He desperately wanted to soothe her alarm, to make her world right again. Despite everything, a part of him still wanted to believe in happy endings.

"I won't let Debby hitch herself to a killer." He touched her cheek. "And I won't let anything happen to you."

"Can you stop either, Nate?"

Nate longed to say, "You can count on me." But could she? Really? "I'll do my best," he vowed.

A lump knotted Nate's throat. He'd tried to do his best before, yet he'd let down those he loved. Would he ever be free from the path he'd taken?

No matter how much he longed to settle down, he couldn't get caught up in the fantasy. The reason he would never share that cottage in the woods.

Chapter Sixteen

Carly slid the needle between threads on the backside of the garment, putting the last tiny, invisible stitch in the hem of the voluminous skirt, then tying a knot and snipping the thread. This was by far the most beautiful ball gown Carly had ever created.

Her gaze swept the shop and the walk beyond. Seeing no one, she hurried to the full-length mirror and held the shimmering red confection in front of her, swaying to the tune of the Blue Danube waltz playing in her head, visualizing Nate's strong arms around her, holding her close. His arms would cherish and protect, exactly as she'd felt during their kiss.

Her mind zipped back to the soft pressure of his lips on hers, the thrilling tingle that raised goose bumps on her arms and warmed her clear to her toes. That kiss suggested tomorrow. A relationship of permanence.

Would he kiss her again?

The bell jingled.

Carly dropped the dress and whirled to the door.

Anna stood in the entrance, smiling. "You should have a dress like that," she said, pointing at the garment in a heap on the floor. "You looked so pretty, just now."

Heat scorched Carly's cheeks; what she deserved for getting caught up in a fantasy. She forced a laugh. "I have no need of such a fancy dress," she said, gathering the garment up and laying it in the waiting box. "How was your visit with Mrs. Watkins?"

"The poor woman's struggling," Anna said, wiping snippets of fabric and thread from the counter and tossing them in the wastebasket. "I mainly listened."

"I'm sure that helped more than you know."

"She's grateful her parents opened their home to her and Bonnie Sue. Too many widows are left with no money, no one to turn to, scrambling for a way to make ends meet."

Anna didn't say the words, but Carly knew Nate's sister was referring to herself. If Carly lost the shop, how would she manage?

"I told Elnora you're doing a wonderful job raising Henry alone. She'll do the same." Anna picked up two pieces of a bodice, then sat and pinned the shoulders together.

"I'm no one to pattern herself after."

"Of course you are. You're a terrific mother and handle a business, too."

"I wouldn't be able to handle this order without your help." Carly struggled for the words she needed to say. "But, more than that, I consider you a friend."

"I feel the same about you."

"Not just a friend. A close friend." Carly picked up a roll of lace for a nightgown and began pinning it to the cuffs. "I haven't had a friend like that in years."

"What do you mean?" Anna's brow puckered. "Everyone in this town likes you."

"I chat with acquaintances at church and in the shop. But I have no one I confide in like I do you."

"Why is that?"

Carly's hand stilled. "When I was married to Max, I

didn't want anyone to know my husband browbeat me. Most weren't fooled." She shrugged her shoulders. "I guess I was ashamed."

"The shame lay at Max's feet, not yours."

"Not entirely." As soon as the words left Carly's mouth, she wanted to pull them back.

"Why would you say that?"

In Anna's eyes Carly saw warmth and acceptance of someone who cared. About her. Someone Carly could trust. "I rushed into marriage," she said, blurting the confession out before she lost her courage. "On our wedding day, I realized I'd made a huge mistake. Max showed me no tenderness, spoke not one affectionate word." Carly returned her gaze to the nightdress in her lap, a pretty frivolous gown promising loving nights with a husband. But, not for her. She quickly looked away. "He rode out the next morning, giving me no idea when he'd return."

Tears welled in Anna's eyes. "What an awful man. I'm so sorry. But don't believe you deserved that treatment," Anna said, her tone without judgment, without criticism.

"There are consequences for what I did, for what Max did." She raised her gaze to Anna. "Before you and I became friends, I pleaded with God to let me keep this shop."

"Of course you did. You have a son to house and feed."

"Max killed your husband—reason enough to lose the store," Carly said in a voice as wobbly as a three-legged table.

"God's not going to punish you for Max's sins."

Tears brimmed in Carly's eyes. "He might."

"Gracious, why would you think that?"

Carly shook her head, unable to admit to Anna why she'd married Max. Carly could barely believe she'd admitted the truth to Nate.

Anna set aside her work and rose to her feet, then lumbered to Carly's side. She laid a gentle hand on Carly's shoulder and looked deep into her eyes. "The Good Lord never forsakes us. Whatever the judge decides with that deed, God has a plan. We may not know what it is, but you and Henry and I will be okay."

Anna saw God's hand in every ordinary thing. She meant to comfort Carly, but what she'd said were mere words. Words would not feed her son or put a roof over his head.

"You know," Anna said, "if the judge rules the deed is legally mine, I'll insist upon sharing the shop right down the middle."

"Nate would never hear of it."

"Not because he's unfeeling about your situation," Anna said. "He thinks the shop won't provide enough income."

"He's right. This big wedding order is unusual."

"Have you thought about expanding? Making hats maybe?"

"I don't know the first thing about creating hats, except that milliners need special equipment I don't have." She nibbled her lower lip, thinking. "But stylish shoes might sell. Ladies in this town might appreciate a choice other than Stuffle Emporium's humdrum clodhoppers."

"Exactly. We're resourceful women. With God's help we can give ourselves a happy ending. Like a fairy tale." Anna gave a confident smile, then picked up the bodice and sat at the sewing machine. Soon the whir of the machine filled the shop.

If only they could find a way to increase sales.

If only Carly could have that happy fairy-tale ending.

The memory of Nate's kiss gripped her, all but cutting off her breath. If only—

She stiffened her spine, refusing to consider the cottage in the woods. Stories of knights rescuing damsels in danger were about as likely as the talking pigs in Henry's storybook. Everyone knew, even her young son, fairy tales were fantasy.

Carly would remember that, too. If she didn't, she might fall in love with Nate. Then what terrible price might she and Henry pay?

Would this be a fool's errand or provide the next lead to Stogsdill's whereabouts? Time would tell.

As the sky bloomed with pink and orange, heralding the rising sun, Nate slapped leather on his horse, its dark coat shining with health; his one white foot the reason Nate called him Maverick.

Lloyd and Lester tromped around the livery, feeding and watering the horses.

"I should return before the first customer arrives," Nate called.

Lester threw up a hand. "If not, you can count on us."

With a nod, Nate led Maverick out of the barn, then swung into the saddle and rode down Main Street, quiet at this early hour. He tugged the brim of his Stetson low and, pressing a heel into Maverick's side, they picked up speed and headed out of town.

He'd missed time in the saddle. Missed the exhilaration of riding with the wind in his face, at one with his horse. But he didn't miss sleeping on the hard ground and meals of hardtack and cold beans. These few weeks he'd spent in Gnaw Bone, he'd grown accustomed to Anna's home cooking, to a soft mattress and a pillow under his head.

His heart stuttered in his chest. Yes…and to the softness of Carly in his arms. And the overpowering need to protect and care for her. When had he ever felt that way before?

He and Rachel would've built a good life together, but he and Carly had walked through the hot coals of difficult pasts and survived. That connection was strong, like a braided whip.

Didn't hurt one bit the woman was beautiful and could hold her own with anyone, including him, and, mothered a boy who'd captured Nate's heart.

A couple miles outside of town, the winding road bordered woods, shooting his thoughts back to the location of that cottage in Carly's dream. Except, these woods were littered with fallen trees and broken limbs, probably the result of a winter ice storm. A hardscrabble reminder woods weren't some fantasy world of perfection. And fairy tales were just that. Myths. Not something to hang anyone's future on.

That truth didn't stop the memory of Carly's lips under his. That truth didn't stop the memory of their powerful attraction that left him shaken. That truth didn't stop the memory of the overpowering yearning to settle down.

Thankfully, before anyone got hurt, she'd headed off a mistake, a happily-ever-after ending doomed to fail. He couldn't jeopardize Carly's safety as he had Rachel's.

Something he should've considered before he'd kissed Carly.

But he could risk stopping Debby from falling into a bad marriage. The sheriff had spent a couple of days looking and had not found any wanted posters on Rory Cummins. Was the man what he claimed, or an outlaw parading as a salesman?

One way to find out. Show Debby the picture of Stogsdill.

Was he about to break a young girl's heart? Not a task he took pleasure in. But better to break her heart now than to see her tied to a robber, a killer. A man who would drag her down with him.

If the two men were one and the same and Debby was as innocent as Carly believed, the price on Rory's head would make Debby break off the engagement. An angry Stogsdill would make it his mission to find out why. He might even retaliate against Debby and her grandparents. Nate's stomach knotted with a pain that burned. More names to add to the growing list of those Nate needed to protect.

But if Debby was in cahoots with the outlaw, she would report the incident to Stogsdill. And Stogsdill would come gunning for Nate. The reason he dared not get caught up in this loco desire for a gentler life with Carly and Henry and let down his guard.

At the Pence farm, an idyllic spot of gently rolling hills tinted green, all seemed right with the world. Nate rode up the lane to the two-story house.

In the barnyard Nate swung from the saddle, slapped the reins around the hitching post and walked to the porch. Had Stogsdill tainted the pristine-white clapboards of this farmhouse with his presence?

Debby opened the door to his knock, looking fresh as a daisy in a blue calico dress. From her fading smile, she was disappointed to see him. Had she expected Rory? Or merely hoped?

"Mr. Sergeant," she said, fiddling with the ruby ring dangling from her neck. "This is a surprise."

Nate doffed his hat. "Good morning, Miss Pence."

"Who is it?" The door opened wider and Debby's grandfather stepped into view, hitching a red suspender over his shoulder.

"Nate Sergeant, Grandpa. He's a friend of Carly Richards."

Would Carly call Nate a friend? Somehow he doubted it. Friends didn't unsettle each other. Friends didn't share kisses that shifted the ground under their feet. Friends didn't erect fences to keep each other out.

"What brings you out here?" Pence said, his tone conveying an unspoken disquiet.

Nate cleared his throat. "Sir, I need to assure myself your granddaughter isn't making a terrible mistake." He paused, plowing a hand through his hair. "By marrying a murderer wanted by the law."

A gasp on her lips, Debby's eyes widened with alarm and then narrowed as red stained her cheeks. "Rory's not an outlaw! He's a salesman."

Mr. Pence laid a gnarled hand on Debby's shoulder and took a step closer. "I ain't all that impressed with Rory. Still… That's a serious accusation," he said, gaze penetrating, suspicious. "Why would you say that, Sergeant?"

"Miss Pence, would you mind me asking where you first met Rory?"

"In St. Louis at Cousin Minnie's church social. Rory's sister attends there and introduced us."

"Shifty Stogsdill is the outlaw I'm referring to. I suspect St. Louis is Stogsdill's home base."

"You're a bounty hunter," Pence said. "I expect you would view every man with suspicion. See every female as a possible sweetheart to this, uh, Shifty person."

"Not every woman." He motioned toward the ruby ring adorning Debby's neck. "I've seen a ruby ring like that on Stogsdill's hand."

Had seen red glinting in the sun mere seconds before Stogsdill gunned down Rachel.

Pence folded his arms across his chest. "Hard to believe my granddaughter would give her heart to a killer."

"Rory wouldn't kill anyone," Debby vowed. "He's got a good job. Plans for our future. He's exciting, makes me laugh."

"Sometimes he makes you cry," her grandfather said, his eyes boring into Debby's.

Debby's chin trembled. "That's not his fault. I get emotional about his leaving and…"

"Deborah Sue, time you—"

"Sir, I have a sketch of Stogsdill." Nate reached inside

his vest. "And information about his height and weight. One look should settle the matter."

"Come inside," Pence said, steering Debby ahead of him.

Nate followed them to a yellow-painted kitchen where the aromas of a hearty breakfast teased his nostrils. He'd left before Anna had awakened. His breakfast a hardboiled egg he'd found in the icebox. But filling his stomach was not the point of his visit.

Gray hair twisted into a knot at her nape, Mrs. Pence stood with her back to him at the blackened mammoth cookstove, scooping fried potatoes from an iron skillet onto a platter.

"Mother," Pence said, "this here's Nate Sergeant, that bounty hunter." Mrs. Pence walked to her husband's side. "He wants us to take a look at the picture of an outlaw he's after."

"Whatever for?" she said, wiping her hands on the apron wrapped around her middle, her wary eyes giving Nate a tongue-lashing. Obviously the woman didn't trust him.

Pence merely pointed to a table in front of the window, then grabbed a magnifying glass lying on the counter beside an open Bible. "Put the paper there where the light's good."

With a nod, Nate strode to the table, the heels of his boots clomping on the wood-planked floor. He unfolded the wanted poster, smoothed the surface with both hands, then stepped aside.

The family edged closer, slowly, as if approaching a venomous snake. Head bent over the poster, Debby looked and then quickly looked away.

Nate held his breath, but didn't have long to wait.

As her gaze traveled back, a horrified gasp rose from Debby's lips, every drop of color leeching from her cheeks. She gripped one of the chairs. "It…it can't be."

Holding the magnifying glass over the picture, Pence leaned closer. As the glass clattered to the table, Pence's mouth moved and his Adam's apple bobbed, but he emitted no sound. Then he turned, his gaze locking with Nate's. "It's him."

"Miss Pence," Nate said gently, "do you agree the man on the wanted poster and your fiancé are one and the same?"

Her lower lip quivering, Debby crumbled into the chair, hunching forward with her elbows on the table, her face in her hands. "I had no idea," she said, then began to cry softly, her shoulders shaking.

Her grandmother bent close, pressing her cheek to Debby's. "There, there," she said.

"That poster says Rory killed a half dozen folks, maybe more. No wonder he wouldn't attend church. Probably feared the wrath of God." Pence sat on his haunches beside his granddaughter's chair and took her hand. "Debby, you know what this means. To make sure that scoundrel won't come near you, you gotta break off the engagement."

"Do you know how to contact him?" Nate said.

Mrs. Pence pulled a hanky from her apron pocket and handed it to her granddaughter.

Debby wiped the square of linen over her cheeks. "He told me to contact his sister. She could get a message to him. Only in an emergency, he said."

"Patricia Schubert."

"Yes." Her face crumpled and a high-pitched wail slid from her lips, shattering the quiet kitchen.

Mrs. Pence pulled her granddaughter to her feet and into her arms, rocking back and forth, crooning softly in her ear.

Nate released the breath he'd been holding. Debby's reaction to that poster either proved her innocence, or she was an amazing actress. Nate tamped down the thought.

Years as a bounty hunter had left him jaded. Even he couldn't deny this young woman was heartbroken.

Pence lurched to his feet, grabbed his hat from the hook by the back door and slapped it on his head. "I'm riding to town. I'll send a wire telling that sidewinder Debby ain't marrying him and he's never to darken our door again."

"I've got a plan I'd like you to consider. A plan that would ensure Stogsdill is caught. For the plan to work, he can't know we're on to him. I'll need your help, if you and your granddaughter are willing to play along."

Her grandfather paused, weighing Nate's words, and then motioned to a chair. "Take the weight off, Sergeant."

Mrs. Pence tilted up Debby's chin. "You up to listening to Mr. Sergeant's plan?"

With a nod, Debby took the chair across from Nate.

"Mother, a cup of your strong coffee may help this plan go down a little easier."

Mrs. Pence served steaming coffee in ironstone mugs, then set sugar and cream on the table. As Nate took a swig of coffee, she took a seat beside her granddaughter. The food grew cold, but no one had an appetite.

This cheerful, orderly kitchen laden with mouth-watering aromas didn't fit the sinister situation. Nate leaned forward and explained his plan, hoping they'd agree to do their part.

Pence looked at Debby. "You must love the man. You okay with this?"

"I thought I loved him, Grandpa, but..." Debby heaved a sigh. "He can be cruel sometimes. Now I know why."

At Debby's words, her grandfather's brow furrowed. He sat studying his hands while the pendulum of the clock clicked its steady beat. "That bruise on your arm last month wasn't from banging into the barn door like you claimed, was it?"

Without a word, Debby hung her head.

"That chicken-livered coward. What kind of man could harm a woman?"

Nate's heart stuttered in his chest. Had Richards left bruises on Carly's arms? Or worse?

"Then it's decided," Pence said. "Someone's got to stop him. We'll do as you suggest, Sergeant. That plan of yours makes sense."

With a nod, Nate set down his half-empty mug. "Thanks for the coffee, ma'am. I'll leave you to your breakfast."

"Mr. Sergeant," Debby said, her sad eyes imploring. "Please tell Carly I'll be in to pay for the dress."

"Knowing Carly, she won't allow it, but I'll tell her."

Nate would pay the bill. The least he could do for Carly and for the young woman Stogsdill had deceived. "Miss Pence, this isn't your fault. The man preys on the defenseless and the innocent."

"That's kind of you to say, but I've been a fool. All I could think about was getting married. I didn't want to examine my misgivings closely."

She reached up and unclasped the chain around her neck, then turned watery eyes to his. "I once thought this ring was beautiful. Do you suppose Rory stole it, even spilled blood to get it?"

"Wouldn't be surprised."

Debby shivered, dropping the ring, chain and all, to the table. "I can't stand the sight of it."

"I'm not expecting the worst, but if Stogsdill should arrive at your door, you should be wearing that ring and call him Rory. Play along. Your lives could depend on it."

Tears sprang to Debby's eyes. "I'm so sorry I brought all this on you," she said to her grandparents in a wobbly voice.

"God will see us through. My Winchester won't hurt none neither."

Pence escorted Nate out, letting the door slam behind

him. And gripped Nate's hand. "I'm beholden to you. Can't bear to think what might've happened to our granddaughter if she'd got herself hitched to a murderer." He exhaled. "I'll keep my guns loaded," he said when they were out of earshot of the house.

"I'll stop by the sheriff's office and tell him our plan." Pence gave a nod.

"Let me know if you see or hear anything suspicious or alarming."

"I will. Can't understand why an outlaw would cotton to a sweet girl like my granddaughter."

The same thought had occurred to Nate. He motioned to the horses grazing in the pasture. "If Debby talked about her life here when she met Stogsdill, maybe those thoroughbreds and this farm enticed him," he said, unhitching his horse and swinging into the saddle. "This would be a good spot to hole up."

"Reckon so."

Nate rode toward Gnaw Bone. No matter what he'd said to Pence, Stogsdill might have seen in Debby a woman he could control, a woman who would give him children and keep her lip buttoned.

If Stogsdill had grown weary of his life, Nate would see that the outlaw didn't get his wish.

He didn't want Stogsdill anywhere near Gnaw Bone, anywhere near those he cared about, but once he got that telegram, Stogsdill would come.

Nate spurred his horse faster. For once, he would have the advantage over Stogsdill and he intended to make use of it, if it was the last thing he did.

Chapter Seventeen

Carly shrugged her shoulders, trying to loosen her tight muscles after hours spent hunched over the sewing machine.

Across the way, Anna hand stitched the opening of the collar she'd turned.

They were making progress, close to completing Vivian's trousseau. The bride had come in that morning for final fittings on several garments. Only two more dresses to make before the Schwartz wedding. Three days to finish, which gave Vivian that week to pack as she'd wanted.

With an hour till closing time, Carly was tempted to lock the door and turn the sign in the window to Closed. But, if she did, her customers might question her reliability. Once the judge arrived, she'd have no choice. Weary as she was, Carly hoped nothing interrupted their progress.

The bell over the door jingled. Maizie rose from the floor, tail wagging, eager to greet the newcomer. Carly stopped pedaling, pasted on a smile and faced the door.

Hat in hand, Nate stood in the entrance, his rugged jaw dark with stubble, his gray eyes probing, his holstered gun riding his hip. He reminded her of their first meeting here in this shop. She'd thought him dangerous then, and he looked dangerous now.

Her heart tripped in her chest. Dangerous and oh, so tempting.

He moved closer, his stride loose, confident, almost a swagger. Carly's traitorous thoughts zinged to his kiss. To the softness of his lips, the hard muscles of his chest beneath her palm, the wild beating of his heart.

As wild as her erratic pulse now. He stopped near her, his smoldering eyes locking with hers, then lowering to her mouth.

He must be thinking of their kiss. That kiss had left her exhilarated, full of yearning, and oh, yes, of trepidation, leaving her as unraveled as a tattered tea towel.

"Nate," Anna said, her alarmed tone jerking Carly's foot on the treadle. "From the look on your face when you came in, I'd say you have bad news."

"I'm afraid so," he said, then explained Debby Pence's fiancé was none other than Stogsdill, the villain he'd been trailing for years.

The news sank to Carly's stomach like a stone. "Poor Debby must be devastated, but at least she won't endure a lifetime of misery." Or what might feel longer than a lifetime.

"Debby's insisting on paying for her wedding dress, but I'd like to take care of the bill."

Nate might look hard and dangerous, but he often showed a softer side, a considerate, even tender side.

"That's kind of you to offer, but once we've finished the Schwartz order, I'll rework the dress so completely, Debby wouldn't recognize it if she met a woman wearing it on the street."

"You're very talented," Nate said, his gaze dropping to her lips and lingering there.

Was he suggesting she had an aptitude for kissing? Heat

flooded Carly's cheeks, and she quickly focused on the fabric under the pressure foot. She stifled a sigh. A crooked seam she'd have to take out and sew again. A reminder that Nate Sergeant would thwart the straight path she'd chosen.

"Will you and Anna have everything stitched by the deadline?"

"Yes, even after taking a couple of hours to drive out to visit Betsy. She and Morris leave Friday. While I was there, I met his sister, Florence. Seemed like a nice woman, able to handle the farm chores."

"That's good to know. Morris came by the livery. He hopes to return to Gnaw Bone when his house or the livery sells. If Betsy's not up to the trip, his sister will handle things."

Henry slammed through the door, a bundle of smiling energy. Carly glanced at her watch. That hour helping the Harders paint the corral fence had flown.

Her son gave not one glance to Anna, not one glance to Carly. All he had eyes for was Nate. He raced to him, the white smears on his cheeks and overalls proof he'd done his part. The ecstatic joy on her son's face confirmed Henry still had Nate on that pedestal, a precarious position. One blunder and Nate would tumble off that lofty perch and shatter her son's heart.

"Hi, buddy," Nate said, squatting in front of her son. "Looks like you tangled with a paintbrush."

Henry stepped into Nate's arms, gazing up at him. "I helped paint a fence. I got some on me, but lots more on the boards."

The smile on Nate's face lavished her son with approval. "You're a good worker."

"I can ride good, too."

"Yes, you can. You and Lady are a team."

"Can we ride to the creek and have a picnic?"

"Soon as I can find time."

"When?" Henry asked, his eyes sparkling with eagerness.

Nate rose to his feet, his expression closed. "Can't say for sure."

Maizie padded over. Henry got down on his knees and hugged the dog's neck, burying his face in the fur, oblivious to the fact Nate had evaded his question.

But Carly had noticed. After being married to Max, she recognized when a man was keeping something from her, from her son, from them all. Like Max, would Nate disappear from their lives one morning? Just leave a note and ride off?

Carly rose from the bench. "Henry, your snack is in the kitchen."

"'Bye, Nate," Henry said, the disappointment in his voice confirmation her son could be easily hurt.

Henry disappeared into the back, Maizie trailing after him.

Nate shifted on his feet. "I'm heading to Kentucky tomorrow. Should be back in a couple days. Three at most."

"Is it a good idea to leave now?" Anna asked. "Once Debby breaks off her engagement, Stogsdill might come here looking for trouble."

"Don't worry." Nate's gaze slid to Carly. "I won't let anything happen to you, I promise."

When had Max protected Carly from anything? Instead he'd been the reason she'd kept alert for trouble. All those years she'd had to protect herself and her son. The reason she'd bought a gun and learned to shoot. The prospect of firing at a human being left her weak in the knees, but Carly knew to save her son's life, she could use it.

Still, Nate couldn't promise to protect them. His intentions were good, but no one was invincible.

Nate stepped closer and laid a gentle hand on Carly's arm. She caught a whiff of soap, sunshine and that fresh manly scent she associated only with Nate.

"You look upset. Are you okay?" he said.

"I'm fine."

But was she really? When her heart raced every time Nate appeared?

"See you at home, Anna," Nate said and strode out without explaining his reason for riding to Kentucky.

What was he hiding?

Carly stiffened. Had another wanted poster lured him to action? Bounty hunting was in Nate's blood. He might care about her and Henry and Anna, but not enough to settle down.

Who or what would protect Carly from making yet another foolish choice, from losing her heart to a man who wouldn't stay?

Circuit Judge Mark Rohlof drove into Gnaw Bone late that evening, news of his arrival spreading through town faster than a prairie fire in August.

By the time Carly opened the shop Thursday morning, three customers had reported the judge's arrival, stating Rohlof had been dust covered, looking for a bath and a good night's sleep.

Sometime today they would learn when and where the hearing was set. She and Anna tiptoed around the subject, both too unsettled to speak the words aloud. Though, with Max losing the deed, did Carly even have a chance?

Either way the judge ruled, the decision would trigger change. Change brought the unknown. Hadn't she learned change could bring hope or bring disaster?

Lester and Lloyd trooped in, tracking dirt on her clean floors.

"This town surely is abuzz," Lester said. "Most folks are taking yer side, Miz Richards. Others are backing Miz Hankins, saying possession of that deed's gotta mean the shop's hers."

Lloyd shrugged. "Can't prove it by me. Only laws I know is the laws Sheriff Truitt says we broke."

"Me and Lloyd ain't never done nothing separately. We got ourselves in a scrape or two, but we're a good team. Leastwise, iffen I can handle his stinky socks and he can put up with me running at the mouth." Lester toed the floor, looking as nervous as a skittish barn cat. "Been thinking," he said. "Could you two ladies do the same and share this here shop?"

"The ownership of the shop is out of our hands now," Carly said, avoiding Anna's eyes.

The bell dinged. Sheriff Truitt entered, doffing his hat. "Morning, ladies," he said, then spotted the Harders twins. "Been a while since I've seen you two in my jail."

"Ain't got no time to shoot up signs, what with working here and at the livery." Lester puffed out his thin chest. "Nate's paying us to muck stalls and care for the horses. Even to drive some of the fancy folks coming to town for the wedding."

Sheriff Truitt reached out a hand. "I'd like to shake you boys' hands. Good to see the change you've made and the men you're becoming."

Wearing sheepish grins, the twins shook with the sheriff.

"Morris Mood even is singing your praises," Sheriff Truitt said. "He's glad Nate has your help. He and Betsy leave for Arizona tomorrow."

"We had a nice send-off for them at the church last night," Anna said.

Carly nodded. "I was so happy Betsy was well enough to come. She promised to write. I'm praying the drier climate will help her."

"Sheriff," Lester said, rocking back on his heels, "have you heard they're placing bets at the saloon on who'll end up with the shop?"

Sheriff Truitt scowled. "What's that you say?"

Lester shook his head. "That's hearsay. We wouldn't step inside."

"And that's a promise," Lloyd affirmed.

Sheriff Truitt scowled at the twins. "Shouldn't you two get moving on that list of chores for Mrs. Richards?"

Lloyd gave a sober nod. "Yes, sir. We're heading out now to till the garden."

With a tip of their hats, the twins sidestepped the sheriff and loped to the back.

As the lawman's gaze swept between Carly and Anna, his amused expression fizzled. He suddenly looked edgier than a greenhorn straddling a bucking bronco, probably feeling trapped in the middle between a longtime resident and the newcomer he'd taken a fancy to.

"Circuit Judge Rohlof stopped at the jail this morning. He asked me to tell you ladies proceedings start tomorrow afternoon at one o'clock."

Carly's mind scrambled for footing. Tomorrow was a Friday. Henry would be in school. If the hearing went two days as the sheriff expected, she would ask Rosalie Harders to watch Henry on Saturday. Easy enough to close the shop both afternoons.

"With all the interest over the shop's ownership, the hearing will be held in the church."

Carly's stomach knotted. Why hadn't she hired legal counsel from Louisville? True, she'd been busy with the Schwartz order, but she'd known this day was coming. She must've suspected, if she didn't have legal ground to stand on, no amount of oratory from a big-city lawyer could impact the outcome.

"Judge Rohlof will give each side time to make your claims. Once he's mulled over the testimony, he'll rule, most likely Saturday afternoon."

In a few minutes' time the judge would pronounce his verdict. Just that quickly, Carly could lose all this.

Her gaze roamed the shop, a tidy place of business with its cupboards filled with bolts of silk, satin, muslin, rolls of ribbon and lace, spools of thread and drawers of notions. The shiny black Singer sewing machine she'd bought with her first year's earnings had increased her efficiency.

Before she'd reopened the shop after more than a year of sitting empty, the place had been a mess. She'd swept up mouse droppings, scrubbed every nook and cranny, stitched curtains, made a dress for the mesh mannequin in the window, hoping to draw in the ladies for a more detailed look at the latest fashion.

With every ounce of a well-honed will, Carly tamped down the panic suddenly swelling within her. Henry had taught her she could trust God's love. But God also loved Anna.

Carly's gaze darted to Nate's sister. With no husband, no children and a brother set on wandering, Anna had no one. A place to put down roots would mean everything to her.

Sheriff Truitt turned to Anna. "The judge wants your brother to testify to what he knows."

"Nate's leaving," Anna said, her voice dismayed. "May already be gone."

Nate banged in, setting the bell into a frantic dance. "Sheriff, Lester said you were here. Judge Rohlof insists on me testifying at the hearing tomorrow. The timing's put a kink in things. Any chance you can get me out of it?"

"'Fraid not. I'll ride out this evening and warn Pence."

The gazes of the two men locked. Then, with a brisk nod, Nate excused himself, saying he needed to get back to the livery.

What was going on? "Sheriff, are Debby or her grandparents in danger?" Carly asked.

Sheriff Truitt shook his head. "No reason to believe that,

but, if they were, old man Pence is good with a gun. Why, a few years back, he shot the highest number of rabbits ever bagged in the county in one day. That record still stands."

Rabbits didn't shoot back. Was there a possibility Mr. Pence would need to protect his wife and granddaughter while Nate and Sheriff Truitt sat in a courtroom? The only threat Carly could think of was Stogsdill. If Stogsdill was nearby, that explained why Nate had vowed to protect her and Anna.

If so, life and death hung in the balance. In comparison, the shop's ownership was of no consequence.

"Well, better get back to the jail." Sheriff Truitt fiddled with the brim of his hat. "Hate to think of either one of you ladies losing out. Judge Rohlof will need the wisdom of Solomon."

As the door swung closed behind the sheriff, Carly and Anna's gazes found each other. Sudden tears brimmed in their eyes. They rose and wrapped each other in a hug.

For surely all those furtive looks and puzzling comments between Nate and Sheriff Truitt implied trouble.

As if they didn't have enough trouble already. By Saturday afternoon the judge would have ruled, and their lives and livelihoods would be forever changed.

Chapter Eighteen

The day of reckoning had arrived. Carly had once found the delay of the circuit judge's arrival irksome. But now? Now her heart pounded in her chest, her stomach a queasy mess, her hands clammy inside her kid gloves.

At least, with Henry in school, she had no concern for her son.

Carly straightened her shoulders and entered Gnaw Bone Christian Church a little before one o'clock, the usual peace she felt inside the house of worship replaced with dread. *Lord, what's Your will in this dispute?*

No matter who won the shop, she and Anna would lose something precious. Shared goals, shared work, shared camaraderie.

The oak pulpit on the platform had been moved, replaced with a small table and chair. Another chair sat off to the side. No doubt an improvised witness stand.

Near the front, Sheriff Truitt stood, his gun belt riding his hips, his badge gleaming. He gave Carly a warm smile, then directed her to the first pew on the left. "Rise when Judge Rohlof enters."

"I will," she choked out, then sat, alone, in the pew.

Across the aisle, Anna shared the pew with Nate, distress plain on her face, her brother's expression unreadable. The man kept his emotions in check, an asset in his occupation.

An urge to shake some sense into him gripped her. If not for Nate, she and Anna could've figured out a solution. But even as the thought came, Carly admitted she had to agree with Nate's assessment. The shop's earnings wouldn't support three.

Behind her, townspeople chatted, their voices rising and falling as they rapidly filled up the pews.

Carly kept her hands clasped in her lap to keep them from trembling. Adept at holding her troubles close to her chest, she would soon be forced to reveal the bad choice she'd made by marrying Max and the debacle that was their marriage. She hadn't fooled many. But no one spoke of such things, at least not in her hearing.

By one o'clock most seats had been taken, as if the whole town had turned out to witness the proceedings. Far more than Pastor Koontz drew for his Sunday sermon. If only all the churchgoers in town could join together for worship instead of for this spectacle.

If she knew for certain she would lose, Carly would've handed the shop over to Anna rather than endure this hearing. But she hadn't been able to release the speck of hope that somehow she would keep her shop, their home, everything solid and familiar.

"All rise," Sheriff Truitt said.

Judge Rohlof entered, took his seat at the table and laid a paper in front of him.

The sound of shifting feet and creaking pews indicated those behind her had also returned to their seats.

Judge Rohlof fiddled with his spectacles, polishing the glass with his handkerchief and letting his steely gaze roam the crowd. "You onlookers are just that. You're not to speak up or interrupt in any way. If you should need to leave, you may not return. Anyone who can't accept those rules will be escorted out by Sheriff Truitt."

The judge put on his spectacles and landed his gaze on Carly. "Tell me your name, please."

"Mrs. Carly Richards."

"Ah, the defendant in this case." He turned toward Anna. "That means you must be Mrs. Anna Hankins, the plaintiff."

"Yes, sir," she said in a voice as shaky as Carly's.

His gaze shifted to Nate. "And I take it you're Mrs. Hankins's brother?"

"Yes. I'm Nate Sergeant, Judge."

Judge Rohlof nodded. "Now that I know who's who, I'll explain procedures. This isn't a criminal case, even a trial, but I'll still ask you to swear on the Bible."

Sheriff Truitt walked to the front, carrying a Bible.

"I'll start with you, Mrs. Richards." Judge Rohlof gave Carly a smile. "Come on up."

On shaky limbs, Carly staggered to Sheriff Truitt, who gave her an encouraging smile, then placed her right palm on the cover of the Bible he held.

"Do you swear the testimony you're about to give is the truth, the whole truth and nothing but the truth?" Sheriff Truitt said.

"I do."

Judge Rohlof waved toward the chair. "Have a seat right here, Mrs. Richards. Tell me about this shop." He glanced at the paperwork on the desk. "Lillian's Alterations and Dressmaking. How'd it get that name?"

"The shop was owned by Lillian Richards. My deceased husband Max Richards inherited the shop from his mother when Lillian died."

"How long ago was that?"

"Ten years ago in March."

"You said she left the shop to your deceased husband.

Were you married to Max Richards at the time of his mother's death?"

Carly swallowed against the sudden lump in her throat. "No. We married a year later."

"So you've run the shop for nine years, give or take."

"Yes, that's right."

"Did the shop come stocked with fabric, thread, whatever a seamstress needs to open her doors?"

"No, sir. The store was empty. Max must've sold all the merchandise. Or perhaps his mother did when her health failed. I bought what I needed."

The judge nodded and wrote on a slip of paper. "Is business good, Mrs. Richards?"

"I keep busy and make enough money to support myself and my son."

"How old is your boy?"

"Seven."

"Young to be without a pa."

Carly bit her lip, then nodded, hoping the judge wouldn't drag Max into this. No matter how miserable Max had made her life, he wasn't on trial. She knew of no law against a man disappearing for weeks at a time. She knew of no law against a man making his family cringe when he walked in the door. She knew of no law against foul breath and an unwashed body.

"Mrs. Richards, I have before me the deed to Lillian's Alterations and Dressmaking." The judge motioned to the paper on the desk. "The name on this deed is Max Richards. Why didn't he add your name to the deed when you married?"

"I never asked him, but I suspect he didn't want to give up control." Her gaze dropped to her lap. "Of the shop."

"And of you, perhaps?"

Carly met Judge Rohlof's shrewd hazel eyes. "That's likely."

"Why wasn't the name on the deed replaced with yours once your husband passed on?"

"I didn't think of it." She inhaled sharply. "But if I had, I couldn't have made the change. The deed was no longer in my possession."

"Who had possession of the deed, Mrs. Richards?"

Carly turned her gaze on Nate and Anna. Anna's brow was puckered. Nate looked angry, as if killing Max once hadn't been enough. "Anna Hankins."

"How did the deed to this shop come into Mrs. Hankins's possession?"

"Anna's husband, Walt Hankins, won the deed from Max during a poker game."

"Did you have knowledge of this poker game?"

"Other than what Anna told me, no. The game was not in Gnaw Bone. But I knew Max gambled."

"Did Mrs. Hankins tell you where the game in question took place?"

"Yes, in a saloon not far from her home in northern Kentucky."

"Did your husband make a practice of being away from home, Mrs. Richards?"

"He was gone more than he was home."

"When your husband returned, did he mention losing the deed in a poker game?"

"No, sir. It wasn't until Nate Sergeant came into my shop about a month after Max's death that I learned the deed wasn't locked up in the shop safe."

"I see." He handed Carly the deed. "Mrs. Richards, please look at the signature on this deed. The name Max Richards has been drawn through and replaced with that of Walter Hankins. And signed by two witnesses. Do you know the two witnesses?"

"No, sir."

"Can you verify that the name Walter Hankins is written in your husband's handwriting?"

Carly stared at the document. "It appears to be Max's handwriting. Though I can't be positive. The only time I saw his signature was on our marriage license."

"Your husband was gone for long periods and never wrote? Not even once?"

"No, sir."

Judge Rohlof reached for the deed and Carly handed it over. "You said the shop earned enough money for you and your son. You have no other help in the shop?"

"Anna Hankins is working there now, until we finish a large order that came in the day we met."

"Is it awkward that the woman claiming your shop is working for you?"

"Not *for* me. *With* me. I consider Anna a friend. I believe she'd say the same about me."

"If more opponents worked together as you and Mrs. Hankins have done, this world would be a better place." The judge made a few notes. "You may return to your seat, Mrs. Richards."

On shaky limbs, Carly rose from the chair and trudged to the first pew.

Beulah Koontz, her pastor's wife, leaned close. "You did a fine job," she whispered, giving Carly a perky smile.

But the smile appeared strained. Mrs. Koontz could tell, as Carly had, the evidence suggested Anna Hankins had possession of the deed and probably legal right to the shop.

"Mrs. Hankins, it's your turn."

As Anna lumbered to the front, a soft murmur ran through the crowd of onlookers. One sweep of Judge Rohlof's fierce gaze quieted the room.

Anna put her hand on the Bible and swore to tell the truth, then sat in the chair Carly had vacated.

"Are you comfortable, Mrs. Hankins?"

"Yes, sir, in this seat, but not with the reason I'm here."

Judge Rohlof's eyes widened as if Anna's statement surprised him, but he made no comment.

Carly wanted to shout amen, but of course didn't. No point in antagonizing the judge who would determine her fate.

"Mrs. Hankins, how did your husband come into possession of the deed to Lillian's Alterations and Dressmaking?"

"Walt won the deed in a poker game, as Mrs. Richards said."

"When did you learn your husband had won the deed?"

"Late that same afternoon."

"Can you be more specific?"

"Yes, sir, the date is seared in my mind. April 1 of this year. April Fools' Day. The day my husband was murdered," she added in a voice that shook.

"Tell me what happened."

Head bent, Anna gripped her gloved fingers in her lap. "Walt came home excited about winning the shop in a poker game, talking a mile a minute, making plans. I'm a seamstress. He saw the shop as a way for us to have a better life." She glanced at the judge with tears in her eyes. "Instead that deed cost him his."

"You say your husband was murdered, Mrs. Hankins. Who killed him?"

"Max Richards. He found out where we lived and rode in, demanding the deed. Walt had hidden it and when—" her shoulders slumped and she seemed to fold into herself "—Walt refused and turned away, Max Richards shot my husband in the back."

Tears brimmed then spilled down Anna's cheeks, the anguish of reliving that nightmare plain on her face. The room was so quiet Carly could hear each ragged breath Anna took.

Carly bit her lip to keep from crying out, from insisting the judge leave Anna alone.

"Are you able to go on?" Judge Rohlof asked, removing a handkerchief from inside his jacket and handing it to Anna.

Anna nodded, wiping her tears. "Max Richards threatened me, but Walt must've hidden the deed before he came inside. I had no idea where. I was so upset and frightened, I couldn't think straight. While my husband bled to death on the kitchen floor, Max Richards tore up the place, then did the same in the barn, but didn't find the deed. Said he'd be back. And if I didn't have the deed, he'd kill me, too." She lifted trembling fingers to her lips. "I believed him."

"Did Max Richards return, as he'd threatened?"

"No, sir, he ended up dead."

"How did he die?"

Anna sucked in a gulp of air. "My brother Nate Sergeant killed him. But Nate didn't have a choice. He—"

"Sheriff Truitt has confirmed your brother arrived at your home shortly after the killing and tracked Max Richards to Gnaw Bone with the intention of bringing him back to Kentucky to stand trial for murdering your husband. I've also seen sworn statements from three witnesses that Richards fired the first shot and Nate Sergeant shot him in self-defense."

"Yes, Nate was absolved of any wrongdoing. He—"

"Mrs. Hankins, the purpose of this hearing is not to determine the guilt or innocence of Max Richards or Nate Sergeant."

Carly wanted to shout that Max had been guilty of pretending he had feelings for her when he'd only wanted someone to provide for him. Guilty when he'd frightened and neglected his family. Guilty when he'd risked the shop.

Didn't that entitle her to the business she'd rebuilt?

"The only reason we're here," the judge went on, "is to determine who is the rightful owner of Lillian's."

"Yes, sir."

"Mrs. Hankins, how did you come into possession of this deed?"

"My brother spent a month looking for it. He finally found the deed hidden under a loose plank in the barn."

"He found it after Max Richards's death?"

"Yes, sir."

"Mrs. Richards says you two are friends. Do you agree with that statement?"

Anna's gaze slid to Carly. She gave a gentle smile that Carly returned. "Yes, I do."

"I've overseen countless hearings and trials, but I can't recall two women forging a friendship after one of their husbands killed the other. How do you explain that, Mrs. Hankins?"

"Carly Richards didn't kill Walt. Her no-good husband did." Anna glanced at the sheriff. "That Bible I put my hand on tells me I'm to forgive my enemies. A tall order for a man like Max Richards. A man so cruel, so callous, he'd devise a scheme, knowing he'd kill to get the deed back. Surely a man to be pitied."

"Indeed. Max Richards is not on trial here, but I don't hesitate to declare him guilty. Guilty of destroying the happiness of two vulnerable women, apparently without remorse, for his own purposes."

Carly exhaled and in that sigh, all the pent-up anger at Max went with it. She could see now she'd been guilty of harboring, even wallowing in, resentment. That resentment had hurt only her. Freed from the heavy burden of bitterness and guilt, she felt lighter, happier. Judge Rohlof had not stamped her guiltless, but God's Son had. Now she truly felt clean, no longer stained by the changes her anger at Max had made in her.

The judge accepted the handkerchief Anna handed back to him. "Thank you, Mrs. Hankins. You may return to your seat."

With a nod, Anna rose and shuffled to her place. Nate gave his sister's shoulder a squeeze.

"I call Nate Sergeant to the stand."

Chapter Nineteen

Nate laid his hand on the Bible. How long since he'd read Scripture? The words used to guide him, used to encourage him, used to fill him with hope. Words he now felt unworthy of reading. What power had he forfeited? What peace had he lost?

He took a breath and swore to tell the truth, then took his seat to testify against Carly, a woman who didn't deserve any of this. Yet Nate had to do what he could to protect his sister.

He'd turned the deed over to Sheriff Truitt to be entered in evidence. The evidence pointed to his sister as the rightful owner. Yet he'd awakened that morning from a night spent tossing and turning, unwilling to testify against the woman capturing his heart.

His gaze locked with Carly's. In those blue depths, he thought he saw a flicker of regret. The outcome of this hearing would surely ring the death knell on the growing affection between them.

If only he'd met Carly under different circumstances. But killing her husband, no matter how despicable Max Richards had been, and claiming her shop for his sister, no matter how badly Anna needed it, had set him and Carly at odds from the first.

"Mr. Sergeant," Judge Rohlof said, raising Nate's head. "Do you live near your sister?"

"No, sir. As a bounty hunter, I'm not in one place very long."

"How did you happen to be there when Walt Hankins was killed?"

"I had intended to bunk with Anna and Walt while I pursued a lead on the whereabouts of an outlaw I was tracking."

"Your sister testified you found the deed. Please tell me how that came about."

A month spent looking for a deed still grated when he'd been used to tracking down every crook he'd sought. All except one. Stogsdill. His hands tightened into fists. Where was the man now?

"Mr. Sergeant, I repeat, how did you find the deed?"

"I searched everywhere I could think of without success. One morning about a month after I started looking, I noticed this ancient feed box in the barn. Too heavy even for a wiry man like Walt. Still, desperation can give a man extraordinary strength. I was able to shove it out of the way and noticed a loose plank. I pried it up and found the deed wrapped in leather and tied with string."

"After you made your sister Anna Hankins aware of its existence, what did you do?"

"I rode to Gnaw Bone again. This time to inform Mrs. Richards the shop no longer belonged to her."

"What was Mrs. Richards's reaction?"

"She didn't believe me. At first. But she opened her safe and found the deed missing."

And then she'd fainted on him. As if it happened yesterday, he remembered Carly cradled in his arms. The soft feel of her against his chest, the fragrance of her hair—

"Mr. Sergeant," Judge Rohlof said, folding his elbows on the table and leaning toward Nate. "What benefit will you gain if Anna Hankins should become the owner of Lillian's?"

"Nothing. Nothing, that is, except peace of mind. My sister's husband was a tenant farmer, barely eking out a living in a remote area in Kentucky. Anna not only lost her husband when Max Richards killed Walt, she lost her home and income. Like Mrs. Richards, Anna's an excellent seamstress. The shop will provide a living. She'll be happy here."

"Your concern for your sister is admirable. Still, I would think as her brother, you'd see her needs were met."

"I would and I have, Judge, but…" Nate's brow furrowed. If Shifty Stogsdill had his way, Nate wouldn't survive. "I'm a bounty hunter. If I should meet an outlaw with a faster draw or better aim, I won't be the one left standing."

"A dangerous occupation. Have you considered another line of work?"

"No. Not until I find Shifty Stogsdill."

"Why are you determined to find this one outlaw?"

"Stogsdill was part of the gang that murdered our parents."

The audience stirred, shifting in their seats and murmuring.

Judge Rohlof scowled at the onlookers. The room quieted. "How long ago was that?" he said.

"Eleven years."

"A long time. I assume you're not even sure this man fired the shot. Why persist in this vendetta?"

"Stogsdill deserves to be brought to justice. He killed someone else in cold blood. An innocent young woman," Nate ground out.

"Who was she?"

Nate shifted in his seat. "I don't see what that has to do with this hearing."

"I find I'm curious and, frankly, Mr. Sergeant, I'm in a position to satisfy that curiosity. Now answer my question."

"Her name was Rachel Reyer."

"Who was she to you?"

"My fiancée."

Across from him, Carly gasped, her hand flying to her mouth, tears filling her eyes.

If only Carly hadn't found out about Rachel this way. She would believe he still loved Rachel. Rachel would always have a special place in his heart, but, like an old tintype, memories of her had faded, his love for her fading with them.

Still he owed her. How naive he'd been to believe he could settle down and live a normal life. He'd make amends for that foolishness by seeing her killer pay for ending her life at the age of twenty.

"I'm sorry about your loss, Mr. Sergeant, but I urge you to remember a man is innocent in this great country of ours until proven guilty in a court of law. No bounty hunter or sheriff has the right to mete out justice." He cocked his head. "Perhaps you could take a lesson from your sister and find a way to forgive your enemy."

Anger welled up inside Nate. "Forgiveness has nothing to do with this. As long as evil roams free, no one is safe."

"Which means you won't remain in town and these women will. They seem harmonious, might even find a way to settle this amicably. I can't help wondering if you're standing in the way of that solution. Yet you appear to have concern for Mrs. Richards's well-being."

Nate rubbed the back of his neck. "From what I've seen, the shop won't support them all. But that doesn't mean I don't care about Mrs. Richards's future. Any man with a thread of decency would rue killing a woman's husband and a son's father, even in self-defense."

"Then perhaps that decency you possess could find a way to settle this between the three of you."

Nate met and held the judge's pointed gaze.

Judge Rohlof gave a curt nod. "I have no more questions. You may take your seat, Mr. Sergeant," he said. He picked up the deed. "I will examine Indiana statutes and my law books. Unless the parties in this dispute come to an agreement first, I will give my ruling tomorrow afternoon at one o'clock. I expect all three of you witnesses to be in attendance."

Nate bit back a protest. The judge seemed determined to keep him in town. Silly, when he had nothing new to add.

Still, even if he left Saturday after the ruling, he should have plenty of time to ride to Louisville before Stogsdill could arrive.

As Nate strode to Anna, he avoided Carly's gaze. He'd just told the judge his concern for Carly was based on killing her husband when everyone in town knew she was better off without Richards.

What did it matter? Carly was strong and would find her way, a way far safer for her and her son than getting tangled up with him.

Wide blue eyes implored Nate, as if his very life depended on her answer. "Mama, can Nate come to supper?"

Carly looked pale, her eyes weary, not in the mood to cook, much less to invite company. Yet Nate yearned to spend time with them just once more before he went after Stogsdill.

"Henry," Nate said. "I'm sure your ma's too tired to cook."

"Did the judge make her work?"

"No, but he asked hard questions, like the teacher does at school sometimes."

Questions that opened wounds. Questions that dug that chasm brought about by the shop's ownership still deeper.

"Oh." The gaze Henry turned on his mom softened with sympathy. "I'm sorry, Mama."

Perhaps Nate knew a way to help them both. "I'd like to treat everyone to supper at Sarah's Café." Staring into Carly's weary eyes, he added, "If you've a mind to go."

"Please, Mama. Say yes. Please."

Carly heaved a sigh. "All right," she agreed reluctantly, probably too tired to fight her son.

Ridiculously happy, Nate turned to his sister. Anna looked droopier than a scarecrow missing its stuffing. "Do you need to rest first, sis?"

"I'm sorry, but I'm not up to going. Remembering that day…" The pain in Anna's voice ricocheted through him. "I'll heat leftover soup and turn in early." She tried for a bright smile. "You go ahead and have a good time."

A closer look revealed Anna's pallor. "If you're not feeling well, I don't want to leave you alone."

"I'm wrung out, is all. A good night's sleep and I'll be fine as a well-tuned fiddle." She tousled Henry's hair. "I know someone who's eager to go."

"Me!" Eyes shining, Henry's head bobbed up and down.

"In that case," Nate said, "let's not keep Henry waiting."

His sister turned away, hobbling toward home, her limp more pronounced, evidence her pain was worse. "Carly, would you and Henry mind going ahead and getting a table? I'd like to see Anna home."

"Of course." She took Henry's hand and they left the shop.

In a few strides, Nate caught up with Anna, wrapping an arm around her for support, then seeing her to the cabin, dodging ruts and uneven ground. Once he'd lit the stove and put the soup on to heat, Anna insisted he join Carly.

"If you're sure you're all right," he said.

She gave him a playful push. "If you don't hurry, Henry will surely burst."

He gave Anna a kiss on the cheek, then loped to the café. As he stepped inside, all chatter ceased. Carly and Henry sat at a table in front of the window. He wound a path through the tables, aware every eye followed him. No doubt speculating on Carly's reaction if she was his target.

Carly sat sipping coffee. At her side, Henry slurped through a paper straw. The dreamy look on his face proved the rarity of the treat.

Nate took the seat across from her, giving him a view of the street and the door, an ingrained practice that had saved his neck more than once. Stogsdill would not have had time to get to Gnaw Bone after he received the wire. Still, a man couldn't be too careful, especially in the company of a defenseless woman and child.

"Mama got me root beer, Nate," Henry said. "The fizzy tickles my nose."

Oblivious to the whisperings of those around them, Henry chattered about his day at school, then focused on his root beer.

"Apparently we're on the menu, judging by the number of folks looking our way," Carly said.

Nate chuckled. "I think they're hoping we'll climb into the boxing ring, Gnaw Bone's version of Sullivan and Ryan."

He could think of far more pleasant ways to resolve the dispute. But Carly would want no part of the image he carried in his mind, of kissing her, of holding her in his arms. He dared not give in to longings that would tie him to anyone, not even Carly, who lured him like a stagecoach carrying gold enticed a robber.

The noise level and the click of silverware suggested the diners had forgotten them and had returned to their meals.

The swinging doors separating the kitchen from the café banged open, and Sarah stepped through. Long and lanky in face and body, her every movement clipped, the café owner exuded no-nonsense efficiency. Face flushed, flyaway strands of hair floating around her face, Sarah toted heaping plates to the next table.

"Hope you enjoy the food," she said, depositing each plate with a plunk.

Then she stepped to Henry's side, pad in hand, spectacles perched on her nose.

"You look shorthanded, Sarah. Where's Lucille?" Carly asked.

"Sick. On the busiest day I've had in ages." Sarah's stern gaze settled on Nate, as if to say, "That's your doing." She glanced at the wall clock. "I'll warn you now. Food's gonna be slow."

"We're in no hurry." Nate smiled, pleased to have more time with Carly and Henry.

"Got fried steak, chicken, stew in the kitchen. What can I get you?" Sarah glanced at Carly.

"Henry will have the small portion of the fried chicken dinner, just a leg with his," Carly said. "I'll have the stew and more coffee."

"Got it." Sarah turned to Nate. "For you?"

"Fried steak and black coffee."

Sarah scrawled the order on the pad, then grabbed the menus and scurried to the kitchen.

As they waited for the food they talked about Henry's riding lessons, the Schwartz wedding, the church ice-cream social scheduled for early June, avoiding the one topic surely on both of their minds: the day of testimony.

Sarah returned with two plates lined up on one arm,

carrying the third in her other hand and set them down in front of them.

The delicious aromas teased Nate's nostrils, reminding him of all the meals his mother had cooked, all the times they'd spent around the table, much like the three of them did now. As they ate and talked, like all the families around them, Nate felt part of the town, part of Carly's family, part of what God had intended from the beginning of time.

A heavy longing pressed against his lungs until he could barely breathe. What he'd give to form a family with Carly and her son. To have a place to call home, to have this woman and child to share each day with, perhaps to be blessed with a second child of their own.

That longing was futile. He'd ridden alone for eight years. The one time he hadn't, he'd caused an innocent woman's death. Maybe one day when his presence no longer put Carly and Henry in jeopardy...

The mere idea was ludicrous. Every time Nate thought he had Stogsdill in his sights, the outlaw would vanish, as if he were made of smoke.

Sarah returned with the pot and refilled their cups, leaving room for cream in Carly's. "How'd the hearing go?"

Carly shrugged. "We each had our say and spoke the truth. The outcome is up to the judge."

The café owner's gaze bored into Nate. "Hate to think what would happen to me if I lost this business," she said, then hurried off with the pot, refilling cups on her way back to the kitchen.

Nate met Carly's eyes. "I'm sorry. I wish—"

She held up her hand. "Let's talk about something else. Something that's good for digestion." She smiled at her son. "Like the A that Henry got on his spelling test."

"Last week I spelled 'monkey' wrong," Henry said, propping his chin in his hand. "I forgetted the *e*."

"You know, we learn the most from the mistakes we make. I doubt you'll misspell monkey again."

"Teacher said there's a key in monkey and that's how we turn him on." He giggled, then leaned toward his mother. "I got two wrong on my 'rithmetic paper today."

"You are a monkey, Henry Austin. The key to doing well in school is to work hard, exactly what you do. But Nate's got a point." A flush bloomed in her cheeks and her gaze fell to her plate. "We do learn the most from our mistakes," she added softly.

Carly had regrets the same as Nate. Somehow that knowledge bonded them, made him yearn to erase the sadness in her sagging shoulders. "Some mistakes bring rewards," he said, then glanced at Henry.

A smile lit her eyes. "You're right. Some mistakes bring all that matters." She reached across the table and laid a gentle hand on Nate's arm. "Thanks."

Sarah dropped off the bill and they rose, scraping the legs of their chairs on the wooden floor.

At the cash register, Nate peeled bills out of his money clip. "Keep the change."

"'Preciate it," Sarah said, the glare she'd fixed on him softening.

Outside he and Carly meandered along the sidewalk toward the shop. Nate had never felt more relaxed, more at ease. This harmony was what it would be like to have Carly and Henry in his life permanently. Henry skipped along in front of them, trying to whistle; a shrill, feeble sound. He'd have to teach the boy.

They reached the shop. Nate scrambled to think of a reason to avoid ending the evening.

"Thank you for supper," Carly said.

"It was my pleasure." He grinned. "That boy can eat."

"He'll be talking about root beer for days." Carly cleared her throat. "I...I meant to ask you something."

"Sure."

"Yesterday Sheriff Truitt said he'd warn Pence. Why? Did Debby write Stogsdill? Tell him the engagement was off?"

"Well, uh, no."

Carly's blue eyes widened. "Why not? Surely she doesn't want to marry the man now that she knows his true identity."

"If Debby had cut things off, who knows when Stogsdill might decide to show up and try to change her mind? I couldn't risk that."

"How could you stop it?"

"I asked Mr. Pence to wire Stogsdill that his delay was giving his granddaughter second thoughts and if he hoped to marry her, he should pay Debby a visit."

With a sharp intake of air, Carly whirled to face him. "You concocted a plan to bring Stogsdill here, to Gnaw Bone?"

"Well, yes, but I'd planned to ride to Louisville yesterday in ample time to meet the train. That is assuming Stogsdill left St. Louis as soon as he received Pence's telegram."

"You believe Stogsdill is coming to Gnaw Bone, and you didn't think you needed to tell me this?"

"I didn't want to worry you. If he was on the train, I'd have gotten the jump on him and turned him in to the authorities there." Nate released a heavy sigh. "But then the judge insisted I testify. I seriously doubt the telegram can be delivered immediately. Still, I should have tim—"

"You concocted a plan that puts my son in danger?" Carly's eyes flashed, icy and cold. "Surely *even you* wouldn't put capturing Stogsdill ahead of a child's safety?"

Carly's gaze darted to Henry, then swept the street. Everything looked routine; a peaceful evening in Gnaw Bone. That peace could be shattered in an instant.

Thanks to Nate.

Never had Carly felt more defenseless. Not even married to Max. "Henry, go inside and get ready for bed."

"Mama, I want to show Nate—"

"Mind me, young man."

Steps lagging, Henry dragged himself onto the porch and inside the kitchen, then took one last look and shut the door.

Once her son was out of sight, Carly shoved a fingertip into Nate's chest. "You didn't think about Henry, did you? All you could think about was getting the reward."

"Surely you know me better than that. Money has nothing to do with this," he said, the muscle in his jaw ticking.

If not the money, then what?

Rachel. The fiancée Nate had reluctantly spoken of at the hearing. Murdered by Stogsdill.

Carly exhaled. "All right, not the money, but admit it. You're obsessed with catching him."

"Try to see this from a lawman's perspective." Nate reached his arms toward her.

This time those arms didn't make her feel safe. This time she had no desire to walk into them.

"Stogsdill wouldn't have taken Debby's rejection lying down. Not knowing when he'd arrive was far more dangerous than my plan."

"Did it ever occur to you, that if not for your telegram, he might not come at all? He's stayed away for weeks."

"All the more reason to believe he'll come. Carly, I understand your concern, but you and Henry are not Stogsdill's target. He doesn't even know you exist."

"Anyone *seen with you* is a target. Doesn't Rachel's death prove that?"

Pain exploded in his eyes, as if she'd hauled back and slapped him.

"I'm sorry, that was cruel. I'm sorry your fiancée was killed. Sorry for the pain that brought."

"I know you are," he murmured. His eyes lowered to his feet. "Rachel was so young. So full of life."

"I let my temper get the better of me. I'm just afraid for my son."

"Do you believe I want to put you and Henry and my sister in harm's way?"

"I don't believe you want us hurt. If anything, my fear for my son makes me understand your desire to make Stogsdill pay. But, anyone in town could tell Stogsdill the bounty hunter and Widow Richards are in a controversy over the ownership of her shop."

"Stogsdill's face is on a wanted poster. He won't risk questioning folks. Still, you make a good point. The less we see of each other, the better."

Carly pulled in a fortifying breath. "You'll stay away? Away from the shop?"

"Yes," he said. "As soon as the hearing ends tomorrow afternoon and I'm free to leave, I'll ride to Louisville. If Stogsdill isn't on the next train from St. Louis, I'll head back here and hole up in the deserted shack in the woods not far from the Pence farm, the perfect spot to lie in wait."

"What if Stogsdill doesn't come that way? Or knows about the shack, too?"

"You'll just have to trust I'm good at my job."

"Good at your job?" she all but shrieked. "Do you believe you're invincible? What if Stogsdill ambushes you first?"

What if he *killed* Nate? The possibility shot through Carly, careening against every muscle and nerve. She couldn't imagine her world without Nate in it. When had he taken root in her heart?

She stifled a sigh. Nor could she imagine her world with

Nate in it, at least permanently. Too much stood between them—his job, the shop, his lack of faith.

Her gaze locked with Nate's. "If Stogsdill should get to Debby first and learns you showed Debby his wanted poster, he won't rest until he gets revenge."

"He's been gunning for me for years. Yet I've managed to survive." He traced her cheek, his fingertips sending a chill down her spine. "I'm grateful you don't want to see me six feet under."

"Don't be silly," Carly huffed. "But admit it. You don't have control of this situation. You don't know what train he'll board. When he'll arrive. All this is speculation.

"Anna and I deserved to know your plan." Carly stepped out of his reach and thrust her hands on her hips. "Once Stogsdill has you in his sights, he'll discover your sister works with me. He'll discover you've been seen with Henry and me."

"Surely you know I care for you. You and Henry. I'll protect you with my life."

Carly wouldn't say what sprang to mind: *Like you protected Rachel.* As frightened as she was, she could never be that cruel and blame Nate for failing the woman he loved. No one could provide absolute protection.

"I'm relieved Debby won't be marrying the man, but this plan of yours puts her life in danger."

"Her grandfather and Sheriff Truitt are prepared to protect Debby and Mrs. Pence, if Stogsdill should get past me."

"When did Mr. Pence send that telegram? How long did you say we have before Stogsdill arrives?"

"He sent the wire late yesterday. If he comes by train, the trip from St. Louis to Louisville takes most of a day."

"That means he could arrive tonight!"

"Carly, I don't believe he could get the wire immediately. If the judge rules tomorrow afternoon, I should be able to arrive in time to meet the first train he can possibly be on."

"I pray you do, Nate, because I can't consider what will happen if you're wrong. Well, I need to put Henry to bed," she said, and then hurried inside.

One day. One day before a monster could arrive in town.

The man she'd feared falling in love with had shown his true colors, as she'd always known he would. He'd put his goal to bring in Stogsdill ahead of his concern for her and Henry.

Why was she surprised? No man had ever put her or her son's well-being first.

Lord, no one has the power to protect us but You.

Not even a fast-draw bounty hunter spouting promises of protection. Promises he'd already failed to keep.

Chapter Twenty

One o'clock Saturday afternoon Carly entered the church, her stomach tied into more knots than a curly headed tot with molasses in its hair.

This was the day the judge would rule. The day she'd learn her fate. One more day, even today, and Stogsdill could arrive in town.

No matter how much Nate claimed to care about her and Henry, did he even want home and hearth? Once he captured Stogsdill, would that satisfy him? Or was bounty hunting in his blood? Vengeance forever in his heart?

The side door opened. Wearing a sober expression and a gun on his hip, Judge Rohlof entered the makeshift courtroom.

Carly rose to her feet, along with a packed sanctuary, then sat once the judge took his seat at the table, this time a single sheet of paper in his hand.

"Sheriff Truitt was called to a ruckus at the saloon. Please follow the same procedure as yesterday. Even with the sheriff away, I'm prepared to toss anyone who can't behave out on his ear."

An already quiet courtroom got quieter still.

"After hearing testimony on the ownership of Lillian's Alterations and Dressmaking and consulting my law books, I'm prepared to rule. The deed to the shop in question was wagered and lost by Max Richards on the afternoon of April 1, 1898, three days before his death on April 4, 1898. Therefore, the deed was not part of Max Richards's estate and would not pass on to his widow." His gaze darted to Carly, then on to Anna. "Therefore, I rule on behalf of the plaintiff. Anna Hankins is now legal owner of Lillian's."

As a muffled gasp rose from those in attendance, Carly closed her eyes, taking deep breaths, fighting for calm. She'd known her chances were not good, but nevertheless she'd clung to hope.

Everything had changed. She'd lost her livelihood. She'd lost their home. She'd lost a future here in Gnaw Bone.

Soon she would lose Anna, who'd become like a sister to her. And the man who had no idea how to put away his pistol and settle down.

"However," the judge went on to say, "my decision does not include the shop's contents. Mrs. Richards purchased every spool of thread and bolt of fabric and lace. Therefore, I instruct Mrs. Richards to give a fair estimate of their value. Mrs. Hankins can either reimburse Mrs. Richards, or return the contents of the shop to her. I've instructed the sheriff to see that this transfer occurs in a timely fashion. With the sensible heads these two ladies possess, I'm sure they will come to a mutually satisfactory solution."

With the buzzing going on in her head, Carly struggled to decipher the judge's words. *Please, Lord, don't let me faint.*

Judge Rohlof tugged off his wire-rimmed spectacles. "I'd like Mr. Sergeant and Mrs. Richards to approach the bench." He gazed at the onlookers. "The rest of you head on home. The show's over."

Carly got to her feet as her neighbors shuffled up the

aisle. Some stopped to pat her hand or to wrap her in a hug. By the time she reached the judge, her throat was clogged with unshed tears.

As she stepped to Nate's side, the misery she saw in his eyes stiffened her spine. He'd gotten what he wanted, hadn't he?

"I'm sorry," he said, then opened his arms.

She sidestepped those arms, arms that might've once brought comfort, but that comfort was merely an illusion. He'd brought all this on them. How dare he pretend the outcome upset him?

Judge Rohlof cleared his throat and turned kind eyes on them. "It's not in my jurisdiction to rule on matters of the heart. However, anyone can see you care about each other. During the hearing, I noticed the furtive glances passing between you. Sheriff Truitt tells me you work at the livery, Mr. Sergeant. Do you earn a decent wage there?"

"Yes, sir."

The judge folded his hands on the sheet of paper detailing his ruling. "Then you can afford to support a wife and child. My suggestion—quit ignoring your feelings and get hitched, thereby keeping the shop in the family and making everyone happy."

Carly tried to work up a smile but failed. "Thank you for your concern, Judge Rohlof, but Mr. Sergeant has a quest and won't be staying."

Nate's gaze met hers and then slid away.

"Well, in that case, Mrs. Richards, I misjudged the situation." He heaved a sigh. "It's never easy to give a ruling that wounds good people."

She thrust back her shoulders. "My son and I will be fine."

"I'm sure you will. I always say the backbone of this great country of ours is our womenfolk. Well, I wish you all the best of luck." He rose and ambled through the side door.

As soon as the door closed, Carly hustled up the aisle, Nate on her heels.

"Carly, please, talk to me."

She whipped around. "What is there to say?"

"I'm sorry."

"So you said. Sorry for what? That I lost the shop or that you're leaving?"

"Both. I've got a job to do." His gaze locked with hers. "You know I don't have a choice."

"In one thing, you do. Admit it, Nate. You don't want to merely capture Stogsdill, you want him dead."

He glanced away, unable to deny her words.

Carly could never accept a man bent on taking a life. "I need to collect my son from Mrs. Harders," she said, then strode outside.

Anna waited and tugged Carly into a hug. "We need to talk."

"Anna, you can't fix this. Henry and I will..."

The bravado Carly had showed in front of the judge, in front of Nate, threatened to crumble. She bit her lower lip and turned away, fighting tears.

She'd lost the business she and Henry had paid dearly for with years under Max's thumb.

Everything she'd endured, everything she'd worked for—

Gone.

Exactly what she deserved.

One look at Carly's pain-racked eyes had Nate taking a step back. As much as he longed to wrap her in his arms, he knew that was the last thing she'd want.

Still, he had to try to make her understand. He stepped between her and his sister. "You and Anna both deserve the shop. I never meant to hurt you, Carly."

"Didn't you?" Carly leaned toward him. "You hurt me

the day you came into my shop and threatened to take it away. Exactly what's happened." Tears flooded her eyes. She wiped at them with the back of her hand. "Our business is concluded, Nate. You got the shop. Now go get your criminal." She lifted her chin. "I have to…figure out what to do next."

He reached for her. "Carly, please—"

"I've got no choice but to move. I'll be out of your way as soon as—"

Henry skidded to a halt in front of them, his young face contorted, tears streaking down his cheeks.

The boy looked up at Nate, his eyes wide, as if seeing him for the first time. "You did it?" he said, his voice soft and broken.

Nate lowered himself to Henry's height. "Did what?"

"You…" Henry's lower lip wobbled, his cheeks flushed. "You killed my pa?" he said with a heartbreakingly hopeful lilt at the end of the question, as if to say, "Please tell me it's not true. Please tell me you didn't do it."

Nate closed his eyes and dragged in a shuddering breath. If only he could lie. If only he could say the words Henry wanted to hear, the words that would stop this little boy from hating him. Nate clung to this second, this too short fraction of time, before the truth detonated like a spark to a stick of dynamite, destroying all the good times they'd shared. "I did, but—"

"You killed him?" Henry's voice broke and the hope drained from his face. Carly laid a hand on Henry's shoulder, but he shook it off. "Wh…wh…why?"

Please, Lord, how to explain this? What words could Nate use to justify his actions? To tell Henry his father was dead because of Nate's gun, Nate's bullet, Nate's sense of right and wrong.

That Henry's father was dead because Max Richards

was a bad man and Nate's job was to stop the bad men in this world.

Nate thought of his parents, of the day Stogsdill or some member of his gang had shot them dead. They'd been good people, decent people, who'd worked hard and loved fiercely. That pain had been like a lance in Nate's chest, a wound that had never fully healed.

This was his legacy to Henry, an unwanted gift that would forever haunt this sweet little boy.

"I didn't want to do it, Henry," Nate said. "I really didn't."

In all the years Nate had done this job, he'd never had to face the son of a man he'd killed. He'd never had to face that grief dead-on. He'd never had to look at the tremble of a little boy's lips, the tears in his eyes, and wish he could go back in time and stop the bullet's course before it entered Richards's heart.

Nate had wanted only to protect, to help the boy. To fill that void, that need for a father.

The terrible truth seeped into his soul. If not for him, Henry would still have his dad, a man who'd failed him, sure, but a man Henry still yearned for.

"I'm sorry."

Carly knelt beside her son and tried to tug him into her arms but his feet remained planted in place. "Sweetie, Nate was just trying to, uh, stop your pa from doing something bad."

"My pa didn't do bad things. He didn't. He didn't," he said a third time, as if that would erase the past, then he lifted his face to Nate's. Pain shimmered in his eyes, colored by disbelief and, worst of all, betrayal. "You—" he sucked in a sob "—you did."

"Henry—"

He shoved his mother's arms away. The Stetson on his head toppled to the ground, tumbling to a stop in a mud puddle.

"I'm really sorry, Henry. I didn't know he was your father and I didn't know…"

How much his death would hurt.

"You did it," Henry said, his voice a harsh, sad whisper. "You did it."

"I'm sorry," Nate said again, but he knew, no matter how many times he said it, his apology wouldn't be enough.

"I don't care!" Henry lunged. His fists hit Nate in the chest, hard, pointed. His voice exploded in wrenching sobs. "I hate you! I hate you!"

Then he ran, his thin legs pumping toward home. A home no longer his. A home Nate had stolen from Henry, too.

He had to do something to make things right between them. "Henry, wait!" Nate started after him.

"Let him go," Carly said, coming up behind him. "Haven't you done enough damage to my family already?"

All the good times he and Henry had shared were gone, along with what was left of a seven-year-old boy's innocence. "Carly, I didn't mean for any of this to happen."

"Whether you meant to or not, you came along and set the wheels in motion. You encouraged Henry's affection, all the while concerned with far more pressing matters than a little boy's happiness. You've hurt my son."

One look at Carly and Nate knew what she didn't say: that he'd hurt her, too.

She wrapped her arms around her chest and looked off in the direction her son had gone. "This town holds too many bad memories. For Henry. And for me." She gathered her skirts and ran toward the shop.

Her soft words clamped against Nate's lungs like a vise. He'd come to Gnaw Bone intent on making life better for his sister. In doing so, he'd killed this beautiful woman's dream and wounded her son.

Nate stared at Henry's Stetson lying there in the mud.

Discarded, soiled, unwanted. He picked up the hat and ran his fingers along the brim, cleaning off the worst of the mud.

Anna hitched closer. From the look of her furrowed brow and damp eyes, she'd heard everything.

He hung his head. "I've made a mess of it, Anna."

"Carly will calm down and explain things to Henry. She'll make him understand what happened with Max."

Nate shook his head. "How can you explain to a child that one bullet, one killing, is different from another?"

"Your entire life you've fought for justice, protected good folks from evildoers. Max Richards killed Walt and tried to kill you. What were you supposed to do, stand there and let him? Who would have been his next victim?" She cupped his jaw in her hand. "You had no choice, Nate. You're a good man and I won't stand by and let you think otherwise."

"Carly doesn't think so."

"She's upset about losing the shop. But I'm going to insist on sharing it with her. May take a while to build up the business, but God won't let us starve."

"She's leaving. She's taking Henry and leaving."

Anna inhaled sharply. "I can't let her go. I'll talk to her." She took his hand. "Remember how upset I was to move to Gnaw Bone? You told me I'd make friends here. That the dresses I made would give women confidence."

He nodded.

"Well, you were right. Carly is my friend. I'm not going to sit back and let her toss that friendship aside. Sometimes it just takes a little convincing to make things right."

He handed Henry's hat to his sister. "Give this to Carly. Maybe Henry will want it…someday."

His sister took the hat and headed toward the shop. Though the limp was no less noticeable, she held herself taller, had a new confidence he hadn't noticed before. Anna had flourished here, using her talent as a seamstress, forging new friendships, especially with Carly and her son. His decision to bring her to Gnaw Bone had been good for her.

But that decision had brought harm to Carly.

No matter what Anna hoped, Carly wouldn't share the shop. She knew same as he did; the shop couldn't support his sister and Carly and her son.

If she followed through on her plan and left town, once he found Stogsdill, he'd go in search of Carly and Henry. He had to know their needs were met. That they were all right. Maybe one day they could find it in their hearts to forgive him.

Henry remained sprawled on his bed, his face buried in his pillow, the elephant Carly had made him tucked in the crook of an arm. A small forlorn figure seeking what comfort he could from a stuffed toy instead of from her.

No matter how much disquiet Henry felt whenever Max was home, her son had still longed for his father's affection. Did Henry believe by shooting Max, Nate had destroyed the last chance to make his father love him?

What child didn't cling to a parent, even a bad parent, always hoping for love and approval?

Even four years after her father's death, she'd still craved his affection. But he'd never declared his love. He'd never declared his approval. He'd never declared Carly anything, except to say she wasn't enough.

Lord, please don't let my son feel unworthy.

She had to try again to make him understand. "Anna dropped off your hat. You might want it the next time you ride Lady."

Though she could tell he wasn't asleep, Henry didn't respond. His silence tore at her. The very thing Carly had feared had happened. Nate had fallen off that pedestal and broken Henry's heart. What could she do to heal his hurt?

Her son had seen Nate as good, pure. Now he saw him as bad, sullied. Life wasn't as black and white as an innocent boy believed. One day, he'd comprehend the shades of gray.

But not too soon, Lord.

Carly laid the hat on Henry's dresser, then sat on the bed and rubbed her son's back. "Who told you what happened to your pa?" she said softly.

Henry rolled over, his eyes bloodshot, his cheeks red and shiny with tears. "I heered Lester and Lloyd talking when Mrs. Harders was watching me."

Leave it to the Harders brothers to shoot off their mouths.

"Mama, wh…what bad thing did Pa do?"

"What?"

"You said Nate was stopping Pa from doing something bad. What was Pa gonna do?"

"Nothing you need to worry about."

"You always lie to me."

"Henry, I don't lie. I—"

"You do, too! You never tell me nuthin'." Fresh tears welled in his eyes. "You smile and smile but your eyes are sad. I can tell you're lying."

"Some things aren't good for children to hear."

"Was Pa gonna hurt you? Was that the bad thing?"

"No."

"But he did. He knocked you down. He called you names. He throwed dishes at you." His chest heaved as he dragged in a ragged breath. "Why didn't we run away, Mama?"

"Well, sweetie, it's complicated."

"You always say that. You never tell the truth!"

Henry scrambled from the bed, still clutching his elephant, and darted from the room.

Henry blamed her for not leaving Max. He didn't understand the risk. She heaved a sigh. Couldn't she be honest, even with herself? The problem stemmed from not dealing with what she and Henry had gone through with Max. Instead she'd lived a lie. Put on a brave face for her son and hidden the truth from everyone. She should've talked with Henry rather than pretend the fear and heartache never happened.

Had she been so naive as to believe she could deceive her son? When he'd lived in this house? When he'd known Max's temper and unpredictable moods? When he'd watched his father's every move with guarded eyes?

She'd told herself she'd kept silent to protect Henry. When the truth was, she'd been afraid her son might ask questions she couldn't bear to answer. It was easier to ignore the ugliness of the past than to admit the mistakes she'd made.

With a moan, Carly picked up Henry's damp pillow and hugged it to her chest, rocking softly, tears she'd refused to shed streaming down her face.

She'd seen her father and Max as bad parents, but she wasn't any better. In her attempt to cover up the truth, she'd failed her son.

One more thing to add to the long list that proved she wasn't good enough. Not even for the son she adored.

Chapter Twenty-One

The streets were deserted. As empty as Nate. He lifted his gaze to the church. Ironic that in a place of worship, a judge had handed down a ruling that rocked his and Carly's fragile relationship.

Then Henry had somehow learned Nate had killed his father, the final blow to a future with the boy and his mother.

Nate gave a strangled laugh. *Lord, I'm sure You aren't happy with me, either. Well, You aren't judging me any harsher than I judge myself.*

Lloyd and Lester skidded to a stop in front of him, gasping for breath, their eyes brimming with alarm.

"Thought you should know we seen a stranger sneaking out of the livery," Lester said, then sucked in a breath. "Looked mighty suspicious, too."

Lloyd nodded. "One of them strings you set was broke."

Surely, there was no way Stogsdill could've had time to get there.

Still…

Every fiber of his being on alert, Nate scanned the street, his hand instinctively going for his gun. And came up empty. Except for his own gun and the sheriff's, Judge

Rohlof hadn't allowed weapons in his court. "I'll get my gun and take a look."

"Iffen you need us, we'll be at the mercantile unloading an order for Stuffle," Lester said. "Everybody in this town's got a job for us."

The twins hustled off.

As he headed to the cabin, the knot in Nate's stomach tightened. If Stogsdill was the stranger skulking around the livery, Nate's plan had backfired. That advantage Nate had believed he had, lost. Once again, he'd underestimated the outlaw and put those he cared about at risk. His worst nightmare.

A thought struck like a bolt of lightning. Had Stogsdill targeted Rachel deliberately? Was Stogsdill playing with him, as a cat toyed with a mouse? Attempting to destroy him by destroying those Nate cared about?

He'd failed Henry and hurt Carly, but he *would* keep them safe or die trying.

At the house, Nate grabbed his weapons, and then ran toward the livery, his gun belt riding his hip, his rifle in hand.

Inside the livery's dim interior, Nate strode toward Maverick's stall, the quiet broken only by the shuffling of hooves and the chirping of a cricket. Some of the horses dozed on their feet. Others greeted him with a nudge of their snouts.

He opened Maverick's stall, slapped leather on his horse, and then led him into the aisle.

Across the way, a slip of paper tacked to a center post caught his attention. Had someone put up an auction bill or—?

A sixth sense flared—a hunch that had kept him alive for years. His gaze sweeping the area, he stepped closer.

The paper was held in place by—

Nate's ebony-handled knife. Someone had been in the cabin.

He ripped the sheet free. In bold, black, stark letters against the pale paper he read, "'The hunter becomes the hunted.'"

Only one man could be responsible for the terse warning.

Energy shot through him, along with hard-nosed determination to protect at any cost. Revenge no longer mattered. All that mattered was protecting Carly, Henry and Anna.

Those he loved.

Yes, *loved*. What a fool he'd been.

He swung into the saddle and rode through the open doors, then nudged his mount. Under him Maverick sprang forward, galloping through the empty streets.

This time Stogsdill wouldn't get past him. This time no one would get hurt. This time Nate would not fail.

Carly couldn't find Henry anywhere. She and Anna had scoured the house, the attic, the shop.

Where could he be? She glanced at the clock. Not an hour ago she'd left his bedroom. Was he so upset he'd run away from home? Her heart tripped in her chest. If he'd run off, she had only herself to blame.

She sucked in a calming breath and tried to tell herself small boys ran away all the time and came trudging back home, safe and sound.

But *this* small boy was her son. Her entire world.

Where would he go? Surely he couldn't get far. Perhaps he'd gone to seek comfort from Lady or even Nate. "Anna, I'm going to the livery."

"Good idea."

"Still, I think… Oh, Anna, I think we need a search party."

Anna wrapped Carly in a hug. "I'm praying for Henry. He'll be all right." She donned her hat. "But it won't hurt to ask Sheriff Truitt for help," she said and hurried out.

Carly ran to the livery, trying to tamp down the panic

putting a stranglehold on her throat. Henry could've gone into a stall and been kicked by a horse. Or perhaps fallen from a tree. Could he be lying somewhere, bleeding, unconscious—

Where was he?

Oh, Father, what a fool I've been to think I could do anything on my own. Help me find my son. Please.

Once she had Henry safely home, she'd change. She'd show her son he could talk to her about anything, by speaking candidly herself. *If* she got the chance.

Fear pressed hard and fast on her lungs, shutting off her air. *Lord, help me stay calm. Help me not to think the worst.*

Inside the livery, her eyes took a moment to adjust. "Henry! Are you in here?" Her voice rose, nearing a screech as she ran to Lady's stall where the gentle mare reached her snout. Carly gave it a perfunctory pat, searching the shadows for her son. "Don't hide from me, sweetie."

No answer. Carly hurried on to the stall where Nate quartered Maverick.

Empty.

He'd already left for Louisville. Once again proving Nate wouldn't be available when she needed him most. Why was she surprised? A bounty hunter was what Nate was and would always be.

Across from Maverick's stall, a crumpled piece of paper lay in the straw. Had Henry left a note?

She snatched it up and smoothed out the wrinkles. "'The hunter becomes the hunted.'"

What did that mean? Who would write such a cryptic message?

Her icy fingers trembled, setting the paper in motion. *Stogsdill. Here. On the hunt for Nate.*

Nate must've gone in search of the outlaw. Instead of organizing a posse, he'd gone alone.

Alone was the way he'd lived his life.

And always would.

Henry's safety was her responsibility. With God's help, she'd find him.

Heart in her throat, she gathered her skirts and ran from the livery. A shadowed figure stepped into her path. A scream slid past her lips. With every ounce of her strength, she shoved her hands against his chest.

He fell back, arms flailing, scrambling for footing. "Miz Richards, it's me, Lester."

"Oh, I'm sorry. I thought you were someone else." Carly laid a trembling hand over her pounding heart. "Henry's missing. I think he's run away. Could you and Lloyd help look for him?"

"We'll turn this town on its side searching for him, Miz Richards. Least we can do. Me and Lloyd feel plum awful Henry overheard our blathering about Nate killing his pa."

"Secrets don't stay hidden forever."

"Reckon so. Oh, I almost forgot." Lester reached inside his vest. "I found this lying in the road."

"Henry's elephant! Where'd you find it?"

"On Second Street near the edge of town."

A boy running away from home would not leave his sleep toy behind. Even if he dropped it, he'd notice.

But if someone had taken him by force…

Energy shot through Carly. "Saddle me a horse, Lester. Then tell Sheriff Truitt that Stogsdill might have Henry."

Carly sprinted toward home. And the gun she kept locked in her safe.

Nate's thoughts raced in rhythm with Maverick's pounding hooves. How had Stogsdill showed up early? Had someone tipped him off? Did the outlaw have spies planted everywhere, enabling him to know Nate's whereabouts? Even if Stogsdill had been at his sister's when the telegram arrived, how had he known Nate was in Gnaw Bone? Was his early arrival merely a coincidence, or part of a plot?

The sun was setting, the glare all but blinding. Nate's gaze swept the woods on his right, the pasture on his left, the road ahead. Stogsdill would expect Nate to look for him at the Pence farm. Instead he might hole up anywhere along this road, lying in ambush.

Something told Nate to slow his horse. Intuition? God at work? He didn't know, but he immediately turned his mount onto the strip of grass bordering the road and the woods.

Every sense alert, he listened, his eyes searching the area, his nostrils pulling in any scent that might carry a clue. Yet he detected nothing out of the ordinary.

A horse whinnied. Maverick's ears pricked. Nate laid a calming hand on his mount's neck, praying Maverick wouldn't answer. The sound appeared to come from a stand of trees up ahead, their trunks thick enough to hide a man.

Nate slid from the saddle then, gripping the butt of his pistol, he moved on silent feet. The tiniest snap of a twig would announce his presence. A few yards away, a small clearing in the woods should expose whoever might be lurking.

The hair on Nate's neck rose. He drew his gun from the holster and inched forward.

"Stop right there, Sergeant!"

Nate froze, gun at the ready, hammer pulled back.

Stogsdill stepped into the clearing, the smirk on his face and his six-shooter visible in the ebbing light.

"Got my gun aimed at your gut, Stogsdill. Give yourself up."

"Ain't likely," Stogsdill said, dragging a small figure

from behind a tree. "Not when this boy makes a mighty fine shield."

"I prayed you'd find me," Henry said, his voice quivery, ending on a sob.

From the frantic look on Henry's face, he was terrified. Panicked. Might try to escape. One long squeeze on the boy's neck would silence his cries. Forever.

If anything happened to that boy, Nate couldn't live with himself. Why had he believed he could prevent tragedies? Why had he believed he could control anything? Only God could.

Lord, help Henry keep his wits. Help me save him, please.

Nate tamped down the alarm rising inside him, fought for calm, the only way to think clearly. "You okay, Henry?"

"Yes, sir," Henry said, tears glistening in his eyes.

"Can't see why you'd trust him, kid, when he shot your dad dead like a dog," Stogsdill said.

A small shudder slid through the boy's slender body, the only indication Henry had heard.

Nate ached to wipe that ugly grin off Stogsdill's face. But with Henry in his clutches, he'd need patience, control.

"I watched you, Sergeant, in that tender scene with this boy. Knew the kid was my trump card. Didn't expect grabbing him to be so easy." Stogsdill cackled. "He just stumbled into my path."

"What do you want, Stogsdill?"

"Why you, of course." His tone turned arctic, threatening. "You're a burr under my saddle, Sergeant. That'll end here, once and for all."

"If you so much as—"

"You're in no position to threaten me." Stogsdill yanked his forearm around Henry's neck.

Henry turned bulging, terrified eyes on Nate.

The desire to rip Stogsdill limb from limb tore through Nate. *Think.* Nate slowed his breathing, fighting for deadly calm.

"Reckon you know I'm gonna win this one. But to keep things *tidier*, I'll free this boy if you throw down your gun and surrender."

Thank You, God. "I will, as soon as Henry's on my horse and safely on his way to town," Nate said. "Agreed?"

"Agreed."

Before the outlaw changed his mind, Nate thrust two fingers into his mouth and whistled. Maverick came trotting into view, then stopped in front of Nate.

"That's the wildest thing I ever did see. Might send the kid off on my horse and keep yours, if I weren't so fond of my tooled saddle."

His gaze riveted on Stogsdill, Nate reached for Maverick's bridle.

"Don't do anything foolish," Stogsdill said, tightening his grip on Henry. "And the kid won't get hurt."

"How can I trust you'll let him go?"

"Doubting my word, are you?" Stogsdill tilted Henry's face toward his. "I ain't keen on hurting youngsters," he said, dropping his arms, releasing his hold. "Get going, kid."

Henry hesitated, as if afraid to turn his back on the outlaw, but then he shot off, legs and arms pumping. Near the road, he tripped and fell face-first in the weeds.

Anna's words echoed in Nate's mind. *Small boys trip, Nate. You didn't do anything wrong.*

Nate took a step toward Henry, intending to help the boy to his feet.

The ominous click of a cocking hammer. "Stay put, Sergeant."

Nate straightened. He would do nothing that might risk Henry seeing Nate gunned down.

"Get up, kid."

Henry scuttled to his feet and hurried to Nate. The fear in his eyes shredded Nate's self-control.

Lord, I don't care what happens to me. Please get Henry safely home.

Nate forced up the corners of his mouth into what he hoped resembled a confident smile. While inside Nate held his breath, praying Stogsdill wouldn't change his mind. "Maverick will take you to town."

Brow furrowed, Henry stared up at the horse. "He's real big, Nate. Bigger'n Lady."

"You can do it. You know how to ride. And Maverick knows you from all those visits to the livery." Nate held out his hands. "Now step on up."

Henry stepped into Nate's cupped hands, first one boot, then the other, and while Nate held him, he gingerly slid his left foot into the stirrup. A gentle push from Nate plopped the boy onto the saddle, his legs dangling over Maverick's broad back.

"I'll turn Maverick in the right direction. Stay on the road. It'll take you home." He handed Henry the reins, then smiled as the boy gripped the leather ribbons properly, exactly as he'd taught him.

With his free hand, Henry grabbed Nate's sleeve, his grip twisting, strong.

Nate gently loosened the boy's grip. "I love you, Henry," he said.

If Nate didn't survive, didn't find a way to be the father to Henry and the husband to Carly he wanted to be, he added, "Take good care of your mom."

Carly's heart stalled in her chest. Up ahead, Nate stood alongside Maverick, Henry on the horse's back. Nate tall and strapping, Henry small but straight as a board, clutching Nate's shirtsleeve.

Was Stogsdill nearby? Had Nate saved her son? Or were they in the sights of Stogsdill's revolver?

She edged Lady off the road, swung from the saddle and led the mare into the woods, out of sight, then tied the reins to a sturdy, low branch. She crept through the underbrush, her skirts catching on brambles, slowing her progress.

As she neared her son and Nate, she could see Henry was stiff, his nod jerky, his gaze darting to the woods. Her son was terrified. Why?

"Shut up the jawing and get the kid out of here before I lose my patience."

Carly's steps faltered and she grabbed at a thorny branch to keep from falling.

The man from the wanted poster—the murderer, Stogsdill, the man Nate had tried to protect them from—stood among the trees.

Gun drawn.

Aimed at Nate and Henry.

God, please protect my son. Protect Nate.

She'd blamed Nate for everything. For losing the shop, for upsetting her son, for luring Stogsdill here. But, if not for her mistakes, Henry would be safely home, eating supper.

Nate laid a palm on Henry's dusty cowboy boot dangling above the stirrups. "Give your mom a message. Tell her I love her."

"Yes, sir."

Tears sprang to Carly's eyes and she wobbled on her feet. Nate *loved* her? The man she'd fought at every turn?

She forced the thought away. She couldn't think about that. Not now. Not when life and death hung in the balance.

With slow, easy steps, as if a gun wasn't aimed at them, Nate turned Maverick and led him onto the road toward town, her little boy on his broad back. Was Stogsdill going to let Henry go? *Oh, please, Lord!*

Nate gave an encouraging smile to her son "Take him home, boy," he said, and sent Henry off with a pat to his horse's rump.

Henry twisted in the saddle, looking back at Nate. "I said I hated you, Nate. I didn't mean it."

"I know you didn't. Now go on," he said, his gaze following their progress.

Even from here, Carly could feel the tension in Nate's shoulders. See his determination to get Henry safely away.

As Henry rode past her hiding spot, his eyes straight ahead, his backbone straight, Carly knew with calm certainty whatever happened here, God had her son in His hands.

"The boy's gone." Stogsdill stepped out of the cover of the trees, his weapon pointed at Nate's midsection. "Time to keep your part of the bargain."

Nate traded his life for Henry's?

Nate straightened, turned toward the outlaw, as if making himself a bigger target than her son. Carly craned her neck. Henry was up the road but still in the rogue's view.

"Toss that pistol into the brush, Sergeant."

"Not until the boy's out of sight."

"Do it now," Stogsdill snarled.

For a fraction of a second Nate hesitated, then tossed his gun. "What's got you so heated up, Stogsdill?"

Stogsdill stepped closer. "First, you killed my spy in this town. Richards was the best mole I had."

What? Max had been an informant for Stogsdill?

Of course. Those unexplained absences, the times he'd stopped at Western Union, his excuses as flimsy as silk organza, the money he'd flaunted, all added up to one thing—Max had aided a killer and profited from it.

"Then you turned my fiancée against me. Not smart."

Stogsdill had murdered Rachel, Nate's fiancée, yet dared to condemn Nate.

"I didn't. You did."

"Liar! Until you interfered, she was a sweet, compliant little thing."

"We both know why. Do you enjoy putting bruises on a defenseless woman, Stogsdill?"

"Shut your trap! Nothing'll give me more pleasure than seeing you dead. And the buzzards picking at your carcass," he said, then cackled.

Devoid of humor, vile, the sound swept a chill through Carly, raising goose bumps on her arms. With hands as cold as ice, stomach tumbling, Carly edged back the hammer on her weapon.

Henry disappeared around the bend. Carly had to do something. Now! *Lord, help me.*

Stogsdill raised his weapon, the barrel pointing at Nate's heart.

Suddenly in a flash of arms and legs, Nate whirled and kicked, his boot slamming into Stogsdill's hand, sending the outlaw's gun flying into the air, then tumbling and disappearing in the high weeds alongside the road.

Bellowing a string of curses, Stogsdill flung himself at Nate. They toppled to the ground, a tangle of thudding fists.

Edging closer, Carly shifted her gun, right, left, trying to take aim at Stogsdill. Nate's hip was in her sights, then Stogsdill's head. Just as she was about to pull the trigger, Nate's back came into view. They moved so quickly, she couldn't get a clear shot.

Oh, Lord, save Nate!

With a roar, Nate heaved. Stogsdill tumbled to the ground. Both men sprang to their feet. They circled and pummeled, chests heaving with the effort of each landed jab.

Stogsdill reared back his hand and slammed his fist into Nate's jaw. Nate's head jerked back, the impact of the blow sending him sprawling. Stogsdill leaped on him, ramming a fist into Nate's gut. Nate fought for air, then bucked, trying to throw Stogsdill off him.

Carly edged still closer.

"Prepare to die, Sergeant," Stogsdill muttered as he bent forward, grunting.

Was he choking Nate?

The gun gripped in her hand, Carly stretched out her arm, her finger on the trigger, the barrel inches from Stogsdill's head. "Unless you want to die, Stogsdill, let him go."

Stogsdill whirled, slamming into the muzzle of the gun. The motion jerked her backward. Her finger slipped in a reflexive squeeze on the trigger.

With a deafening boom, the Smith and Wesson fired.

Chapter Twenty-Two

A bullet whizzed past Nate's ear.

Too close.

Then he saw her—Carly, gun in her hands, her eyes wide with fear.

If only he could whisk her away from danger, but logic kicked in, springing him into action. He launched himself at Stogsdill.

The outlaw tumbled and rolled, scuttling for the weapon Nate had kicked out of his hand and into the weeds.

With his eyes focused on the spot where he'd tossed his own gun, Nate spied the glint of metal. He dove for his revolver and lurched to his feet, aiming it at Stogsdill crouching in front of him, the outlaw's weapon inches from his outstretched fingers.

Heart pounding, breath coming in spurts, Nate's hand wobbled. He clenched the gun tighter, sucked in a steadying breath. "One move, Stogsdill, and you're dead."

Exactly what the villain deserved.

Kill him, his mind raged. *Kill him for murdering your parents. Kill him for murdering Rachel.*

Vengeance is mine, saith the Lord.

While Nate warred with his conscience, Stogsdill

lurched for his gun, reared to his knees and stretched out his hand. As fast as a blink, he aimed the pistol at Nate's heart.

As if from a great distance, Nate heard Carly's "Watch out!" and he squeezed the trigger.

A high-pitched, ear-piercing cry of pain.

Stogsdill writhed on the ground, holding his shooting hand, moaning.

The sound of hoofbeats. Someone was coming.

Could it be a member of Stogsdill's gang?

"Carly, leave. Now!"

"I'm staying." Her weapon aimed at Stogsdill, Carly's eyes never left the outlaw. "You okay?"

In that moment Nate knew he'd loved Carly from that very first day when she'd fainted in his arms. Seeing her now, strong and in charge, a woman not to be trifled with, he'd never loved anyone more.

This petite woman, who had endured both a father and a husband's tyranny, and the pain Nate had brought her, had saved *him*. A man who'd thought he was beyond saving.

"Where did you get that gun?" he asked.

"It's mine. Just because I dislike guns doesn't mean I can't use one."

"You never cease to surprise me," he said, his own weapon pointed toward those thundering hoof beats. He exhaled a gust as Sheriff Truitt galloped in.

The sheriff swung from his horse, weapon drawn. "Heard the shot. Was afraid I was too late." Then, as he took in Carly poised for trouble, a grin stole over his face. "Looks like you've got things well in hand, Mrs. Richards," he said, "but, since I'm here, might as well do my job."

Truitt grabbed up Stogsdill and pulled his hands behind his back to cuff him.

"Watch my hand!"

"You're lucky that's the only hole in you, Stogsdill,"

Truitt said as the handcuffs closed with a clank. He turned to Carly and smiled. "Maybe you can talk Nate into splitting the reward money."

"She deserves it all," Nate said. "I'd be dead if she hadn't distracted Stogsdill."

"Sheriff, don't listen to him. Nate deserves it for nearly sacrificing his life to save my son," she said, her weapon still aimed at Stogsdill. "Do you know if Henry arrived in town?"

"Can't say. Left town as soon as Lester warned me Stogsdill was in the area."

"Maverick will get him back safely." Nate wiped his sweaty face on his forearm, leaving a smear of blood on his sleeve. "If you left immediately, Truitt, I gotta wonder what took you so long," he said, grinning.

"Took a roundabout route to the Pence farm, figuring that's where Stogsdill would head."

Carly's brow furrowed. "Are Debby and the Pences okay?"

"They're fine. Guess Stogsdill didn't want to argue with a sawed-off shotgun and a grandfather itching to use it."

"Oh, thank you, God," Carly said.

"Where's your horse, Stogsdill?" Truitt asked. When Stogsdill didn't answer, the sheriff gave him a shake. "Not smart for a man who'll be spending time in my jail."

"Just beyond the clearing," Stogsdill muttered.

Nate led the animal to the sheriff. "Put your foot in the stirrup, Stogsdill," Nate said. When the outlaw complied, his cuffed hands behind his back, Nate heaved Stogsdill onto the horse. Stogsdill wobbled, but then righted himself in the saddle.

Truitt took a rope hanging from his saddle and trussed Stogsdill like a Thanksgiving turkey. "Can't imagine he can cause any trouble, but I'll keep a gun at the ready in case he tries something stupid."

Nate turned to Carly. "Where's your horse?"

"Just up the road."

Nate found his Stetson and plopped it on his head. Side by side yet not touching, they walked to where Lady waited. Fireflies danced in the grass. Daylight was waning. On such a peaceful spring evening, Nate found it hard to believe they'd had to fight for their lives.

Though Nate loved Carly with everything in him, the words she'd spoken, *Haven't you done enough damage to my family?* echoed through him. Still, he wouldn't let Carly leave town until he'd had his say.

Carly tucked her gun into a drawstring bag looped over the saddle horn, then turned to him. "Do you want to ride double?"

Nothing would please him more than having Carly in front of him, tucked in his arms. "Thanks, but Lady's getting up in years and is too small to carry us both."

If not for this courageous woman, would he have survived Stogsdill's squeezing hands on his throat? As he helped her mount, he said, "Thanks for saving my life back there." He gazed into her soft eyes of cornflower blue. "I thought the knight was supposed to save the day, not the other way around."

"Sometimes the damsel has to take matters into her own hands, especially when the knight's face looks like raw beefsteak."

"That bad?" he said, chuckling.

Her smile was tender. "Worse." She fluttered a touch along his brow. "Does it hurt?"

"I've had worse."

"You could have been killed." Her touch stilled. "Thank you."

He quirked his split lip into a grin. "Just doing my job, ma'am."

"Please don't make a joke, Nate. You saved my son. Me. Maybe even the town. I can't thank you enough."

"God was with us back there."

"I know you're right. I'll be thanking Him on the ride home." A smile curved across her face. "I can't wait to hug and hold my son."

For a moment Nate had hoped she'd say she wanted to hug him, too, but she didn't. He wouldn't push her. Not when he'd been the reason Henry had run away. "Henry wouldn't have needed saving if not for me."

"I was to blame more than you." Her eyes welled with tears. "The question is, Nate, can you save yourself?"

"What do you mean?"

"Maybe you need to think about what you want out of life," she said, then nudged her horse.

Without a backward glance, she rode out to meet Truitt waiting in the road, Stogsdill's horse trailing behind, and guided Lady to the back of the line.

"Sergeant, I'll send a horse for you," Truitt said, as they headed off and picked up speed.

Stogsdill swayed, fighting for balance on that fancy saddle he prized. Soon the outlaw would be behind bars where he belonged.

With Nate's mission over, what would the next years bring? That decision rested with the beautiful, courageous woman disappearing around the bend.

And with God.

Nate couldn't wait another day, another minute, to start over, to be clean, to be forgiven. He removed his Stetson and knelt beside the road, then closed his eyes and breathed the words he needed to say and he hoped God wanted to hear, "I'm sorry, Lord, for my need for revenge, for believing I was somehow invincible, able to protect and overcome anything when…"

He sucked in a shaky breath. "When I'm a mere man.

I see now I'd put myself in Your seat. I'm climbing down now, Lord." An emotional sigh slid from his lips. "I want to change. Help me throw off the shackles of anger and guilt and find new life, Your purpose, Your peace."

Tears slid down his face as the oppressive weight of sin and guilt he'd carried slipped from his shoulders, replaced with the certainty that God loved and had forgiven him.

Joy bubbling up inside him, he rose. He was free. Free from the mistakes of his past. Free to begin anew.

Free to settle down with Carly. If she would have him.

Tucked in his bed, his sleep toy at his side, Henry smiled up at Carly. Finally she could let down her guard. The nightmare was over. *Thank You, Lord, for saving us.*

Nate had pretended to give Carly the credit for saving him, but when Stogsdill had reared back against the barrel of her gun, her finger had wobbled on the trigger and fired, the bullet barely missing Nate. Another few inches…

"Mama, one more drink. Please."

Carly complied. She couldn't think of a time when she'd been happier for her son to invent excuses to postpone his bedtime.

Henry drank a few sips of water, then handed her the cup. She kissed him on the cheek. He appeared relaxed, no worse for his ordeal.

Would his abduction create problems later? If so, she'd encourage him to talk about his worries. And no longer ignore trouble and pretend all was well when it wasn't.

Henry yawned. "Nate said he loves you, Mama."

Nate *loved* her. She'd heard his claim, yet hearing it now, the words zinged through her, producing a mixture of anticipation and alarm. Was she ready for love, for such a huge step?

What if Henry wouldn't accept Nate in their life? "Are you still mad at Nate?"

"Nope, he saved me from the bad man." His brow furrowed. "Is that why Nate shot Pa? 'Cause Pa was a bad man?"

She peered into her son's innocent eyes. She would not tell Henry that his father was bad. But she would answer his questions and let the conversation go wherever he led.

"Nate shot your father because he was going to shoot him." She studied her son, recalling his tearful assertion that Max didn't do bad things. Surely the claim of a distraught, hurting boy. "Henry, you know your pa did bad things, don't you?"

Eyes troubled, he nodded. "He scared me."

"Me, too." She glanced at the small soiled Stetson on the bureau. "I'm sorry you had to find out about your pa like you did." She brushed a lock of hair off his forehead. "I'm sorry I didn't talk with you about a lot of things."

Max's outbursts paraded across her mind, of Max throwing food, knocking her to the floor, yelling at her and Henry, shaking her son.

"Things like your pa's temper that made him say and do cruel things. You were right when you said I wasn't truthful. Can you forgive me?"

"I forgive you, Mama." The peaceful expression on Henry's face proved he did.

"I promise you can talk to me about anything and I'll be honest. No secrets between us."

"Did Nate kill that bad man that catched me?"

"No, he didn't. Stogsdill's in jail. The courts will punish him, not Nate. God's Word says life is precious and we're not to kill." Yet for Henry, for Nate, she'd have pulled that trigger. She thanked God she hadn't needed to. "Lawmen sometimes use weapons to protect people. But they're not to shoot unless there's no other way."

"I don't wanna be a lawman. I wanna take care of horses."

Nate's influence no doubt. "You would be a good liveryman."

"Maverick taked me to town, Mama. People was shouting and cheering. Nate's horse didn't spook."

"Everyone in Gnaw Bone is happy you're safe." Carly adjusted the collar on Henry's pajamas. "Me, most of all," she said, inhaling his fresh-washed scent.

"Mama, I'm sorry I runned away."

"Running away isn't a good solution. Next time you're upset, talk to me about it." She pulled Henry onto her lap. "Are you still mad about anything?"

"That bad man scared the mad outta me."

Carly nodded, understanding how life-and-death events put things in perspective. After their encounter with Stogsdill, she now understood Nate's quest was important; the only way to ensure his survival and the survival of anyone he cared about.

"I told Nate I was sorry for saying I hate him." Tears welled in his eyes. "I don't hate him, Mama. I love Nate."

"And he loves you."

"He does. He told me." Henry smiled up at her. "Mama, marry Nate so I can get me a new pa."

Her mind racing with possibilities, with uncertainties, with all the eventualities, Carly tucked Henry under the covers.

What if she and Nate couldn't work out their differences? What if he wouldn't give up chasing after outlaws? What if he'd declared his love for her in a moment of high tension and didn't mean it?

Did that openness she'd promised include discussing romance with a seven-year-old? "We'll see. It's almost ten. Far too late to be planning our lives, you little monkey. Now go to sleep."

"The key turns on the monkey. M-o-n-k-e-y." Another yawn. This time his mouth opened so wide it all but swallowed Henry's face. "I'm sleepy, Mama. I'll ask for a new pa tomorrow."

With one final kiss on Henry's forehead, Carly rose, the knot in her stomach bigger than Henry's Stetson across the way. Nothing in her life had prepared her to reach for happiness. If she wanted to give her son his wish, she'd have to face and conquer her fear of trusting her heart to a man.

Perhaps, just perhaps, she would be enough for a good man.

A good man like Nate, a quiet voice said inside her.

She turned out the lamp and left the room, wondering what tomorrow would bring.

The worst was over. Stogsdill was behind bars. Henry was found. Nate had made peace with God. So why didn't he feel reassured?

How could he, when things were still unsettled between him and Carly? Why not be honest? Things between them were a mess. He'd clean up that mess if it was the last thing he did. Nothing mattered if he didn't have Carly in his life.

Carly opened the door to his rap. "Nate." She smiled, easing the tension inside him. "I'm relieved you're back."

Did she care? About him? A faint glimmer of hope slid through him. "Sheriff Truitt sent Lester out with Maverick. On the ride into town, Harders nearly talked me to death." Nate grinned. "I suspect all those words Lloyd doesn't say end up coming out of Lester's mouth."

Carly chuckled. "Could be."

They needed to talk. Not about such frivolous stuff as the Harders. About *them*. That couldn't wait until tomorrow. *Please, Lord, let her say yes.*

"I know it's late, but I've got a few words of my own that need saying."

She hesitated for a moment, then nodded.

Thank You, Lord. Now if he could only make amends.

"Let's sit on the porch. Henry's asleep and I don't want to risk waking him." She smiled. "Though he's so worn out, I doubt John Philip Sousa's band marching through his bedroom would rouse him."

"That's tired."

She stepped out onto the porch and eased the door closed behind her. The full moon, the gentle breeze, the quiet street, all spoke of a serene spring night. But, inside, Nate's stomach flipped faster than tumbleweed in a windstorm.

Carly sat on the wicker settee, leaving room for him.

As if taking a seat on a prickly cactus, Nate eased down beside her, unsure how to get to the reason for his visit. "How's Henry after his abduction?"

"He may have some bad dreams, but he'll be fine."

Nate reached for her hand and she allowed him to take it. "You were a courageous woman tonight." He studied her. "How are *you*?"

"Grateful. Grateful to you and to God for keeping Henry safe."

God had seen to the boy's safety. Nate knew that now. No mere mortal could control the uncontrollable, as he'd tried to do. "As evil as Stogsdill is, he didn't have it in him to harm a child. The only explanation is God."

The smile she gave him was a gift.

"Thanks to you and God, Carly, we've rid the world of a menace. A task I'd set out to do as an eighteen-year-old boy, almost eight years ago. After all those years pursuing him, having him in jail is a huge relief, but it also feels strange, almost unreal."

"You were young for such an enormous task."

"We both had to grow up quickly." He had to know. "Are you still planning to leave town?"

"Anna will pay for my supplies. With my half of the fees from the Schwartz order, I'll have funds to start a new business in a new town. This time the name on the sign out front will be mine."

"What it should've been all along."

"Max wouldn't have allowed that. But now I'm making my own decisions and a new start."

"Please don't leave, Carly." He ran his thumb over the back of her hand. "Give us a chance."

Her gaze locked with his. "Today, when you had the chance, why didn't you shoot to kill?"

He cupped her hand with his. "I discovered I couldn't kill Stogsdill in cold blood, unless I had no choice."

"You've changed. In more ways than one." The tender look in her eyes was almost a caress. "You just gave God the credit for Stogsdill not harming Henry."

"Today taught me that I can't handle this life without God in it. I asked Him to forgive me for the life I've lived. For the mistakes I've made." He swallowed hard. "And I think He has. I'm finally free of the guilt and hate I've carried."

"Oh, Nate…"

"I've always believed in God, but I was angry with Him for allowing evil to flourish." Tears welled in his eyes, threatening to undo him. Carly squeezed his hands, enabling him to continue. "I didn't believe God could love someone like me."

"I've known you were a good man for quite a while. I'm relieved you now see that, too."

Carly watched the play of emotion on Nate's face. With every particle of her being, she knew this man, toughened by the terrible tragedies in his life, had released all that stood between him and a forgiving God.

Nate loved God. And she believed he loved her and Henry. He'd shown his love for them, time and time again, but vengeance—that need to bring down Stogsdill—had stood in the way, along with his fear he'd bring disaster down on their heads.

Now nothing stood in the way. Certainly not losing the shop to Anna. God was their security, not the business she'd paid a terrible price for. God had her and Henry in His grip and would provide for their needs. Had he already done that when He'd brought Nate to town? Had He known that together she and Nate would heal their wounds and find love? Had He known Nate would be the dad Henry had prayed for?

Why had she taken so long to understand the truth? Tears flooded her eyes. She loved Nate. Heart and soul.

Did she have the courage to tell him? She'd prayed about her feelings for Nate on the ride into town. Would he put down his gun and prove he was part of God's plan for her and Henry? Could Nate be a man who stayed? A man to settle in one town, committed to a family?

She wouldn't continue living in the shadow of her own life. She'd speak up. Set things in motion. Take action, as she'd done when she'd ridden out to save her son.

She motioned to the gun belt riding Nate's hips. "Are you giving that up?"

Without one word, Nate released the buckle and tossed his gun belt onto the floor, then pulled her close. "Only a fool would choose a six-shooter over an amazing woman like you."

Tears stung her eyes. "I love you, Nate. Goodness knows I've fought it with everything in me. But there it is." She raised her chin. "So what are you going to do about it?"

He grinned. "I like a woman who knows her own mind. Guess it's time to buy a livery."

"What?" she said, swatting at him.

"Appears my feisty seamstress's apt to stitch a nip or a tuck in my hide if I don't get it said."

He dropped to the floor on one knee and took her hand, gazing up at her. What she saw in the depths of his smoky-gray eyes spoke the words she longed to hear and knew were coming.

"I love you, Carly, with all my being. Will you do me the great honor of becoming my wife?"

"Yes, I'll marry you!" She rose, pulling him to his feet and into her arms. Nothing had ever felt so right.

He lowered his head and kissed her. She gently cupped Nate's jaw and returned that kiss, her heart hammering wildly in her chest.

"I don't want to wait long to get married," he said.

"Anna helped Vivian dress for her wedding tonight. The Harders handled delivering the guests. Now I'm free to make my wedding dress." She cocked her head at him. "Will we marry in church?"

"Of course. Where else?"

She'd have the wedding she'd always dreamed of.

"You know, Carly, after we're married, Anna could move into the quarters behind the shop and we could rent the cabin to Lloyd and Lester. They're old enough to be out on their own."

"Where would we live?"

"How would you like to take the reward money and build that house in the woods you've been wanting with the white picket fence and a shade tree for Henry to climb?"

"You'd do that for me?"

"I'd do anything for you." He smiled. "I have an ulterior motive for wanting Lester and Lloyd close to the livery."

"Why? Won't you be working there?"

"Yes, but I'll be a new father and bridegroom. That's going to keep me mighty busy."

His words heated her cheeks. "I'll miss working in the shop."

"I want to provide for you and Henry. But you can work as much or as little as you want. You and Anna can figure it out."

"That'll give me more time with Henry, something I've always wanted."

"Just Henry?"

"No, silly. More time with both of the men in my life."

He took her in his arms. "I intend to spend a lifetime showing you dreams do come true." He smiled down at her. "Do you know how I know?"

"How?"

"God brought me you."

Tears stung her eyes. "That's what I told Henry." She inhaled deeply. The stench of her past now smelled as sweet as the honeysuckle growing on the trellis at the end of the porch. "When has this world ever smelled sweeter?"

The screen door squeaked. Henry appeared in the doorway, clutching his stuffed elephant. "Mama, I had a bad dream." Then he raced across the porch and slammed against Nate's legs. "Nate! You saved me."

"Hi, buddy. God saved us all."

Nate sat on his haunches and gathered Henry close. "Is it okay with you if I marry your mama?"

"Would I be your boy?"

"Yes, you would."

"Hurray!" Henry darted out of Nate's arms and raced around in a circle, like a puppy chasing its tail. "I got me a new pa, Mama." He looked up at Nate. "A good pa."

"The only kind of father for a good boy like you." Nate gathered Henry in his arms, then stood and tugged Carly close in the other, kissing both their cheeks. A kiss with the promise of now and forevermore.

Henry took Nate's cheeks in his hands. "You aren't gonna leave town, are you?"

"No, my boy. I'd never leave a town where I found myself, found my family, found God. All waiting on a bounty hunter to find his way home."

Epilogue

The hot, sticky days of summer gave way to the first cool night of fall. Life had settled into a routine, a new routine where Carly woke up with the man she loved every morning and fell asleep in his arms every night.

As Henry counted stars, his arm around Maizie, Carly ambled up to the porch where Nate sat on the swing, relaxing. The welcoming smile on his face said he'd found his place in the world and was never leaving.

She slipped in beside him and nestled into the crook of his arm. "I love you, Nate Sergeant."

Nate leaned down. "You've made me a very happy man, Mrs. Sergeant," he whispered near her ear, sending a shiver cascading down her spine.

This loving man had healed Carly's wounded heart. And brought Anna into her life, a woman she'd come to love like a sister during long days of cutting fabric and stitching hems. The last couple of weeks, Sheriff Truitt had come courting Anna, putting a perpetual smile on her face, as if it had been stitched in place.

At times life seemed so perfect, so wonderful, Carly wanted to pinch herself to ensure she wasn't dreaming.

She leaned back, studying Nate's face in the light of the moon. Was he as content running the livery? "Do you miss chasing outlaws?"

"Nope. I love being a family man with my wonderful wife and son and a baby on the way." He kissed her forehead. "I thank God each day for the peace of my life."

She ran a hand over her belly. "In about five months that peace you esteem will be interrupted with a squalling baby."

"Nothing sounds sweeter than to walk the floor with my son or daughter tucked in my arms," he said, covering her hand with his.

Carly's gaze settled on Henry's small figure, lying sprawled on his back, his face lifted to the sky. "After years of being an only child, I hope the baby doesn't make Henry jealous and demanding."

"We'll take one day at a time and learn as we go. But, knowing Henry, he'll be a terrific big brother." Nate pulled Carly to him, encircling her with his arms. "When I entered your shop that day in April, I had no idea God had far bigger plans for me than I could have imagined. I'm a slow learner, but I'm not about to forget our great God redeemed a lost bounty hunter, then turned him inside out into a family man."

Henry clomped up the porch step, raced toward the swing, then wiggled between them. "Then how come your insides aren't on the outside, Pa?"

Nate chuckled. "You make a good point, son."

Carly ran her fingertips through Henry's hair. "Are you done counting stars, little man?"

"There're so many, Mama, I kept losing my place." He patted Carly's belly. "Hi, baby sister. What you doing in there?"

"What if your baby sister turns out to be a brother?"

Nate said, his eyes shining with love for her son. "Wouldn't you like a boy to play with?"

"Mama needs a girl for her when you and me go fishing."

Carly met Nate's amused gaze. He gave her a wink.

"You're a thoughtful son to think of me," Carly said.

"The next one can be a brother for me. Then the next one—"

"Whoa, cowboy, let's not get too far ahead with those plans."

"Yeah, better save some babies for Aunt Anna and Sheriff Truitt."

Carly exchanged a smile with Nate. "Maybe we should give them time to marry first."

"Okay." Henry leaned back and looked up at Nate. "Pa, can I help finish building the cradle?"

"I could use the help of a big boy like you. But for now, what do you say we try counting those stars one more time before I tuck you into bed with a story?"

"Will you tell the story again about the prince saving the princess?"

"That should be easy for your pa since he's the prince in my real-life story," Carly said, her voice husky with emotion.

"You're his princess, Mama. Pa said so."

Nate lifted Henry in his arms, then walked to the step and sat with Henry in his lap. The two most important people in Carly's world gazed up at the clear night sky.

"One, two…" Henry said, his voice getting sleepier as he rattled off a growing tally.

One hand resting on her belly, embracing the child who would join them in a few months, Carly counted her blessings as Nate and Henry counted the stars. Though she had far too many to number, Carly intended to spend the rest of her life thanking God for the wonderful gifts He had given her, the fragrance of the future sweeter than anything she could have imagined.

But, wasn't that exactly what she would expect from their loving God?

* * * * *

Dear Reader,

I hope you enjoyed *The Bounty Hunter's Redemption*. Gnaw Bone, the setting of this novel, is a real, unincorporated community in Brown County, Indiana. I couldn't resist using the unique name for my fictional town, which in no way is intended to resemble the real place or its residents. Intrigued by the origins of the name, I found a couple theories in Wikipedia. Some say the town's name derives from the original French settlement in the area, Narbonne, which early English settlers heard as "Gnaw Bone." Another theory suggests that someone was looking for a man and was told, "I seed him over at the Hawkins place a gnawin' on a bone." I favor the latter folksy explanation.

I'm often asked where story ideas come from. The idea for *The Bounty Hunter's Redemption* came from a sentence that popped into my mind one morning. I quickly grabbed the pen and pad that writers keep nearby and recorded the words I feel God gave me: *When you've been married to a polecat, it takes a while to get rid of the stench.* From that cryptic sentence sprang the seeds for Carly's story. Whatever way the ideas come, I'm privileged to pen stories I hope bring glory to God and provide a "happily-ever-after ending," what God wants for each of us.

I love to hear from readers. Please write me at my website janetdean.net.

Blessings,

Janet Dean

REQUEST YOUR FREE BOOKS!

2 FREE INSPIRATIONAL NOVELS
PLUS 2 *FREE* MYSTERY GIFTS

Love Inspired HISTORICAL

SPECIAL EXCERPT FROM

Love Inspired **HISTORICAL**

*Can a grieving woman find happiness with a man who
can't remember his own name?*

Read on for a sneak preview of
RECLAIMING HIS PAST,
an exciting new entry in the series,
SMOKEY MOUNTAIN MATCHES.

October 1885
Gatlinburg, Tennessee

It wasn't easy staying angry at a dead man.

Jessica O'Malley hesitated in the barn's entrance, the tang of fresh hay ripening the air. The horses whickered greetings from their stalls, beckoning her inside, probably hoping for a treat. She used to bring them carrots and apples. She used to enjoy spending time out here.

This place had become the source of her nightmares. Her gaze homed in on the spot where the man she'd loved had died defending her. The bloodstain was long gone, but the image of Lee as she'd held him during those final, soul-wrenching moments would be with her for as long as she lived.

If he'd been honest with her, if he'd made different choices, she wouldn't be living this lonely, going-through-the-motions half-life. She wouldn't be a shadow of her former self, clueless how to reclaim the fun-loving girl she once was.

Lost in troubling memories, a weak cry for help wrenched her back to the present with a thud. Her empty milk pail slipping from her fingers, Jessica hurried to investigate. She surged around the barn's exterior corner and had to grope the weathered wall for support at the unexpected sight of a bruised and battered man near the smokehouse.

Hatless and looking as if he'd romped in a leaf pile, his golden-blond hair was messy. "Can you help me?"

"Who are you? What do you want?"

He dropped to his knees, one hand outstretched and the other clutching his side. Jessica belatedly noticed the blood soaking through his tattered shirt. Bile rose into her throat. Lee's gunshot wound had done the same to his clothing. There'd been so much. It had covered her hands. Her dress. Even the straw covering the barn floor had been drenched with it.

"Please…ma'am…"

The distress in his scraped-raw voice galvanized her into action. Searching the autumn-draped woods fanning out behind her farm's outbuildings, she hurried to his side and ducked beneath his arm. She barely had time to absorb the impact of his celestial blue eyes on hers. "What happened to you?"

"I…don't remember."

Don't miss
RECLAIMING HIS PAST
by Karen Kirst,
available February 2016 wherever
Love Inspired® Historical books and ebooks are sold.

SPECIAL EXCERPT FROM

Love Inspired®

*As a young woman seeks a better life for herself
and her son in Amish country, will she find happiness
and love with an Amish carpenter?*

*Read on for a sneak preview of
A HUSBAND FOR MARI,
the second book in the new series
THE AMISH MATCHMAKER.*

"That's James," Sara the matchmaker explained in English. "He's the one charging me an outrageous amount for the addition to my house."

"You want craftsmanship, you have to pay for it," James answered confidently. He strode into the kitchen, opened a cupboard, removed a coffee mug and poured himself a cup. "We're the best, and you wouldn't be satisfied with anyone else."

He glanced at Mari. "This must be your new houseguest. Mari, is it?"

"*Ya*, this is my friend Mari." Sara introduced her. "She and her son, Zachary, will be here with me for a while, so I expect you to make her feel welcome."

"Pleased to meet you, Mari," James said. The foreman's voice was pleasant, his penetrating eyes strikingly memorable. Mari felt a strange ripple of exhilaration as James's strong face softened into a genuine smile, and he held her gaze for just a fraction of a second longer than was appropriate.

LIEXP0116R

Warmth suffused her throat as Mari offered a stiff nod and a hasty "Good morning," before turning her attention to her unfinished breakfast. Mari didn't want anyone to get the idea that she'd come to Seven Poplars so Sara could find her a husband. That was the last thing on her mind.

"Going to be working for Gideon and Addy, I hear," James remarked as he added milk to his coffee from a small pitcher on the table.

Mari slowly lifted her gaze. James had nice hands. She raised her eyes higher to find that he was still watching her intently, but it wasn't a predatory gaze. James seemed genuinely friendly rather than coming on to her, as if he was interested in what she had to say. "I hope so." She suddenly felt shy, and she had no idea why. "I don't know a thing about butcher shops."

"You'll pick it up quick." James took a sip of his coffee. "And Gideon is a great guy. He'll make it fun. Don't you think so, Sara?"

Sara looked from James to Mari and then back at James. "I agree." She smiled and took a sip of her coffee. "I think Mari's a fine candidate for all sorts of things."

Don't miss
A HUSBAND FOR MARI
by Emma Miller,
available February 2016 wherever
Love Inspired® books and ebooks are sold.